The River Prophet

by

Raymond S. Spears

Double 9 Books

The River Prophet
by Raymond S. Spears

ISBN: 978-93-71813-36-5

Published by

DOUBLE 9 BOOKS
2/13-B, Ansari Road
Daryaganj, New Delhi – 110002
info@double9books.com
www.double9books.com
Tel. 011-40042856

ABOUT THE AUTHOR

Raymond Smiley Spears was an American writer known for crafting western and adventure stories. He was born on August 2, 1876, in Belleview, Ohio, to John Randolph Spears, a noted naval historian, and Celestia Colette Smiley Spears, who worked as a teacher. Raised in a household shaped by intellectual curiosity and historical awareness, Spears developed a strong interest in storytelling from an early age. He pursued his education in Philadelphia, New York, where he deepened his knowledge of American history and frontier life. Drawing from this background, Spears began to write fiction that vividly depicted life in rugged terrains and untamed landscapes. His stories often focused on themes of survival, courage, and the pioneering spirit, and were widely read during the early 20th century. He was particularly known for creating narratives that blended historical detail with fast-paced action. Over the course of his career, Spears produced numerous works that contributed to the popular imagination of the American West. He passed away in 1950 at the age of 74, leaving behind a substantial legacy in the genre of frontier fiction.

CONTENTS

CHAPTER I

Elijah Rasba lived alone in a log cabin on Temple Run. He was a long, lank, blue-eyed young man, with curly brown hair and a pale, almost livid complexion. His eye-brows were heavy and dark brown, and the blue steel of his gaze was fixed unwaveringly upon any object that it distinguished.

Two generations before, Old Abe Rasba had built a church on a little brook, a tributary of Jackson River, away up in the mountains. The church was laid up of flat stones, gathered in fields, from ledges of rock and up the wooded mountain side. It was large enough to hold all the people for miles around, and the roof was supported by massive hewn timbers, and some few attempts had been made to decorate the structure.

Old Abe had called his church "The Temple," had preached from a big hollow oak stump, and laid down the Law of the Bible, which he had memorized by heart, and expounded from experience. Elijah Rasba, grandson of Old Abe, thus came honestly by reverence and religion, but the strange glory which had surrounded the old Temple had departed from the ruin, and of all the congregation, only Elijah remained.

Land-slips had ruined a score of farms cleared on too-steep hills; lightning had destroyed the overshot grist mill, and the two big stones had been cracked in the hot flames; a feud had opened graves before the allotted time of the victims. It seemed to Elijah, sitting there in his cabin, as though damnation had visited the faithful, and that death was the reward of belief.

The ruins of the old Temple stood melancholy where the heavy stone wall, built by a man who believed in broad, firm foundations, had split an avalanche, but without avail, for the walls had given way and let the roof beams drop in. No less certain had been the fate of the congregation; they, too, were scattered or dead. There remained but one dwelling in the little valley, with a lone occupant, who was wrestling with his soul, trying to understand, for he knew in his heart that he must read the truth and discover the meaning of all this trouble, privation, disaster, and death.

He was quite practical about it. He had a field of corn, and a little garden full of truck; over his fireplace hung a 32-20 repeating rifle, and in one corner were a number of steel traps, copper and brass wire for snares, and a home-made mattock with which a rabbit could be extricated from a burrow, or a skunk-skin from its den.

An Almanac, a Bible, and a "Resources of Tennessee" comprised the library on the shelf. The Almanac had come by mail from away off yonder, about a hundred miles, perhaps—anyhow, from New York. The "Resources of Tennessee" had come down with a spring freshet in Jackson River, and was rather stained with mountain clays. The Bible was, of course, an inheritance.

It was a very small article, apparently, to create all the disturbances that seemed to have followed its interpretations there on Temple Run. Elijah would hold it out at arms length and stare at it with those sharp eyes of his, wondering in his soul how it could be that the fate of nations, the future of humanity, the very salvation of every soul rested within the compass of that leather-covered, gilt-edged parcel of thin paper which weighed rather less than half as much as a box of cartridges.

Elijah did not spare himself in the least. He toiled at whatever task appeared for him to do. As he required for his own wants fifty bushels of corn for a year, he planted enough to shuck a hundred bushels. Once, in the fervour of the hope that he was called upon to raise corn for humanity, he raised five hundred bushels, only to give it all away to poor white trash who had not raised enough for themselves.

Again he felt the call to preach, and he went forth with all the eagerness of a man who had at last discovered his life's calling. He went on foot, through storms, over mountains, and into a hundred schoolhouses and churches, showing his little leather-skinned Bible and warning sinners to repent, Christians to keep faith, and Baal to lower his loathly head.

He had returned from his five months' pilgrimage with the feeling that his utmost efforts had been futile, and that for all his good will, it had not been vouchsafed him to leave behind one thought in fertile soil. The matter had been brought home to him by an incident of the last meeting he had addressed, over on Clinch.

In the Painted Church he had volunteered a sermon, and no sermons had been preached there in years. Feuds, inextricably tangled, had involved five different families, and members of all those families were in the church, answering to his challenge.

They sat there with rifles or shotguns between their knees, with their pistols on their hips, and eternal vigilance in their eyes. While listening to his sermon they kept their gaze fastened upon one another, lest an unwary moment bring upon them the alert shot of an enemy.

As he had stood there, gaunt in frame, famished of soul, driven by the torments of an ambition to see the right, to do it, it seemed to him as though the final burden had been heaped upon him, and that he must break under the weight on his mind.

"What can I say to you all?" he burst out with sudden passion. "Theh yo' set with guns in yo' hands an' murder in yo' souls—to listen to the word of God! How do yo' expect the Prince of Peace to come to yo' if yo' set there thataway?"

His indignation rose as he saw them, and his scorn unbridled his tongue, so that in a few minutes the congregation watched one another less, the preacher more, and all settled back, to listen and blink under his accusations and his declarations. It really seemed, for the time, as though he had caught and engaged their attention. But when the sermon ended and he had taken his departure, before he was a hundred yards down the road he heard loud words, angry shouts, and then the scream of a woman.

The next instant there came a salvo of gun and pistol shots and in all directions up and down the cross-roads people fled on horseback. Three men had been killed, five wounded and a dozen become fugitives from justice at the end of the church service.

Elijah Rasba fled homeward, his will and hopes broken, and sank dejectedly into a slough of despondency. All his good intentions, all the inspiration of his endeavour, his very spiritual exaltation had terminated in a tragedy, as inexplicable as it was depressing.

His conscience would neither let him rest nor work. He looked at his Bible, inside and out, the very fibres of his brain struggling by reason, by effort, by main strength, to discover what his duty was. No answer soothed his waking hours or gave him rest from his dreams. On him rested a kind of superstitious scorn and fear, and he began to believe the whisperings of his neighbours which reached his ears. They said:

"He's possessed!"

To his own freighted mind the statement seemed to be true. He did not know what new sin he had committed, nor could he look back on long years of his youth and young manhood and discover any sin which he had not already expiated, over and over again. He had obeyed the scriptural injunctions to the best of his knowledge, and the reward was this daily and nightly torment, the scorn of his fellows, and the questioning of his own soul.

Worst of all, constructively, he had given feud fighters the chance to do murder upon one another. Under the guise of preaching for them for the good of their souls, he had enabled them to meet in antagonism, watch in wrath, and kill without mercy. Too late he realized that he should have foreseen the tragedy, and that he should have provided against it by going first to each faction, preaching to each family, and then, when he had brought them to their knees, united them in the common cause of religion.

"On me is Thy wrath!" he cried out in the anguish of his soul. "Give thy tortured slave something good to do, ere I go down!"

There was no reply, immediate or audible; he was near the limits of his endurance; he drew his arm back to throw the Bible into the flames of his fireplace, but that he could not do. He tossed it upon the shelf, drew his hat down upon his ears and at the approach of night started over the ridges to the Kalbean stillhouse.

He stalked down a ridge into that split-board shack of infamy. He found five or six men in the hot, sour-smelling place. They started to their feet when they saw the mountain preacher among them.

"Gimme some!" he told Old Kalbean. "I'm a fool! I'm damned. I'll go with the rest of ye to Hell! Gimme some!"

"Wha—What?" Old Kalbean choked with horror. "Yo' gwine to drink, Parson?"

"Suttinly!" Rasba cried. "Hit ain' no ust for me to preach! I preach, an' the congregation murders one anotheh! Ef I don't preach, I cayn't live peaceable! They say hit makes a man happy—I ain' be'n happy, not in ten, not in twenty yeahs!"

He caught up the jug that rested on the floor, threw the tin cup to one side, up-ended the receptacle, and the moonshiner and his customers stared.

"Theh!" Rasba grunted, when he had to take the jug down for breath. He reached into his pocket, drew out a silver dollar, and handed it to the amazed mountain man.

"Theh!" he repeated, defiantly. "I've shore gone to Hell, now, an' I don't give a damn, nuther. S'long, boys! D'rectly, yo'l heah me jes' a whoopin', yas suh! Jes' a whoopin'!"

He left them abruptly and he went up into the darkness of the laurels. They heard him crashing away into the night. When he was gone the men looked at one another:

"Yo' 'low he'll bring the revenuers?" one asked, nervously.

"Bring nothin'!" another grinned. "No man eveh lived could drink fifteen big gulps, like he done, an' git furder'n a stuck hog, no, suh!"

They listened for the promised whoops; they strained their ears for the cries of jubilation; but none came.

"Co'rse," the stiller explained, as though an explanation were needed, "Parson Rasba ain' used to hit; he could carry more, an' hit'll take him longer to get lit up. But, law me, when hit begins to act! That's three yeah old, boys, mild, but no mewl yo' eveh saw has the kick that's got, apple an' berry cider, stilled down from the ferment!"

CHAPTER II

Virtue had not been rewarded. This much was clear and plain to the consciousness of Nelia Carline. Looking at herself in the glass disclosed no special reason why she should be unhappy and suffering. She was a pretty girl; everybody said that, and envy said she was too pretty. It seemed that poor folks had no right to be good-looking, anyhow.

If poor folks weren't good-looking, then wealthy young men, with nothing better to do, wouldn't go around looking among poor folks for pretty girls. Augustus Carline had, apparently, done that. Carline had a fortune that had been increased during three generations, and now he didn't have to work. That was bad in Gage, Illinois. It had never done any one any good, that kind of living. One of the fruits of the matter was when Nelia Crele's pretty face attracted his attention. She lived in a shack up the Bottoms near St. Genevieve, and he tried to flirt with her, but she wouldn't flirt.

In some surprise, startled by his rebuff, he withdrew from the scene with a memory that would not forget. The scene was a wheat field near the Turkey bayou, where he was hunting wild ducks with a shotgun. She had been gathering forty pounds of hickory nuts to eke out a meagre food supply.

Poor she might be; ill clad was her strong young figure; her face showed the strain of years of effort; her eyes had the fire of experience in suffering; and she stood, a supple girl of heightened beauty while the hunter, sure of his welcome, walked up to her, and, as both her hands held the awkward bushel basket, ventured to tickle her under the chin.8

She dropped the basket and before it reached the ground she caught the rash youth broad-handed from cheek to back of the ear, and he stumbled over a pile of wheat sheaves and fell headlong. As he had dropped his shotgun, she picked it up and with her thumb on the safety, her finger on the trigger, and her left hand on the breech, showed him how a $125 shotgun looks in the hands of one who could and would use it on any further provocation.

He took his departure, and she carried the gun and hickory nuts home with her. Thus began the inauspicious acquaintance of Nelia Crele and

Augustus Carline. The shotgun was very useful to the young woman. She killed gray and fox squirrels, wild turkeys, geese and ducks, several saleable fur-bearers, and other game in her neighbourhood. She told no one how she obtained the weapon, merely saying she had found it; and Augustus Carline did not pass any remarks on the subject.

By and by, however, when the tang of the slap and the passion of the moment had left him, he knew that he had been foolish and cowardly. He had some good parts, and he was sorry that he had been precipitate in his attentions. After that encounter, he found the girls he met at dances lacked a certain appearance, a kindling of the eye, a complexion, and, a figure.

He ventured again into the river bottoms across from St. Genevieve and fortune favoured him while tricking her. He apologized and gave his name.

Nelia was poor, abjectly poor. Her father was no 'count, and her mother was abject in suffering. One brother had gone West, a whisky criminal; a sister had gone wrong, with the inheritance of moral obliquity. Nelia had, somehow, become possessed with a hate and horror of wrong. She had pictured to herself a home, happiness, and a life of plenty, but she held herself at the highest price a woman demands.

That price Augustus Carline was only too willing to pay. He had found a girl of high spirits, of great good looks, of a most amusing quickness of wit and vigour of mentality. He married her, to the scandal of everybody, and carried her from her poverty to the fine old French-days mansion in Gage.

There he installed her with everything he thought she needed, and—pursued his usual futile life. Too late she learned that he was weak, insignificant, and, like her own father, no 'count. Augustus Carline was a brute, a creature of appetites and desires, who by no chance rose to the heights of his wife's mental demands.

Nelia Carline regarded the tragedy of her life with impatience. She studied the looking glass to see wherein she had failed to measure up to her duty; she ransacked her mind, and compared it with all the women she met by virtue of her place as Gus Carline's wife. Those women had not proved to be what she had expected grand dames of society to be.

"I want to talk learning," she told herself, "and they talk hairpins and dirty dishes and Bill-don't-behave!"

Now one of those women, a kind of a grass widow, Mrs. Plosell, had attracted Gus Carline, and when he came home from her house, he was always drunk. When Nelia remonstrated, he was ugly. He had thrown her down and gone back to the grass widow's the night before. Nelia considered that grim fact, and, having made up her mind, acted.

In her years of poverty she had learned many things, and now she put into service certain practical ideas. She had certain rights, under the law, since she had taken the name of Augustus Carline. There were, too, moral rights, and she preferred to exercise her moral rights.

Part of the Carline fortune was in unregistered stocks and bonds, and when Gus Carline returned from the widow's one day he found that Nelia was in great good humour, more attractive than he had ever known her, and so very pleasant during the two days of his headache that he was willing to do anything she asked.

She asked him to have a good time with her, and put down on the table before him a filled punch bowl and two glasses. He had never known the refinements of intoxicating liquors. Now he found them in his own home, and for a while forgot all else.

He sang, danced, laughed and, in due course, signed a number of papers, receipts, bills and checks to settle up some accounts. These were sort of hit-or-miss, between-the-acts affairs, to which he paid little attention.

To Nelia, however, they represented a rite as valid as any solemn court procedure could be, for to her river-trained instinct there was no moral question as to the justice of her claim upon a part of Carline's fortune. Her later experience, her reading, had taught her that society and the law also held with the principle, if not the manner of her primitive method, for obtaining her rights to separate support.

When Carline awakened, Nelia was gone. Nelia had departed that morning, one of the servants said. The girl did not know where she had gone. She had taken a box of books, two trunks, two suitcases and was dressed up, departing in the automobile, which she drove herself.

He had a feeling of alarm, which he banished as unworthy. Finally toward night he went down to the post office where he found several letters. One seared his consciousness;

> Gus:
>
> Don't bother to look for me. I'm gone, and I'm going to stay gone. You have shown yourself to be a mere soak, a creature of appetite and vice, and with no redeeming mental traits whatever. I hate you, and worse yet, I despise you. Get a divorce get another woman—the widow is about your calibre. But, I give you fair warning, leave me alone. I'm sick of men.
>
> Nelia.

CHAPTER III

Elijah Rasba stalked homeward from the still in the dark, grimly and expectantly erect. Now he was going to have that period of happiness which he knew was the chief reason for people drinking moonshine whiskey. He looked forward to the sensation of exuberant joy very much as a man would look forward to five hours of happiness, to be followed by hanging by the neck, till dead.

The stars were shining, and the over-ridge trail which he followed was familiar enough under his feet, once he had struck into it from the immediate vicinity of the lawbreakers. He saw the bare-limbed oak trees against the sky, and he heard rabbits and other night runners scurrying away in the dead leaves. The stars fluttering in the sky were stern eyes whose gaze he avoided with determined wickedness and unrepentance.

Arriving at his own cabin, he stirred up the big pine-root log, and drew his most comfortable rocking chair up before the leaping flames. He sat there, and waited for the happiness of mind which was the characteristic of his idea of intoxication.

He waited for it, all ready to welcome it. If it had come into his cabin, all dressed up like some image of temptation or allurement, he would not have been in the least surprised. He rather expected a real and tangible manifestation, a vision of delight, clothed in some fair figure. He sat there, rigidly, watching for the least symptom of unholy pleasure. He had no clock by which to tell the time, and his watch was thoroughly unreliable.

Again and again he poked up the fire. He was surprised, at last, to hear a far-away gobble, the welcome of a wild turkey for the first false dawn. By and by he became conscious of the light which was crowding the fire flare into a subordinate place.

Day had arrived, and as yet, the delight which everybody said was in moonshine whiskey had failed to touch him. However, he knew that he was not properly in a receptive mood for happiness. His soul was still stubborn against the allurements of sin. He stirred from his chair, fried a rabbit in a pan, and baked a batch of hot-bread in a dutch oven, brewing strong coffee and bringing out the jug of sorghum molasses.

He ate breakfast. He was conscious of a certain rigidity of action, a certain precision of motion, ascribing them to the stern determination which he had that when he should at last discover the whiskey-happiness in his soul, he would let go with a whoop.

"Some hit makes happy, and some hit makes fightin' mad!" Rasba suddenly thought, with much concern, "S'posen hit'd make me fightin' mad?"

A fluttering trepidation clutched his heart. The bells ringing in his ears fairly clanged the alarm. He hadn't looked for anything else but joy from being drunk, and now suppose he should be stricken with a mad desire to fight—to kill someone!

No deadlier fear ever clutched a man's heart than the one that seized Elijah Rasba. Suppose that when the deferred hilarity arrived, he was made fighting drunk instead of joyous? The thought seized his soul and he looked about himself wondering how he could chain his hands and save his soul from murder, violence, fighting, and similar crimes! No feasible way appeared to his frightened mind.

He dropped on his knees and began to pray for happiness, instead of for violence, when the drink that he had had should seize him in its embrace. He prayed with a voice that roared like thunder and which made the charcoal fall from the log in the fireplace, and which alarmed the jays and inquisitive mockingbirds about the little clearing.

He prayed while his voice grew huskier and huskier, and his head bowed lower and lower as he wrestled with this peril which he had not foreseen. All he asked was that when the moonshine began to operate, it make him laugh instead of mad, but terrible doubts smote him. A glance at his rifle on the wall made him fairly grovel on the floor, and he knew that in his hands the andirons, the axe, the very hot-bread rolling pin would be deadly weapons.

He hoped that he would not be able to shoot straight, but this hope was instantly blasted, for a flock of wild turkeys came down into the cornfield about ninety yards from his cabin, and although he seldom shot anything in his own clearing, he now tried a shot at the turkey gobbler and shot it dead where it strutted. If he should be stricken with anger instead of with joy, no worse man could possibly live! There was no telling what he would do if the liquor would work "wrong" on him. He could kill men at two hundred yards!

He determined that he would see no human beings that day. Few people ever visited him in his cabin, but he took no chances. He crept up the mountain and skulking through the woods found an immense patch of laurels. He crawled into it, and sat down there for hours and hours, so that no one should have an opportunity to speak to him and stir the latent devil of violence.

He returned to his cabin long after dark, and raking some hot coals out of the ashes, whittled splinters and started a blaze. He was assailed by hunger, and he baked corn pones and dry-salted pork, then added a great flapjack of delicious sage sausage to the meal. He brought out cans of fruit, whose juice assuaged his increasing thirst. Having eaten heartily he resumed his vigil before the fireplace, and then he noticed that some one had tied something on the stock of his rifle.

It was a letter which a passer-by had brought up from the Ford Post Office, and when he opened it and looked at the writing, remorse assailed him:

> Dear Parsun:
>
> Ever senct you preched here I ben sufrin count of my boy JocK. You know Him for he set right thar, frade of no man, not the Tobblys, nor the Crents. When tha drawed DOWN to shoot, he stud right thar an shot back shoot fer shoot, an now he has goned awa down the Rivehs an I am worited abot his soul because he is a gud boy an neveh was no whars in all his borned days an an i hear now he is gettin bad down thataway on Misipy rivch where thas all Bad Peple an i wisht yud prey fer him so's he wont get bad. Mrs. drones panted church on Clinch.

Rasba read the letter for the words at first. Then he went back after the meaning, and the meaning struck him like a blow in the heart.

"Me pray fo' any man again," he gasped. "Lawse! Lawse!"

He didn't feel fit to pray for himself, let alone for any other sinner, but there came to his memory a picture of Mrs. Drones, a motherly little woman who had taken him home to a dinner at which seven kinds of preserved fruit were on the table, and where the family laughed around the fireplace—only to see Jock a fugitive the next night, and the terrors of a feud war upon them.

"And Jock's getting bad down the Mississippi River!" Rasba repeated to himself, striving to grapple with that fact. He could not think clearly or coherently. The widow's voice, however, was as clearly speaking in his thoughts as though she stood there, instead of merely having written to him. He took to walking up and down the floor, back and forth, on one plank.

He had forgotten that there was such a thing for humans as sleep. The incongruity of his having been wide awake for two days and two nights did not occur to him till suddenly his eyes turned to the bed in the corner of the room and its purpose was recalled to his mind. He blinked at it. His eyes opened with difficulty. He threw chunks on the fire and went toward the bed, but as he stood by it the world grew black before his eyes and clutching about him, he sank to the floor.

CHAPTER IV

Nelia Carline would not return to that miserable little river-bottom cabin where she had grown up in unhappy privation. She had other plans. She drove the little automobile down to Chester, put it in the Star Garage, then walked to the river bank and gave the eddy a critical inspection.

For years she had lived between the floods of the river and the poverty of the uplands. Her life had often crossed that of river people, and although she had never been on the river, she had frequently gone visiting shanty-boaters who had landed in for a night or a week at the bank opposite her own shack home. She knew river men, and she had no illusions about river women. Best of all now, in her great emergency, she knew shanty-boats, and as she gazed at the eddy and saw the fleet of houseboats there her heart leaped exultantly.

No less than a score of boats were landed along the eddy bank, and instantly her eyes fell upon first one and then another that would serve her purpose. She walked down to the uppermost of the boats, and hailed from the bank:

"U-whoo!"

A lank, stoop-shouldered woman emerged from the craft and fixed the well-favoured young woman with keen, bright eyes.

"You-all know if there's a shanty-boat here for sale—cheap?" Nelia asked, without eagerness.

The woman looked at the bank, reflectively.

"I expect," she admitted at last. "This un yaint, but theh's two spo'ts down b'low, that's quittin' the riveh, that blue boat theh, but theh's spo'ts."

"I 'lowed they mout be," Nelia dropped into her childhood vernacular as she looked down the bank, "Likely yo' mout he'p me bargain, er somebody?"

"I 'low I could!" the river woman replied. "Me an' my ole man he'ped a feller up to St. Louis, awhile back, who was green on the river, but he let us kind of p'int out what he'd need fo' a skift trip down this away. Real friendly feller, kind of city-like, an' sort of out'n the country, too. 'Lowed he was a writin' feller, fer magazines an' books an' histries an' them kind of things. Lawsy! He could ask questions, four hundred kinds of questions, an' writin' hit all down into a writin' machine onto paper. We shore told him a heap an' a passel, an' he writes mornin' an' nights. Lots of curius fellers on Ole Mississip'. We'll sort of look aroun'. Co'se, yo' got a man to go 'long?"

"No."

"Wha-a-t! Yo' ain' goin' to trip down alone?"

"I might's well."

"But, goodness, gracious sake, you're pretty, pretty as a picture! I 'lowed yo' had a man scoutin' aroun'. Why somethin' mout happen to a lady, if she didn't have a man or know how to take cyar of herse'f."

Nelia shrugged her shoulders. Mrs. Tons, the river woman, gazed for a minute at the pretty, partly averted face. It was almost desperate, quite reckless, and by the expression, the river woman understood. She thought in silence, for a minute, and then looked down the eddy at a boat some distance away.

"Theh's a boat. Like the looks of it?"

"It's a fine boat, I 'low," Nelia said. "Fresh painted."

"Hit's new," the woman said.

"Is it for sale?"

"We'll jes walk down thataway," the river woman suggested. "Two ladies is mostly safe down thisaway."

"My name's Nelia Crele. We used to live up by Gage, on the Bottoms—"

"Sho! Co'se I know Ole Jim Crele, an' his woman. My name's Mrs. Tons. We stopped in thah 'bout six weeks ago. I hearn say yo'd—yo'd married right well!"

"Umph!" Nelia shrugged her shoulders, "Liquor spoils many a home!"

"Yo' maw said he was a drinkin' man, an' I said to myse'f, from my own 'sperience.... Yo' set inside yeah, Nelia. I'll go down theh an' talk myse'f. We come near buyin' that bo't yistehd'y. Leave hit to me!"

Nelia sat down in the shanty-boat, and waited. She had not long to wait. A tall, rather burly man returned with the woman, who introduced the two;

"Mis' Crele, this is Frank Commer. His bo't's fo' sale, an' he'll take $75 cash, for everything, ropes, anchor, stoves, a brass bedstead, an' everything and I said hit's reasonable. Hit's a pine boat, built last fall, and the hull's sound, with oak framing. Co'se, hit's small, 22 foot long an' 7 foot wide, but hit's cheap."

"I'll take it, then," Nelia nodded.

"You can come look it over," the man declared. "Tight hull and tight roof. We built it ourselves. But we're sick of the river, and we'll sell cheap, right here."

The three went down to the boat, and Nelia handed him seventy-five dollars in bills. He and his partner, who came down from the town a few minutes later, packed up their personal property in two trunks. They left the dishes and other outfit, including several blankets.

The four talked as the two packed up. One of them suddenly looked sharply at Nelia:

"You dropping down alone?"

She hesitated, and then laughed:

"Yes."

"It's none of my business," the man said, doubtfully, "but it's a mean old river, some ways. A lady alone might get into trouble. River pirates, you know."

It was a challenge. He was a clear-eyed, honest man, hardly twenty-five years of age, and not an evil type at all. What he had to suggest he did boldly, sure of his right at such a time, under such circumstances, to do. He was entirely likeable. In spite of herself, Nelia wavered for a moment. She knew river people; the woman by her side would have said she would be safer with him than without his protection. There was only one reason why Nelia could not accept that protection.

"I'll have to take care of myself," she shook her head, without rebuke to the youth. "You see, I'm running away from a mean scoundrel."

"Hit's so," the river woman approved, and the men took their departure without further comment.

The two women, disapproving the men's housekeeping, scrubbed the boat and washed all the bedding. Nelia brought down her automobile and the two carried her own outfit on board. Then Nelia took the car back to the garage, and said that she would call for it in the morning.

"All right, Mrs. Carline," the garage man replied, without suspicion.

Back at the landing, Nelia bade the river woman good-bye.

"I got to be going," she said, "likely there'll be a whole pack after me directly—"

"Got a gun?" the woman asked.

"Two," Nelia smiled. "Bill gave me a goose rifle and Frank let me have this—he said it's the Law down Old Mississip'!"

"The Law" was a 32-calibre automatic pistol in perfect condition.

"Them boys thought a heap of yo', gal!" The river woman shook her head. "Frank'd sure made you a good man!"

"Oh, I know it," replied Nelia, "but I'm sick of men—I hate men! I'm going to go droppin' along, same's the rest."

"Don't let go of that pistol. Theh's mean, bad men down thisaway, Nelia!"

Nelia laughed, but harshly. "I don't give a damn for anything now; I tell you that!"

"Don't forget it. Shoot any man that comes."

Nelia, who could row a skiff with any one, set her shanty-boat sweeps on their pins, coiled up the two bow lines by which the boat was moored to the bank, and which the river woman untied, then rowed out of the eddy and into the main current.

"It's good floating right down," Mrs. Tons called after her, "till yo' git to Grand Tower Rock—thirty mile!"

The river rapidly widened below Chester, and the little houseboat swung out into mid-stream. Nelia knew the river a little from having been down on a steamer, and the misery she left behind was in contrast to the sense of freedom and independence which she now had.

Stillness, peace, the sense of vast motion in the river torrent comforted her. The moment of embarking alone on the river had been full of nervous tenseness and anxiety, but now those feelings were left behind and she could breathe deeply and confront the future with a calm spirit. The veil that the blue mist of distance left behind her was penetrable by memory, but the future was hidden from her gaze, as it was hidden from her imagination.

The determination to dwell in the immediate present caught up her soul with its grim, cold bonds, and as the sun was setting against the sky beyond the long, sky-line of limestone ledges, she entered the cabin, and looked about her with a feeling of home such as she had never had before.

"I'll stand at the breech of my rifle, to defend it," she whispered to herself. "Men are mean! I hate men!"

She found a flat book on a shelf which held a half hundred magazines. The book was bound in blue boards, and backed with yellow leather. When she opened it, out of curiosity, she discovered that it was full of maps.

"Those dear boys!" she whispered, almost regretfully. "They left this map book for me, because they knew I'd need it; knew everybody down thisaway needs a map!"

They had done more than that; they had left the equally indispensable "List of Post Lights," and when dusk fell and she saw a pale yellow light revealed against a bank the little book named it "Wilkinson Island." She pulled toward the east bank into the deadwater below Lacours Island, cast over her anchor, and came to rest in the dark of a starless night.

CHAPTER V

In mid-afternoon, the man who had so desperately and as a last resource tested the efficiency of moonshine whiskey as a palliative for mental misery awaked gradually, in confusion of mind and aching of body. Noises filled his ears, and streaking lights blurred the keenness of his eyes. Reason had but little to do with his first thoughts, and feelings had nearly everything. There did not seem to be any possible atonement for him to make. Too late, as it seemed, he realized the enormity of his offence and the bitterness of inevitable punishment.

There remained but one thing for him to do, and that was go away down the rivers and find the fugitive Jock Drones, whose mother feared for him. No other usefulness of purpose remained in his reach. If he stood up, now, before any congregation, the imps of Satan, the patrons of moonshiners, would leer up at him in his pulpit, reminding him that he, too, was one of them.

He went over to the corner of his cabin, raised some planks there and dug down into the earth till he found a jug. He dragged the jug into the cabin and out of it poured the Rasba patrimony, a hidden treasure of gold, which he put into a leather money belt and strapped on. There was not much in the cabin worth taking away, but he packed that little up and made ready for his departure.

It was but a few miles over to Tug River, and he readily engaged a wagon to carry him that far. On the wooded river bank he built a flatboat with his own hands, and covered one end of it with a poplar-wood cabin, purchased at a near-by sawmill. He floated out of the eddy in his shack-boat and began his journey down the rivers to the Mississippi, where he would perform the one task that remained for him to do in the service of God. He would find Jock, give him his mother's message, and after that expiate his own sins in the deserved misery of an exiled penitent.

Tug River was in flood, a heavy storm having cast nearly two inches of rainfall upon part of the watershed. On the crest of the flood it was fast running and there was no delay, no stopping between dawn and dusk. Standing all day at the sweeps Rasba cleared the shore in sharp bends, avoided the obstacles in mid stream, and outran the wave crests and the racing drift, entering the Big Sandy and emerging into the unimaginable breadths of the Ohio.

He had no time to waste on the Ohio. The object of his search was on the Mississippi, hundreds of miles farther down, and he could not go fast enough to suit him. But at that, pulling nervously at his sweeps and riding down the channel line, he "gain-speeded," till his eyes were smarting with the fury of the changing shores, and his arms were aching with the pulling and pushing of his great oars, and he neither recognized the miles that he floated nor the repeated days that ensued.

Long since he had escaped from his own mountain environment. The trees no longer overhung his course; railroad trains screamed along endless shores, bridges overhung his path like menacing deadfalls, and the rolling thunder of summer storms was mingled with the black smoke of ten thousand undreamed-of industries. The simplicity of the mountain cornfields of his youth had become a mystery of production, of activity, of passing phenomena which he neither knew nor understood. In his thoughts there was but one beacon.

His purpose was to reach the Mississippi, take the young man in hand, and redeem him from the evils into which he had fallen. His object was no more than that, nor any less. From the confusion of his experiences, efforts, and humiliations, he held fast to one fact: the necessity of finding Jock Drones. All things else had melted into that.

The river banks fell apart along his course; the river ridges withdrew to wide distances, even blue at times; mere V-gullies or U-gorges, widened into vast corn fields. A post-office store-house at a rippling ford gave way to smoking cities, rumbling bridges, paved streets, and hurrying throngs. The lone fisherman in an 18-foot dugout had changed insensibly to darting motorboats and to huge, red-wheeled, white-castled monsters, whose passage in the midst of vast waters was attended by the sighs of toiling engines and the tossing of troubled seas.

Except for that one sure demand upon him, Elijah Rasba long since would have been lost in the confusion and doubts of his transition from narrow wooded ridges and trembling streamlets to this succession of visions. But his soul retained its composure, his eyes their quickness to seize the essential detail, and he rode the Tug River freshet into the Ohio flood tide bent upon his mission of redeeming one mountain youth who had strayed down into this far land, of which the shores were washed by the unimaginable sea of a river.

When at the end of a day he arrived in a way-side eddy and moored his poplar-bottom craft against a steep bank and the last twilight had faded from his vision, he would eat some simple thing for supper, and then, by lamp-light, try to read his exotic life into the Bible which accompanied him on his travels. He knew the Book by heart, almost; he knew all the rivers told about in it; he knew the storms of the various biblical seas; he knew the Jordan, in imagination, and the Nile, the Euphrates, the Jabbok, and the Brook of Egypt, but they did not conform in his imagination with this living tide which was carrying him down its course, over shoal, around bend and from vale to vale of a size and grandeur beyond expression.

Elijah was speechless with amazement; the spies who had gone into Canaan, holding their tongues, and befriended by women whose character Elijah Rasba could not identify, were less surprised by the riches which they discovered than Rasba by the panorama which he saw rolled out for his inspection day by day.

Other shanty-boaters were dropping down before the approach of winter. Sometimes one or another would drift near to Rasba's boat and there would be an exchange of commonplaces.

"How fur mout hit be, strangeh?" he would ask each man. "'Low hit's a hundred mile yet to the Mississippi?"

A hundred miles! They could not understand that this term in the mountain man's mind meant "a long ways," if need be a thousand or ten thousand miles. When one answered that the Mississippi was 670 miles, and another said it was a "month's floating," their replies were equally without meaning to his mind. Rasba could not understand them when they talked of reaches, crossings, wing dams, government works, and chutes and islands, but he would not offend any of them by showing that he did not in the least understand what they were talking about. He must never again hurt the feelings of any man or woman, and he must perform the one service which the Deity had left for him to perform.

Little by little he began to understand that he was approaching the Mississippi River. He saw the Cumberland one day, and two hours later, he was witness to the Tennessee, and that long, wonderful bridge which a railroad has flung from shore to shore of the great river. The current carried him down to it, and his face turned up and up till he was swept beneath that monument to man's inspiration and the industry of countless hands.

Rasba had seen cities and railroads and steamboats, but all in a kind of confusion and tumult. They had meant but incidents down the river; this bridge, however, a structure of huge proportions, was clearly one piece, one great idea fixed in steel and stone.

"How big was the man who built that bridge?" he asked himself.

While yet the question echoed in his expanding soul he hailed a passing skiff:

"Strangeh! How fur now is it to the Mississippi River?"

"Theh 'tis!" the man cried, pointing down the current. "Down by that air willer point!"

CHAPTER VI

Those first free days on the Mississippi River revealed to Nelia Crele a woman she had never known before. Daring, fearless, making no reckoning, she despised the past and tripped eagerly into the future. It was no business of any one what she did. She had married a man who had turned out to be a scoundrel, and when fate treated her so, she owed nothing to any one or to anything. Even the fortune which she had easily seized through the alcoholic imbecility of her semblance of a man brought no gratitude to her. The money simply insured her against poverty and her first concern was to put that money where it would be safe from raiders and sure to bring her an income. This, watchfulness and alertness of mind had informed her, was the function of money.

She dropped into Cape Girardeau, and sought a man whom she had met at her husband's house. This was Duneau Menard, who had little interest in the Carlines, but who would be a safe counsellor for Nelia Crele. He greeted her with astonishment, and smiles, and told her what she needed to know.

"I was just thinking of you, Nelia," he said, "Carline's sure raising a ruction trying to find you. He 'lows you are with some man who needs slow killing. He telephoned to me, and he's notified a hundred sheriffs, but, shucks! he's a mean scoundrel, and I'm glad to see yo'."

"I want to have you help me invest some money," she said. "It's mine, and he signed every paper, for me. Here's one of them."

He took the sheet and read:

> I want my wife to share up with me all my fortune, and I hereby convey to her stocks, bonds, and cash, according to enclosed signed certificates, etc.
>
> Augustus Carline.

"How come hit?" the man asked.

"He was right friendly, then," she replied, grimly. "For what you-all said about the daughter of my mother I come here to claim your help. You know about money, about interest and dividends. I want it so I can have money, regular, like Gus did—"

"I shall be glad to fix that," he said, wiping his glasses. "What you wish is a diversified set of investments. How much is there?"

She stacked up before him wads, rolls, briquettes, and bundles. He counted it, slip by slip and when he had completed the tally and reckoned some figures on the back of an envelope, he nodded his approval.

"I expect that this will bring you around twelve or fifteen hundred dollars a year, safe, and a leetle besides, on speculation."

"That'll do," she said, approvingly.

No one in town connected her with the sensation up around Gage. She was just one of those shanty-boat girls who come down the Mississippi every once in a while, especially below St. Louis. In a hundred cities and towns people were looking for Mrs. Augustus Carline, supposed to be cutting a dashing figure, and probably in company with a certain Dick Asunder, who had been seen in Chester, with his big black automobile on the same day that Mrs. Carline abandoned her husband's automobile there.

Of course, the shanty-boaters did not tell, if they knew; the River tells no tales. Certainly, of all the women in the world this casual visitor at Attorney Menard's need not attract attention. Menard always did have strange clients, and it was nothing new to see a shanty-boat land in and some man or woman walk up to his corner office and sit down to tell him in legal confidences things more interesting to know than any one not of his curiosity and sympathy would ever dream.

Attorney Menard kept faith with river wastrels, floating nomads who are akin to gypsies, but who are of all bloods—tramps of the running floods. He listened to narratives stranger than any other attorney; in his safe he had documents of interest to sweethearts and wives, to husbands and sons, to fugitives and hunters. Letters came to him from all parts of the great basin, giving him directions, or notifying him of the termination of lives whose passing had a significance or a meaning.

Nelia's mother knew him, and Nelia herself recalled his good-humoured smile, his weathered face, his appeal to a girl for her confidence, and the certainty that her confidence would be respected. She had gone to him as naturally as she would have gone to a decent father or a wise mother. She took from him his neatly written receipt, but with the feeling that it was superfluous. In a little while she returned to the shanty-boat and dropped out of the eddy on her way down the river. She floated under the big Thebes Bridge, and landed against the west bank before dark, there to have the luck to shoot a wild goose. The maps showed that she was approaching the Lower Mississippi.

When she had left Cape Girardeau, she had noticed a little brick-red shanty-boat which landed in just below her own. Without looking up, she discovered that a man leaned against the roof of his low cabin whose eyes did not cease to watch her every motion while she cast off, coiled her ropes, and leaned to the light sweeps.

When she was a safe distance down the river, she ventured to look up stream, and saw that the little red shanty-boat had left its mooring, and that the man was coming down the current astern of her. It was a free river; any one could go whither he pleased, but the certainty that she had attracted the man's attention revealed to her the necessity of considering her position there alone and dependent on her own resources.

She remembered the two market hunters, and their warnings. The man astern was a patient, lurking, menacing brute, who might suspect her of having property enough to make a river piracy worth while; or he might have other designs, since she was unfortunately good-looking and attractive. Night would surely be his opportunity and the test of her soul.

She could have landed at Commerce, where there were several shanty-boats and temporary safety; she could have floated on down at night and slipped into the shore in the dark, her lights out; she could have tried flight down the river hoping to lose the brick-red boat; she decided against all these.

Boldly she pulled into an eddy just before sunset, and had made fast to a snag and a live root when the little boat came dropping down in the edge of the current hardly forty feet distant, with the man leaning on his sweeps, watching her every motion, especially fastening his gaze upon her trim figure.

As he came opposite she turned and faced him; her jaws set.

"Hello, girlie!" he called, leaning upon his sweeps to carry his skiff-like boat into the same eddy.

On the instant she snatched the automatic pistol from her bosom and, dropping the muzzle, fired. The man stumbled back with a cry. He stood grabbing at his shoulder, his florid face turning white, his eyes starting with terror and pain. She saw him reel and fall through the open hatch of his cabin and his boat go drifting on into the crossing below. It occurred to her numbed brain that she was delivered from that peril, but as dusk fell she hated the misery of her loneliness.

CHAPTER VII

The Ohio had the Mississippi eddied. The rains that had fallen over the valleys of Kentucky and southern Ohio, Indiana, and Illinois had brought a tide down the big branch and as there was not much water running out of the Missouri and Upper Mississippi, the flood had backed up the Mississippi for a little while, stopping the current almost dead.

Elijah Rasba, running full tilt in the mid Ohio current, looked ahead that afternoon, and he had a full view of the thing to which he had come, seeking the wandering son of Mrs. Drones.

He arrived at the moment when the Mississippi, having been banked up long enough, began to feel the restraint of the Ohio and resent it. The gathered waters moved down against the Ohio flood and pressed them back against the Kentucky side. Once more the Mississippi River resumed its sway. On the loosed waters was a little cigar-box of a shanty-boat, and Rasba rowed toward it across the saucer-like sucks and depressions where the two currents of different speeds dragged by each other.

He pulled alongside, hailed, and, for answer, heard a groan, a weak cry:

"Help!"

He carried a line across to the stranger's deck and made it fast. Then he saw, stretched upon the floor, a stricken man, from whose side a pool of blood had run. Working rapidly, Elijah discovered the wound and as gunshot injuries were only too familiar in his mountain experience he well knew what he should do. Examination showed that it was a painful and dangerous shoulder shot. He cleared away the stains, washed the hole, plucked the threads of cloth out of it, turned the man on his face and, with two quick slashes of a razor, cut out the missile which had done the injury.

Healing liniment, the inevitable concoction of a mountaineer's cabin, soothed while it dressed the wound. Pads of cotton, and a bandage supplied the final need, and Rasba stretched his patient upon the cabin-boat bunk, then looked out upon the world to which he had drifted.

It was still a vast river, coming from the unknown and departing into the unknown. He knew it must be the Mississippi, but he acknowledged it with difficulty.

He did not ask the man about the bullet. Born and bred in the mountains, he knew that that would be an unpardonable breach of etiquette. But the wounded man was uneasy, and when he was eased of his pain, he began to talk:

"I wa'nt doin' nothing!" he explained, "I were jes' drappin' down, up above Buffalo Island, an' b'low Commerce, an' a lady shot me—bang! Ho law! She jes' shot me thataway. No 'count for hit at all."

"A lady you knowed?" Rasba asked.

"No suh! But she's onto the riveh, into a shanty-boat, purty, too, an' jes' drappin' down, like she wa'nt goin' no wheres, an' like she mout of be'n jes' moseyin'. I jes 'lowed I'd drap in, an' say howdy like, an' she drawed down an' shot—bang!"

"Was she frightened?"

"Hit were a lonesome reach, along of Powerses Island," the man admitted, whining and reluctant. "She didn't own that there riveh. Hain't a man no right to land in anywheres? She shot me jes' like I was a dawg, an' she hadn't no feelin's nohow. Jes' like a dawg!"

"Did you know her?"

"No, suh. We'd be'n drappin' down, an' drappin' down—come down below Chester, an' sometimes she'd be ahead, an' sometimes me, an' how'd I know she wouldn't be friendly? Ain't riveh women always friendly? An' theh she ups an' shoots me like a dawg. She's mean, that woman, mean an' pretty, too, like some women is!"

Rasba wondered. He had been long enough on the Ohio to get the feeling of a great river. He saw the specious pleading of the wounded wretch, and his quick imagination pictured the woman alone in a vast, wild wood, at the edge of that running mile-wide flood.

"Of co'rse!" he said, half aloud, "of co'rse!"

"Co'rse what?" the man demanded, querulously.

"Co'rse she shot," Rasba answered, tartly. "Sometimes a lady jes' naturaly has to shoot, fearin' of men."

Rasba landed the two boats in at the foot of a sandbar, and made them fast to old stakes driven into the top of the low reef. He brought his patient some hot soup, and after they had eaten supper, he sat down to talk to him, keeping the man company in his pain, and leading him on to talk about the river, and the river people.

In that first adventure at the Ohio's forks Rasba had discovered his own misconceptions, and the truth of the Mississippi had been partly revealed to him. What the Tug was to the Big Sandy, what the Big Sandy was to the Ohio, the Ohio was to the Mississippi. What he had looked to as the end was but the beginning, and Rasba was lost in the immensity of the river that was a mile wide, thousands of miles long, and unlike anything the mountain preacher had ever dreamed of. If this was the Mississippi, what must the Jordan be?

"My name's Prebol," the man said, "Jest Prebol. I live on Old Mississip'! I live anywhere, down by N'Orleans, Vicksburg—everywhere! I'm a grafter, I am—"

"A grafter?" Rasba repeated the strange word.

"Yas, suh, cyards, an' tradin' slum, barberin' mebby, an' mebby some otheh things. I can sell patent medicine to a doctor, I can! I clean cisterns, an' anything."

"You gamble?" Rasba demanded, grasping one fact.

"Sho!" Prebol grinned. "Who all mout *yo'* be?"

"Elijah Rasba," was the reply. "I am seeking a soul lost from the sheepfold of God. I ask but the strength to find him."

"A parson?" Prebol asked, doubtfully, his eyes resting a little in their uneasy flickerings. "One of them missionaries?"

"No, suh." Rasba shook his head, humbly. "Jes' a mountang parson, lookin' for one po'r man, low enough fo' me to he'p, maybe."

Prebol made no reply or comment. His mind was grappling with a fact and a condition. He could not tell what he thought. He remembered with some worriment, that he had cursed under the pain of the dressing of the wound. He knew that it never brought any man good luck to swear within ear-range of any parson.

He could think of nothing to do, just then, so he pretended weariness, which was not all pretense, at that. Rasba left him to go to sleep on his cot, and went over to his own boat, where, after an audible session on his knees, he went to bed, and fell into a sound and dreamless sleep.

In the morning, when the parson awakened, his first thought was of his patient, and he started out to look after the man. He looked at the face of the sandbar reef against which the little red shanty-boat had been moored. The boat was gone!

Rasba, studying the hard sand, soon found the prints of bare feet, and he knew that Prebol had taken his departure precipitately, but the reason why was not so apparent to the man who had read many a wild turkey track, deer runway, and trails of other game.

From sun-up till nearly noon, while he made and ate his breakfast, and while he turned to the Scriptures for some hint as to this river man's mind, his thoughts turned again and again to the pictures which Prebol's tales, boastings, whinings, and condition had inspired.

He felt his own isolation, strangeness, and ignorance. He could not understand the man who had fled from assistance and succour; at the same time the liveliness of his fancy reverted again and again to the woman living alone in such a desolation, shooting whoever menaced.

That type was not new to him. Up in his own country he had known of women who had stood at their rifles, returning shot for shot of feud raiders. The pathetic courage of the woman who had shot Prebol appealed to him.

The wounded man, wicked beyond measure, and the woman assailed, he realized, were like hundreds of other men and women whose shanty-boats he had seen down the Ohio River, and which lurked in bends and reaches on both sides of the Mississippi.

"Give thyself no rest!" he read, and he obeyed. He believed that he had a black sin to expiate, and he dared not begin what his soul was hungering to do, because knowing wickedness, he had deliberately sinned.

Alternately, he read his Bible and prayed. Late in the day he dropped out of the eddy and floated on down.

"I 'low I can keep on huntin' for Jock Drones," he told himself. "I shore can do that, yes, indeed!"

CHAPTER VIII

Having rid herself of the leering river rat, Nelia Crele trembled for a time in weak dismay, the reaction from her tense and fiery determination to protect herself at all costs. But she quickly gathered her strength and, having brewed a pot of strong coffee, thrown together a light supper, and settled back in her small, but ample, rocking chair, she reviewed the incidents of her adventure; the flight from her worthless husband and her assumption of the right to protect herself.

After all, shooting a man was less than running away from her husband. She could regard the matter with a rather calm spirit and even a laughing scorn of the man who had thought to impose himself on her, against her own will.

"That's it!" she said, half aloud, "I needn't to allow any man to be mean to me!"

She had given her future but little thought; now she wondered, and she pondered. She was free, she was independent, and she was assured of her living. She had even been more shrewd than old Attorney Menard had suspected; the money she had left with him was hardly half of her resources. She had another plan, by which she would escape the remote possibility of Menard's proving faithless to his trust, as attorneys with his opportunities sometimes have proved.

Nelia Crele could not possibly be regarded as an ordinary woman, as a mere commonplace, shack-bred, pretty girl. Down through the years had come a strain of effectiveness which she inherited in its full strength; she was as inexplicable as Abraham Lincoln. Her stress of mind relieved, she regarded the shooting of the man with increasing satisfaction, since by such things a woman could be assured of respect.

Gaiety had never been a part of her childhood or girlhood; she had withstood the insidious attacks and menaces that threatened her down to the day when Gus Carline had come to her. Courted by him, married, and then living in the clammy splendour of the house of a back-country rich man, she had found no happiness, but merely a kind of animal comfort. She had had the Carline library to read, and she had brought with her the handy pocket volumes which had been her own and her delight. She was glad of the foresight which enabled her to put into a set of book shelves the companions which had, alone, been her comfort and inspiration during the few years of her wedded misery.

Now, on the Mississippi, in the shanty-boat, she need consult only her own fancy and whim. Mistress of her own affairs, as she supposed, she could read or she could think.

"I do what I please!" she thought, a little defiantly. "It's nobody's business what I do now; what'd Mrs. Plosell care what people said about her? I'll read, if I want to, and I'll flirt if I want to—and I'll do anything I want to—"

She reckoned without the Mississippi. Everybody does, at first. Her money was but a means to an end. She knew its use, its value, and the perfect freedom which it gave her; its protection was not underestimated.

At the same time, sloth was no sin of hers. Living on the river insured physical activity; her books insured her mental engagement.

She had lived so many years in combat with grim necessity that the lesson of thrift of all her resources had been brought home to her. Having been waylaid by circumstance so often, she took grim care now to count the costs, and to insure her getting what she was seeking. The trouble was she could not disassociate her feelings from her ideas. They were inextricably interwoven. The brief years of her wedlock had been in one way a disillusionment, in another a revelation.

She had found her own hunger for learning, her own strength and weakness, and while she had lost to the Widow Plosell, she had clearly seen that it was not her fault but Gus Carline's meagreness of mind and shallowness of soul. Instead of losing her confidence, she had found her own ability.

For hours she debated there by her pretty lamp, with the curtains down, and the comforting and reassuring weight of the automatic pistol in her lap. She knew that she must never have that weapon at arm's length from her, but as she remembered where it had come from she wondered to think that she had so easily refused the suggestion of Frank, the market hunter.

"It's all right, though," she shrugged her shoulders, "I can take care of myself, and being alone, I can think things out!"

In mid-morning she cut loose from the bank and floated away down stream. The river was very wide, and covered with crossing-ripples. She looked down what the map showed was the chute of Hacker Tow Head, and then the current carried her almost to the bank at the head of Buffalo Island.

Here there was a stretch of caving bank; the earth, undercut by the river current, was lumping off in chunks and slices. Her boat bobbed and danced in the waves from the cave-ins, and the rocking pleased her fancy.

The names along this bit of river awakened her interest; Blackbird Island was clearly described: Buffalo Island harked back many years into tradition; Dogtooth Island was a matter of river shape; but Saladin, Tow Head and Orient Field stirred her imagination, for they might reveal the scene of steamboat disasters or some surveyor's memory of the Arabian Nights. Below Dogtooth Island, under Brooks Point, were a number of golden sandbars and farther down, in the lower curve of the famous S-bends she read the name "Greenleaf," which was pretty and picturesque.

She was living! Every minute called upon some resource of her brain. She had read in old books things which gave even the name Cairo, at the foot of the long, last reach of the Upper Mississippi, a significance of far lands and Egyptian mysteries. Gratefully she understood that the Mississippi was summoning ideals which ought to have been called upon long since when in the longings of her girlhood she had been circumspect and patient, keeping her soul satisfied with dreams of fairies playing among the petals of hill-side flowers, or gnomes wandering among the stalks of toll-yielding cornfields.

Mature, now; fearless—and, as the word romped through her mind in all its changes, free—free!—she played with her thoughts. But below Greenleaf Bend, as another day was lost in waning evening, she early sought a sandbar mooring at the foot of Missouri Sister Island, where there were two other shanty-boats, one of them with two children on the sand. She need not dread a boat where children were found. Possibly she would be able to talk to another woman, which would be a welcome change, having had so much of her own thoughts!

This other woman was Mrs. Disbon, out of the Missouri. She and her husband had been five years coming down from the Yellowstone, and they had fished, trapped, and enjoyed themselves in their 35-foot cabin-boat home. Of course, taking care of two children on a shanty-boat was a good deal of work and some worry, for one or the other was always falling overboard, but since they had learned to swim it hadn't been so bad, and they could take care of themselves.

"You all alone?" Mrs. Disbon asked.

"I'm alone," Nelia admitted, having told her name as Nelia Crele.

"Well, I don't know as I blame you," Mrs. Disbon declared, looking at her husband doubtfully. "Seems to me that on the average, men are more of a nuisance than they're worth. It's which and t'other about them. I see you've had experience?"

Nelia looked down at her wedding ring.

"Yes, I've had experience," she nodded.

"Going clear down?"

"You mean—?"

"N'Orleans?"

"Why, I hadn't thought much about it."

"The Lower River's pretty bad." Disbon looked up from cleaning his repeating shotgun. "My first trip was out of the Ohio and down to N'Orleans. I wouldn't recommend to no woman that she go down thataway, not alone. Theh's junker-pirates use up from N'Orleans, and, course, there's always more or less meanness below Cairo. Above St. Louis it ain't so bad, but mean men draps down from Little Klondike."

"I haven't made up my mind," Nelia said, adding, with a touch of bitterness, "I don't reckon it makes so much difference!"

"Lots that comes down feel thataway," Mrs. Disbon nodded, with sympathy, "Seems like some has more'n their share, and some considerable less!"

Nelia remained there three days, for there was good company, and a two-day rain had set in between midnight and dawn on the following morning. There was no hurry, and she was going nowhere. She had the whole family over to supper the second night, and she ate two meals or so with them.

The other shanty-boat, about a hundred yards down stream, was an old man's. He had a soldier's pension, and he lived in serene restfulness, reading General Grant's memoirs, and poring over the documents of the Rebellion, discovering points of military interest and renewing his own memories of his part in thirty-odd battles with Grant before Vicksburg and down the line with the Army of the Potomac.

Nelia could have remained there indefinitely, but restlessness was in her mind, as long as she had so much money on board her little shanty-boat. Disbon knew so many tales of river piracy that she saw the wisdom of settling her possessions, either at Cairo or Memphis, whichever should prove best.

Landing against the bank just above the ferry, she walked over to Cairo and sought for a man who had hired her father to help him hunt for wild turkeys. He was a banker, and would certainly be the right kind of a man to help her, if he would.

"Mr. Brankeau," she addressed him in his office, "I don't know if you remember me, but you came hunting to the River Bottoms below St. Genevieve, one time, and you and Father went over into Missouri, hunting turkeys."

"Remember you?" he exclaimed. "Why—you—of course! Mrs. Carline—Nelia Crele!"

She met his questioning gaze unflinchingly.

"I know I can trust you," she said, simply. "If you'd known Gus Carline!"

"I knew his father," Brankeau said. "I reckon as faithless a scoundrel as ever lived. Old man Carline left his first wife and two babies up in Indiana—I know all about that family! I saw by the newspapers—"

"I want some railroad stocks, so I can have interest on my money," she said by way of nature of her presence there. "When we separated, he let me have this paper, showing he wanted me to share his fortune—"

"He was white as that?" Brankeau exclaimed, astonished at the paper Carline had signed.

"He was that white," she replied, her eyes narrowing. Brankeau from the wideness of his experience, laughed. She, an instant later, laughed, too.

"So you settled the question between you?" he suggested, "I thought from the newspapers he hadn't suspicioned—this paper—um-m!"

"It's not a forgery, Mr. Brankeau," she assured him. "He was one of those gay sports, you know, and, for a change, he sported around with me, once. I came away between days. You know his failing."

"Several of them, especially drink," the man nodded "It's in cash?"

"Every dollar, taken through his own banks, on his own orders."

"And you want?"

"Railroads, and some good industrial or two. Here's the amount—"

She handed him a neatly written note. He took out a little green covered book, showing lists of stocks, range of prices, condition of companies, and, together, they made out a list. When they had finished it, he read it into the telephone.

Within an hour the stocks had been purchased, and a week later, he handed her the certificates. She rented a safe deposit box and put them into it, subject only to her own use and purposes.

"Thank you, Mr. Brankeau," she said, and turned to leave.

"Where are you stopping?" he asked.

"I'm a shanty-boater."

"You mean it? Not alone?"

"Yes," she admitted.

"I wish I were twenty years younger," he mourned.

"Do you, why?" she looked at him, and, turning, fled.

He caught up his top-coat and hat, but he went to the Ohio River, instead of to the Mississippi, where Nelia stood doubtfully staring down at her boat from the top of the big city levee.

At last, she cast off her lines and dropped on down into The Forks.

She sat on the bow deck of her boat, looking at the place where the pale, greenish Ohio waters mingled with the tawny Missouri flood.

A gleam of gold drew her attention, as she glanced downward and she was startled to see her wedding ring, with its guard ring, still on her left hand; it had never been off since the day her husband placed it there.

For a minute she looked at it, and then deliberately, with sustained calmness, removed the thin guard, and slipped the ring from its place. She put it upon the same finger of her right hand, where it was snug and the guard was not necessary.

vast and powerful that it dwarfed the senses of mortals to a feeling of the proper proportion of their affairs in the workings of the universe.

Insensibly, but surely, his pride began to fade and his selfishness began to give way to better understanding and kindlier counsels. That much the River Spirit had done for him. He would not give up the search, but rather would he increase its thoroughness, and redouble his efforts. But he would never again be quite without sympathy, quite without understanding of sensations and experiences which were not of his own heart and soul.

The river was a mile wide; its current surged from the deeps; it flowed down the bend and along the reach with a noiselessness, a resistlessness, a magnitude that seemed to carry him out of his whole previous existence—and so it did carry him. Still human, still finite, prone to error and lack of comprehension, nevertheless Augustus Carline entered for the moment upon a new life recklessly and willingly.

CHAPTER IX

A whisper, that became a rumour, which became a report, reached Gage and found the ears of Augustus Carline, whose wife had disappeared sometime previously. After two wild days of drinking Carline suddenly sobered up when the fact became assured that Nelia had gone and really meant to remain away, perhaps forever.

The thing that startled him into certainty was the paper which he found signed by himself, at the bank. He had forgotten all about signing the papers that night when Nelia had shown herself to be the gayest sport of them all. Now he found that he had signed away his stocks and bonds, and that he had given over his cash account.

The amount was startling enough, but it did not include his real estate, of which about two thirds of his fortune had been composed. If it had been all stocks and bonds, he thought he would have been left with nothing. He considered himself at once fortunate and unlucky.

"I never knew the old girl was as lively as that!" he told himself, and having tasted a feast, he could not regard the Widow Plosell as more than a lunch, and a light lunch, at that.

Nelia had been easily traced to Chester. Beyond Chester the trail seemed to indicate that Dick Asunder had eloped with her, but ten days later Asunder returned home with a bride whom he had married in St. Louis.

Beyond Chester Nelia had left no trace, and there was nothing even to indicate whether she had taken the river steamer, the railroad train, or gone into flight with someone who was unknown and unsuspected. When Carline, sobered and regretful, began to make searching inquiries, he learned that there were a score, or half a hundred men for whom Old Crele had acted as a hunter's and fisher's guide. These sportsmen had come from far and wide during many years, and both Crele and her wistful mother admitted that many of them had shown signs of interest and even indications of affection for the girl as a child and as a pretty maid, daughter of a poor old ne'er-do-well.

"But she was good," Carline cried. "Didn't she tell you she was going—or where she'd go?"

"Never a word!" the two denied.

"But where would she go?" the frantic husband demanded. "Did she never talk about going anywhere?"

"Well-l," Old Crele meditated, "peahs like she used to go down an' watch Ole Mississip' a heap. What'd she use to say, Old Woman? I disremember, I 'clar I do."

"Why, she was always wishing she knowed where all that river come from an' where all it'd be goin' to," Mrs. Crele at last recollected.

"But she wouldn't dare—She wouldn't go alone?" Carline choked.

"Prob'ly not, a gal favoured like her," Old Crele admitted, without shame. "I 'low if she was a-picking, she'd 'a' had the pick."

Cold rage alternated with hot fear in the mind of Gus Carline. If she had gone alone, he might yet overtake her; on the other hand, if she had gone with some man, he was in honour bound to kill that man. He was sensitive, now, on points of honour. The Widow Plosell, having succeeded in creating a favourable condition, from her viewpoint, sought to take advantage of it. She was, however, obliged to go seeking her recent admirer, only to discover that he blamed her—as men do—for his trouble. She consulted a lawyer to see if she could not obtain financial redress for her unhappy position, only to learn of her own financial danger should Mrs. Carline determine upon legal revenge.

Carline, between trying to convince himself that he was the victim of fate and the innocent sufferer from a domestic tragedy brought upon himself by events over which he had no control, fell to hating liquor as the chief cause of his discomfiture.

Then a whisper that became a rumour, which at last seemed to be a fact, said that Nelia Carline was somewhere down Old Mississip'. Someone who knew her by sight was reported to have seen her in Cape Girardeau, and the husband raced down there in his automobile to see if he could not learn something about the missing woman, whose absence now proved what a place she had filled in his heart.

There was no doubt of it. Nelia had been there, but no one had happened to think to tell Carline about it. She had landed in a pretty shanty-boat, the wharf-master said, and had pulled out just before a river man in a brick-red cabin-boat of small size had left the eddy. The river man had dropped in just behind her, and, according to the wharf-master:

"I shore kept my eyes on that man, for he was a riveh rat!"

The thought was sickening to Carline. His wife floating down the river with a river rat close behind presented but two explanations: she was being followed for crime, or the two were just flirting on the river, together.

He bought a pretty 28-foot motorboat, 22-inch draft with a 7-foot beam and a raised deck cabin. Having stocked up with supplies, he started down the Ohio to find his woman.

He could not tell what his intention was, not even to himself; his mind, long weakened and depraved by liquor, lacked clarity of thought and distinctiveness of purpose. One hour he raged with anger, and murder blackened his heart; another minute, his shattered nerves left him in a panic of fears and remorse, and he hoped for nothing better than to beg his wife and sweetheart for forgiveness. At all times dread of what he might find at the end of the trail tormented him from terror to despair.

His anguish overcame all his other sensations. It even overcame his lust for liquor. He grew sturdier under his affliction, so that when he arrived at Cairo, and swung his craft smartly up to the wharf-boat, his eyes were clear and his skin was honestly coloured by sunshine and pure winds. Here fortune favoured him with more news of his wife. The engineer of the Cairo-Missouri ferryboat had seen a young and pretty woman moored at the bank some distance from the landing. She had remained there upward of a week, having no visitors, and making daily visits over the levee into the little city.

"One day she stood there, I bet half an hour, looking back, like she wa waiting," the engineer said. "I seen her onto the levee top. Then she com down, jumped aboard with her lines, an' pulled out to go on trippin' dow I wondered then wouldn't some man be following of her."

When Carline passed below the sandbar point, at which the Ohio Mississippi mingle their waters, and the human flotsam from ten thou towns is caught by swirling eddies, he found himself subdued by a sh that fell athwart his course, dulling the fire of his own spirit with a and an awe which he had never before known.

His wife had gone past the Jumping Off Place; he had heard a tl jests about that fork of the rivers, without comprehending it meaning, till in his own experience he, too, was flung down th forces now beyond his control, though he himself had set them His suffering was no less acute, his mind was no less active, but slowly on him that, after all, the acute pain which was in hi no greater than the sorrow, the suffering, the poisoned deli thousands who had given themselves to this mighty flood,

CHAPTER X

For a minute Elijah Rasba, as the Mississippi revealed itself to him, contemplated a greater field for service than he had ever dreamed of. Then, humbled in his pride at the thought of great success, he felt that it could not be; for such an opportunity an Apostle was needed, and Rasba's cheeks warmed with shame at the realization of the vanity in his momentary thought.

He was grateful for the privilege of seeing the panorama that unrolled and unfolded before his eyes with the same slow dignity with which the great storm clouds boiled up from the long backs of the mountains of his own homeland. He missed the elevations, the clustered wildernesses, and ledges of stone against a limited sky, but in their places he saw the pale heavens in a dome that was uninterrupted from horizon to horizon. There seemed to be hardly any earth commensurate with the sky, and the river seemed to be flowing between bounds so low and insignificant that he felt as though it might break through one side or the other and fall into the chaos beyond the brim of the world.

Instinctively he removed his hat in this Cathedral. Familiar from childhood with mountains and deep valleys, the sense of power and motion in the river appealed to him as the ocean might have done. He looked about him with curiosity and inquiry. He felt as though there must be some special meaning for him in that immediate moment, and it was a long time before he could quite believe that this thing which he witnessed had continued far back beyond the memory of men, and would continue into the unquestionable future.

He floated down stream from bend to bend, carried along as easily as in the full run of time. He looked over vast reaches, and hardly recognized other houseboats, tucked in holes along the banks, as craft like his own. The clusters of houses on points of low ridges did net strike him as veritable villages, but places akin to those of fairyland.

All the rest of the day he dropped on down, not knowing which side he should land against, and filled with doubts as to where his duty lay. Once he caught up his big oars and began to row toward a number of little shanty-boats moored against a sandbar, close down to a wooded bank, only to find that the river current carried him away despite his most muscular endeavours, so he accepted it as a sign that he should not land there.

For a time Rasba thought that perhaps he had better just let the river carry him whither it would, but upon reflection he remembered what an old raftsman, who had run strands of logs down Clinch and Holston, told him about the nature of rivers:

"Come a falling tide, an' she drags along the banks and all that's afloat keeps in the middle; but come a fresh an' a risin' tide, an' the hoist of the water is in the mid-stream, and what's runnin' rolls off to one side or the other, an' jams up into the drift piles."

The philosophy of that was, for this occasion, that if Old Mississip' was falling, Elijah Rasba might never get ashore, not in all the rest of his born days, unless he stirred his boots. So catching up his sweep handles he began to push a long stroke toward the west bank, and his boat began to move on the river surface. Under the two corners of his square bow appeared little swirls and tiny ripples as he approached the bank and drifted down in the edge of the current looking for a place to land.

Before he knew it, a big patch of woods grew up behind him, and when he felt the current under the boat slacken he discovered that he had run out of the Mississippi River and was in a narrow waterway no larger than Tug Fork.

"Where all mout I be?" he gasped, in wonderment.

He saw three houseboats just below him, moored against a sandbar, with hoop nets drying near by, blue smoke curling out of tin pipes, and two or three people standing by to look at the stranger.

He rowed ashore and carried out a big roped stone, which he used as anchor; then he walked down the bar toward the man who watched his approach with interest.

"I am Elijah Rasba," he greeted him. "I come down out of Tug River; I am looking for Jock Drones; he's down thisaway, somewheres; can yo' all tell me whichaway is the Mississippi River?"

"I don't know him," the fisherman shook his head. "But this yeah is Wolf Island Chute; the current caught you off of Columbus bluffs, and you drifted in yeah; jes' keep a-floatin' an' d'rectly you'll see Old Mississip' down thataway."

"It's near night," Rasba remarked, looking at the sun through the trees. "I'm a stranger down thisaway; mout I get to stay theh?"

"Yo' can land anywhere's," the man said. "No man can stop you all!"

"But a woman mout!" Rasba exclaimed, with sudden humour. "Yistehd'y evenin', up yonway, by the Ohio River, I found a man shot through into his shanty-boat. He said he 'lowed to land along of the same eddy with a woman, an' she shot him almost daid!"

"Ho law!" the fisherman cried, and another man and three or four women drew near to hear the rest of the narrative. "How come hit?"

Rasba stood there talking to them, a speaker to an audience. He told of his floating down into the Mississippi, and of his surprise at finding the river so large, so without end. He said he kind of wanted to ask the way of a shanty-boat, for a poor sinner must needs inquire of those he finds in the wilderness, and he heard a groan and a weak cry for help.

"I cyard for him, and he thanked me kindly; he said a woman had shot him when he was trying to be friendly; a pretty woman, young and alone. Co'rse, I washed his wound and I linimented it, and I cut the bullet out of his back; law me, but that man swore! Come night, an' he heard say I was a parson, he apologized because he cursed, and this mo'nin' he'd done lit out, yas, suh! Neveh no good-bye. Scairt, likely, hearin' me pray theh because I needed he'p, an' 'count of me being glad of the chanct to he'p any man in trouble."

"Sho! Who all mout that man be, Parson?"

"He said his name were Jest Prebol—"

"Ho law! Somebody done plugged Jest Prebol!" one of the women cried out, laughing. "That scoundrel's be'n layin' off to git shot this long time, an' so he's got hit. I bet he won't think he's so winnin' of purty women no more! He's bad, that man, gamblin' an' shootin' craps an' workin' the banks. Served him right, yes, indeedy. But he'd shore hate to know a parson hearn him cussin' an' swearin' around. Hit don't bring a gambler any luck, bein' heard swearin', no."

"Nor if any one else hears him; not if he thinks swearin' in hisn's heart!" Rasba shook his head gravely. "How come hit yo' know that man?"

"He's used down this riveh ten-fifteen years; besides, he married my sister what's Mrs. Dollis now. Hit were a long time ago, though, 'fore anybody knowed he wa'n't no good. I bet we hearn yo' was comin', Parson. Whiskey Williams said they was a Hallelujah Singer comin' down the Ohio—said he could hear him a mile. I bet yo' sing out loud sometimes?"

"Hit's so," Rasba admitted. "I sung right smart comin' down the Ohio. Seems like I jest wanted to sing, like birds in the posey time."

"Prebol shore should git to a doctor, shot up thataway. He didn't say which lady shot him, Parson?" a woman asked.

"No; jes' a lady into an eddy into a lonesome bend." Rasba shook his head. "A purty woman, livin' alone on this riveh. Do many do that?"

"Riveh ladies all do, sometimes. I tripped from Cairo to Vicksburg into a skift once," a tall, angular woman said. "My man that use to be had stoled the shanty-boat what I'd bought an' paid for with my own money. I went up the bank at Columbus Hickories, gettin' nuts; I come back, an' my boat was gone. Wa'n't I tearin' an' rearin'! Well, I hoofed hit down to Columbus, an' I bought me a skift, count of me always havin' some money saved up."

"I bet Vicksburg's a hundred mile!" Rasba mused.

"A hundred mile!" the woman said with a guffaw. "Hit's six hundred an' sixty-three miles from Cairo to Vicksburg, yes, indeed. A hundred mile! I made hit in ten days, stoppin' along. I ketched it theh."

"You found yo' man?"

"Shucks! Hit wa'n't the man I wanted, hit were my boat—a nice, reg'lar pine an' oak-frame boat. I bet me I chucked him ovehbo'd, an' towed back up to Memphis. Hit were a good $300 bo't, sports built, an' hits on the riveh yet—Dart Mitto's got hit, junkin'. You'll see him down by Arkansaw Old Mouth if yo's trippin' right down."

"I expect to," Rasba replied, doubtfully. Never in his life before had he talked in terms of hundreds of miles, cities, and far rivers,

"Yo'll know that boat; he's went an' painted hit a sickly yeller, like a railroad station. I hate yeller! Gimme a nice light blue or a right bright green."

"Hyar comes anotheh bo't!" one of the men remarked, and all turned to look up the chute, where a little cabin-boat had drifted into sight.

No one was on deck, and it was apparent that the Columbus banks had shunted the craft clear across the river and down the chute, just as Rasba himself had been carried. The shadow of the trees on the west side of the chute fell across the boat and immediately brought the tripper out of the cabin.

A shadow is a warning on wide rivers. It tells of the nearness of a bank, or towhead, or even of a steamboat. In mid-stream there is little need for apprehension, but when the current carries one down into a caving bend and close to overhanging trees or along the edges of short, boiling eddies, it is time to get out and look for snags and jeopardies.

Seeing the group of people on the sandbar, the journeyer, who was a woman, took the sweeps of her boat and began to work over to them.

"Hit handles nice, that bo't!" one of the fishermen said. "Pulls jes' like a skift. Wonder who that woman is?"

"I've seen her some'rs," the powerful, angular woman, Mrs. Cooke, said after a time. "Them's swell clothes she's got on. She's all alone, too, an' what a lady travels alone down yeah for I don't know. She's purty enough to have a husband, I bet, if she wants one."

"Looks like one of them Pittsburgh er Cincinnati women," Jim Caope declared.

"No." Mrs. Caope shook her head. "She's off'n the riveh. Leastwise, she handles that bo't reg'lar. I cayn't git to see her face, but I seen her some'rs, I bet. I can tell a man by hisns walk half a mile."

In surprise she stared at the boat as it came nearer, and then walked down to the edge of the bar to greet the newcomer.

"Why, I jes' knowed I'd seen yo' somers! How's yer maw?" she greeted. "Ho law! An' yo's come tripping down Ole Mississip'! I 'clare, now, I'd seen yo', an' I knowed hit, an' hyar yo' be, Nelia Crele. Did yo' git shut of that up-the-bank feller yo' married, Nelia?"

"I'm alone," the girl laughed, her gaze turning to look at the others, who stood watching.

"If yo' git a good man," Mrs. Caope philosophized, "hang on to him. Don't let him git away. But if yo' git somebody that's shif'less an' no 'count, chuck him ovehbo'd. That's what I b'lieve in. Well, I declare! Hand me that line an' I'll tie yo' to them stakes. Betteh throw the stern anchor over, fo' this yeah's a shallows, an' the riveh's eddyin', an' if hit don't go up hit'll go down, an'—"

"Theh's a head rise coming out the Ohio," someone said. "Yo' won't need no anchor over the stern!"

"Sho! I'm glad to see yo'!" Mrs. Caope cried, wrapping her arms around the young woman as she stepped down to the sand, and kissing her. "How is yo' maw?"

"Very well, indeed!" Nelia laughed, clinging to the big river woman's hand. "I'm so glad to find someone I know!"

"You'll know us all d'rectly. Hyar's my man, Mr. Caope—real nice feller, too, if I do say hit—an' hyar's Mrs. Dobstan an' her two darters, an' this is Mr. Falteau, who's French and married May, there, an' this feller—say, mister, what is yo' name?"

"Rasba, Elijah Rasba."

"Mr. Rasba, he's a parson, out'n the Tug Fork of the Big Sandy, comin' down. Miss Nelia Crele, suh. I disremember the name of that feller yo' married, Nelia."

"It doesn't matter," Nelia turned to the mountain man, her face flushing. "A preacher down this river?"

"I'm looking for a man," Rasba replied, gazing at her, "the son of a widow woman, and she's afraid for him. She's afraid he'll go wrong."

"And you came clear down here to look for him—a thousand, two thousand miles?" she continued, quickly.

"I had nothing else to do—but that!" he shook his head. "You see, missy, I'm a sinner myse'f!"

He turned and walked away with bowed head. They all watched him with quick comprehension and real sympathy.

CHAPTER XI

Jest Prebol, sore and sick with his bullet wound, but more alarmed on account of having sworn so much while a parson was dressing his injury, could not sleep, and as he thought it over he determined at last to cut loose and drop on down the river and land in somewhere among friends, or where he could find a doctor. But the practised hand of Rasba had apparently left little to do, and it was superstitious dread that worried Prebol.

So the river rat crept out on the sandbar, cast off the lines, and with a pole in one hand, succeeded in pushing out into the eddy where the shanty-boat drifted into the main current. Prebol, faint and weary with his exertions, fell upon his bunk. There in anguish, delirious at intervals, and weak with misery, he floated down reach, crossing, and bend, without light or signal. In olden days that would have been suicide. Now the river was deserted and no steamers passed him up or down. His cabin-boat, but a rectangular shade amidst the river shadows, drifted like a leaf or chip, with no sound except when a coiling jet from the bottom suckled around the corners or rippled along the sides.

The current carried him nearly six miles an hour, but two or three times his boat ran out of the channel and circled around in an eddy, and then dropped on down again. Morning found him in mid-stream, between two wooded banks, as wild as primeval wilderness, apparently. The sun, which rose in a white mist, struck through at last, and the soft light poured in first on one side then on the other as the boat swirled around. Once the squirrels barking in near-by trees awakened the man's dim consciousness, but a few minutes later he was in mid-stream, making a crossing where the river was miles wide.

He passed Hickman just before dawn, and toward noon he dropped by New Madrid, and the slumping of high, caving banks pounded in his ears down three miles of changing channel. Then the boat crossed to the other side and he lay there with eyes seared and staring. He discovered a grave stone poised upon the river bank, but he could not tell whether it was fancy or fact that the ominous thing bent toward him and fell with a splash into the river, while a wave tossed his boat on its way. He heard a quavering whine that grew louder until it became a shriek, and then fell away into silence, but his senses were slow in connecting it with one of the Tiptonville cotton gins. He heard a voice, curiously human, and having forgotten the old hay-burner river ferry, worried to think that he should imagine someone was driving a mule team on the Mississippi. For a long time he was in acute terror, because he thought he was blind, and could not see, but to his amazed relief he saw a river light and knew that another night had fallen upon him, so he went to sleep once more.

Voices awakened him. He opened his eyes, and the surroundings were familiar. He smelled iodine, and saw a man looking over a doctor's case. Leaning against the wall of the cabin-boat was a tall, slender young man with arms folded.

"How's he comin' Doc'?" the young man was saying.

"He'll be all right. How long has he been this way?"

"Don't know, Doc; he come down the riveh an' drifted into this eddy. I see his lips movin', so I jes' towed 'im in an' sent fo' yo'!"

"Just as well, for that wound sure needed dressing. I 'low a horse doctor fixed hit first time," the physician declared. "He'll need some care now, but he's comin' along."

"Oh, we'll look afteh him, Doc! Friend of ourn."

"I'll come in to-morrow. It's written down what to do, and about that medicine. You can read?"

"Howdy," Prebol muttered, feebly.

"He's a comin' back, Doc!" the young man cried, starting up with interest.

"Well, old sport, looks like you'd got mussed up some?" the doctor inquired.

"Yas, suh," Prebol grinned, feebly, his senses curiously clear. "Hit don't pay none to mind a lady's business fo' her, no suh!"

"A lady shot you, eh?"

"Yas, suh," Prebol grinned. "'Peahs like I be'n floatin' about two mile high like a flock o' ducks. Where all mout I be?"

"Little Prairie Bend."

"Into that bar eddy theh?"

"Yas, suh—the short eddy."

"Much obliged, Doc. Co'se I'll pay yo'—"

"Your friend's paid!"

"Yas, suh," Prebol whispered, sleepily, tired by the exertion and excitement.

"Sleep'll do him good," the doctor said, and returned to his little motorboat.

The young man went on board his own boat which was moored just below Prebol's. As he entered the cabin, a burly, whiskered man looked up and said:

"How's he coming, Slip?"

"Doc says he's all right. Jest said a woman shot him for tryin' to mind her business, kind-a laughed about hit."

"Theh! I always knowed a man that'd chase women the way he done'd git what's comin'. A woman'll make trouble quicker'n anything else on Gawd's earth, she will."

"Sho! Buck, yo's soured!"

"Hit's so 'bout them women!" Buck protested.

"If a man'd mind his business, an' not try to mind their business, women'd be plumb amusin'," Slip laughed.

"Wait'll yo've had experience," Buck retorted.

"Shucks! Ain't I had experience?"

"Eveh married?"

"No-o."

"Eveh have a lady sic' yo' onto some'n bigger'n yo' is?"

"No-o; reckon I pick my own people to scrap."

"Theh! That shows how much yo' don't know about women. Never had no woman yo' 'lowed to marry?"

"Huh! Catch me gittin' married—co'se not."

"Sonny, lemme tell yo'; hit ain't yo'll do the catchin', an' hit won't be yo' who'll be decidin' will yo' git married. An' hit won't be yo' who'll decide how long yo'll stay married, no, indeed."

"Peah's like yo' got an awful grouch ag'in women, Buck."

"Why shouldn't I have?" Buck started up from shuffling and throwing a book of cards. "Look't me. If Jest Prebol's shot most daid by a woman, look't me. Do you know me—where I come from, where the hell I'm goin'?

Yo' bet you don't. I've been shanty-boatin' fifteen years, but I ain't always been a shanty-boater, no, I haven't. Talk to me about women. When I think what I've took from one woman—Sho!"

He stared at the floor, his teeth clenched and his strong face set. Slip stared. His pal had disclosed a new phase of character.

Buck turned and glared into Slip's eyes.

"I'll tell you, Slip, you're helpless when it comes to women. They've played the game for ten thousand years, practised it every day, wearing down men's minds and men never knew it. Read history, as I've done. Study psychology, as I have. Go down into the fundamentals of human experience and human activities, and learn the lesson. Fifteen years I've been up and down these rivers, from Fort Benton to the Passes, from the foothills of the Rockies to the headwaters of Clinch and Holston in the Appalachians. Why? Because one woman sang her way into my heart, and because she tied my soul to her little finger, and when she found that I could not escape—when she had—when she had—What do you know about women?"

Slip stared at him. His pal, partner in river enterprises, an old river man, who talked little and who played the slickest games in the slickest way, had suddenly emerged like a turtle's head, and spoken in terms of science, education, breeding—regular quality folks' talk—under stress of an argument about women. And they had argued the subject before with jest and humour and without personal feeling.

Buck turned away, bent and shivering.

"I 'low I'll roast up them squirrels fo' dinner?" Slip suggested.

"They'll shore go good!" Buck assented. "I'll mux around some hot-bread, an' some gravy."

"I got to make some meat soup for that feller, too."

"Huh! Jest Prebol's one of them damned fools what tried to forget a woman among women," Buck sneered.

At intervals during the day Slip went over and gave Prebol his medicine, or fed him on squirrel meat broth; toward night they floated their 35-foot shanty-boat out into the eddy, and anchored it a hundred yards from the bank, where the sheriff of Lake County, Tennessee, no longer had jurisdiction. In the late evening Slip lighted a big carbide light and turned it toward the town on the opposite bank.

Pretty soon they heard the impatient dip of skiff oars, a river fisherman came aboard, and stood for a minute over the heater stove, warming his fingers. He soon went to the long, green-topped crap table in the end of the room, and Slip stood opposite, to throw bones against him. A tiny motorboat crossed a little later; and three men, two heavy set and one a slim youth, entered, to sit down at one of the little round tables and play a game.

One by one other patrons appeared, and soon there were fourteen or fifteen. Slip and Buck glided about among them quietly, their eyes alert, their hats drawn down over their eyes, taking a hand here, throwing bones there, poking up the coal fire, putting on coffee, making sandwiches, every moment on the *qui vive*, communicating with each other by jerks of the hand, lifting of shoulders, or the faintest of whisperings.

A jar against the side of the boat sent one or other of the two out to look, to greet a newcomer or to fend off a drift log. A low whistle from the stern took Buck through the aisle between the staterooms to the kitchen where a rat-eyed little man waited him on the stern deck,

"Lo, Buck! I'm drappin' down in a hurry; I learn yo' was heah. Theh's a feller drapping down out the Ohio; he's lookin' fo' a feller name of Jock Drones—didn't hear what for. Yo' know 'im?"

"Nope, but I'll pass the word around."

"S'long!"

"Jock Drones—huh!" Buck repeated, turning into the lamp-lit kitchen where Slip was sniffing the coffee pot.

"Friend of mine just stopped," Buck whispered. "There's a detective coming down out of the Ohio. Told me to pass the word around. He's after somebody by the name of Drones, Dock or Jock Drones."

Slip started, turned white, and his jaws parted. Buck's eyes opened a little wider.

"S'all right, Slip! Keep your money in your belt, to be ready to run or swim. It's a long river."

Slip could not trust himself to speak. Buck, patting him on the shoulder, went on into the card room and closed the kitchen door behind him, drawing the aisle curtains shut, too, so that no one would go back until Slip had recovered his equilibrium.

CHAPTER XII

Augustus Carline instinctively slowed down his motorboat and took to looking at the wide river, its quivering, palpitating surface; its vistas at which he had to "look twice to see the end," as the river man says with whimsical accuracy.

Negligent and thoughtless, he could now feel some things which had never occurred to him before: his loneliness, his doubts, his very helplessness and indecision. His wife had been like an island around which he sailed and cruised, sure in his consciousness that he could return at any time to that safe mooring. He had returned to find the island gone, himself adrift on a boundless ocean, and he did not know which way to turn. The cays and islets, the interesting rocks and the questionable coral reefs supplied him with not the slightest semblance of shelter, support, or safety.

He did not even know which side of the river to go to, nor where to begin his search. He was wistful for human companionship, but as he looked at the distant shanty-boats, and passed a river town or two, he found himself diffident and shamed.

He saw a woman in a blue mother-hubbard dress leaning against the cabin of her low, yellow shanty-boat, a cap a-rake on her head, one elbow resting on her palm, and in the other a long-stemmed Missouri meerschaum. Her face was as hard as a man's, her eyes were as blue and level as a deputy sheriff's in the Bad Lands, and her lips were straight and thin. How could a man ask her if she had seen his wife going down that way?

He stopped his motor and let his boat drift. He wondered what he could or would say when he overtook Nelia. There struck across his imagination the figure of a man, the Unknown who had, perhaps, promised her the care he had never given her, the affection which she had almost never had from him. Having won her, this Unknown would likely defy him down there in that awful openness and carelessness of the river.

He found a feeling of insignificance making its way into his mind. He had been vain of his looks, but what did looks amount to down there? He had been proud of his money, but what privilege did money give him on that flood? He had rejoiced in his popularity and the attention women paid him, but the indifferent gaze of that smoking Amazon chilled his self-satisfaction. He cringed as he seemed to see Nelia's pretty eyes glancing at him, her puzzled face as she apparently tried to remember where she had seen him. The river wilted the crumpling flower of his pride.

As his boat turned like a compass needle in the surface eddies he saw a speck far up stream. He brought out his binoculars and looked at it, thinking that it was some toy boat, but to his astonishment it turned out to be a man in a skiff.

It occurred to Carline that he wished he could talk to someone, to any one, about anything He had no resources of his own to draw on. He had always been obliged to be with people, talk to people, enjoy people; the silences of his wife's tongue had been more difficult for him to bear than her edged words. The skiff traveller, leisurely floating in that block of river, drew him irresistibly. He kicked over the flywheel and steered up stream, but only enough partly to overcome the speed of the current. The sensation of being carried down in spite of the motor power, complicated with the rapid approach of the stranger in his skiff, was novel and amusing. When he stopped the motor, the rowboat was within a hundred feet of him, and the two men regarded each other with interest and caution.

The traveller was unusual, in a way. On his lap was a portable typewriter, in the stern of the boat a bundle of brown canvas; a brass oil stove was on the bottom at the man's feet; behind him in the bow were a number of tins, cans, and boxes.

Neither spoke for some time, and then Carline hailed:

"Nice, pretty day on the river!"

"Fine!" the other replied. "Out the Ohio?"

"No—well, yes—I started at Evansville, where I bought this boat, but I live up the Mississippi, at Kaskaskia—Gage, they call it now."

"Yes? I stopped at Menard's on my way down from St Louis."

"When was that?"

"About ten days ago—tell you in a minute—Monday a week!" A big quarto loose-leaf notebook had revealed the day and date.

"Well, say—I—?" Carline's one question leaped to his lips but remained unasked. For the minute he could not ask it. The thing that had been his rage, and then his wonder, suddenly drew back into his heart as a secret sorrow.

"Won't you come over?" Carline asked, "it'd be company!"

"Yes, it'll be company," the other admitted, and with a pull of his oars brought the skiff alongside. He climbed aboard, painter in hand, and making the light line fast to one of the cleats, sat down on the locker across from his host.

"My name's Carline."

"Mine's Lester Terabon; a newspaper let me come down the river to write stories about it; it's the biggest thing I ever saw!"

"It's an awful size!" Carline admitted, looking around over his shoulder, and Terabon watched the face.

"Are you a river man?" the visitor asked.

"No. My father was a big farmer, and he made some money when they put a railroad through one of his places."

"Just tripping down to see the river?"

"No-o—well—" Carline hesitated, looking overside at the water.

"That must be Wolf Island over there?" the reporter suggested.

Carline looked at the island. He looked down the main river and over toward the chute toward which the Columbus bluffs had shunted them. Then he started the motor and steered into the main channel to escape the rippling shoals which flickered in the sunshine ahead of them, past an island sandbar.

"I don't know if it's Wolf Island." Carline shook his head. "I'm looking for somebody—somebody who came down this way."

The traveller waited. He looked across the current to the bluffs now passing up stream, Columbus and all.

"I don't suppose you find very much to write about, coming down?" Carline changed his mind.

For answer Terabon drew his skiff alongside and reached for his typewriter. As he began to write, he said: "I write everything down—big or little. A man can't remember everything, you know."

"Make good money writing for the newspapers?"

"Enough to live on," Terabon replied, "and, of course, it's living, coming down Old Mississip'!"

"You like it travelling in that skiff? Where do you sleep?"

"I stretch that canvas between the gunwales in those staples; I put those hoops up, and draw a canvas over the whole length of the boat. I can sleep like a baby in its cradle."

"Well, that's one way," Carline replied, doubtfully. "If I owned this old river, you could buy it for two cents."

Terabon laughed, and after a minute Carline joined in, but he had told the truth. He hated the river, and he was cowed by it; yet he could not escape its clutches.

"I fancy it hasn't always treated you right," Terabon remarked.

"Treated me right!" Carline doubled his fists and stiffened where he sat. "It's!—it's—"

He could not speak for his emotion, but his little pointed chin trembled a minute later as he relaxed and looked over his shoulder again. The typewriter clicked along for minutes, Terabon's fingers dancing over the keys as he put down, word for word, and motion for motion, the man who was afraid of the river and yet was tripping down it. It seemed as though the man afraid must have some kind of courage, too, because he was going in spite of his fears.

"It's passing noon, and I think I'll get something to eat," Terabon suggested; "I'll get up my—"

"I forgot to eat!" Carline said. "I've got everything, and that knob there is a three-burner oil stove. We'll eat on board. Never mind your stuff, I've got so much it'll spoil—but I ain't much of a cook!"

"I'm the original cook the Cæsars wanted to buy for gold!" Terabon boasted. "I got some squirrels, there, I killed up on Buffalo Island, and we'll fry them."

Nor did he fail to make his boast good, for he soon had hot-bread, gravy browned in the pan, boiled sweet potatoes, and canned corn ready for the table. When they sat down to eat, Carline confessed that he hadn't had a real meal for a week except one he ate in a Cairo restaurant.

"I could have got a kind of a meal," he admitted, "but you see I was worried a good deal. Did you stop at Stillhouse Island?"

"Where's that?"

"Just above Gage, kind of across from St. Genevieve."

"Let's see—oh, yes. There was an old fellow there, what's his name? He told me if I happened to see his daughter I should tell her to write him, for her mother wanted to hear."

"He said that! And you—it was Crele, Darien Crele said that?"

"That's the name—Nelia, his daughter."

"Yes, sir. I know. I guess I know! She's my wife—she was—It's her—"

"You're looking for?"

"Yes, sir; she ran away and left me. She came down here."

"Kind of a careless girl, I imagine?"

"Careless! God, no! The finest woman you ever saw. It was me—I was to blame. I never knew, I never knew!"

For a minute he held up his arms, looking tensely at the sky, struggling to overcome the emotion that long had been boiling up in his heart, rending the self-complacency of his mind. Then he broke down—broke down abjectly, and fell upon the cabin floor, crying aloud in his agony, while the newspaper man sitting there whispered to himself:

"Poor devil, here's a story! He's sure getting his. I don't want to forget this; got to put this down. Poor devil!"

CHAPTER XIII

"And he says he's a sinner himself," Nelia repeated, when she returned on board her cabin-boat in the sheltering safety of Wolf Island chute, with Mamie Caope, Parson Rasba, and the other shanty-boaters within a stone's toss of her.

Till she was among them, among friends she trusted, she had not noticed the incessant strain which she endured down those long, grim river miles. Now she could give way, in the privacy of her boat, to feminine tears and bitterness. Courage she had in plenty, but she had more sensitiveness than courage. She was not yet tuned to the river harmonies.

Something in Rasba's words, or it was in his voice, or in the quick, full-flood of his glance, touched her senses.

"You see, missy, I'm a sinner myse'f!"

What had he meant? If he had meant that she, too, was a sinner, was that any of his business? Of course, being a parson—she shrugged her shoulders. Her thoughts ran swiftly back to her home that used-to-be. She laughed as she recalled the deprecatory little man who had preached in the church she had occasionally attended. She compared the trim, bird-like perspicuity and wing-flap gestures of Rev. Mr. Beeve with the slow, huge turn and stand-fast of Parson Rasba.

She was glad to escape the Mississippi down this little chute; she was glad to have a phrase to puzzle over instead of the ever-present problem of her own future and her own fate; she was glad that she had drifted in on Mrs. Mame Caope and Jim and Mr. Falteau and Mrs. Dobstan and Parson Rasba, instead of falling among those other kinds of people.

Mrs. Caope was an old acquaintance of her mother who had lived all her life on the rivers. She was a better boatman than most, and could pilot a stern-wheel whiskey boat or set hoop nets for fish.

"If I get a man, and he's mean," Mrs. Caope had said often, "I shift him. I 'low a lady needs protection up the bank er down the riveh, but I 'low if my cookin' don't pay my board, an' if fish I take out'n my nets ain't my own, and the boat I live in ain't mine—well, I've drapped two men off'n the stern of my boat to prove hit!"

Mrs. Caope had not changed at all, not in the years Nelia could recall, except to change her name. It was the custom, to ask, perfectly respectfully, what name she might be having now, and Mrs. Mame never took offence, being good natured, and understanding how hard it was to keep track of her matrimonial adventures, episodes of sentiment but without any nonsense.

"Sho!" Mrs. Caope had said once, "I disremember if I couldn't stand him er he couldn't stand me!"

Nelia, adrift in her own life, and sure now that she never had really cared very much for Gus Carline, admitted to herself that her husband had been only a step up out of the poverty and misery of her parents' shack.

"You see, missy, I'm a sinner myse'f!"

Her ears had caught the depths of the pathos of his regret and sorrow, and she pitied him. At the same time her own thoughts were ominous, and her face, regular, bright, vivacious, showed a hardness which was alien to it.

Nelia went over to Mrs. Caope's for supper, and Parson Rasba was there, having brought in a wild goose which he had shot on Wolf Island while going about his meditations that afternoon. Mrs. Caope had the goose sizzling in the big oven of her coal range—coal from Pittsburgh barges wrecked along the river on bars—and the big supper was sweeter smelling than Rasba ever remembered having waited for.

Mrs. Caope told him to "ask one of them blessin's if yo' want, Parson!" and the four bowed their heads.

Jim Caope then fell upon the bird, neck, wings, and legs, and while he carved Mrs. Caope scooped out the dressing, piled up the fluffy biscuits, and handed around the soup tureen full of gravy. Then she chased the sauce with glass jars full of quivering jellies, reaching with one hand to take hot biscuits from the oven while she caught up the six-quart coffee pot with the other.

"I ain't got no patience with them women that don't feed their men!" she declared. "About all men want's a full stomach, anyhow, an' if you could only git one that wa'n't lazy, an' didn't drink, an' wasn't impedent, an' knowed anything, besides, you'd have something. Ain't that so, Nelia?"

"Oh, indeed yes," Nelia cried, from the fullness of her experience, which was far less than that of the hostess.

After they had eaten, they went from the kitchen into the sitting room, where Rasba turned to Nelia.

"You came down the river alone?" he asked.

"Yes," she admitted.

"I wonder you wouldn't be scairt up of it—nights, and those lonesome bends?"

"It's better than some other things." Nelia shook her head. "Besides, you've come alone down the Ohio yourself."

He looked at her, and Mrs. Caope chuckled.

"But—but you're a woman!" Rasba exclaimed.

"Suppose a mean man came aboard your boat, and—and tried to rob you," Nelia asked, level voiced, "what would you do?"

"Why, course, I'd—I'd likely stop him."

"You'd throw him overboard?"

"Well—if hit were clost to the bank an' he could swim, I mout."

Nelia and the Caopes laughed aloud, and Rasba joined in the merriment. When the laughter had subsided, Rasba said:

"The reason I was asking, as I came by the River Forks I found a little red boat there with a man on the cabin floor shot through—"

"Dead?" Nelia gasped.

"No, just kind of pricked up a bit, into one shoulder. He said a lady shot him because he 'lowed to land into the same eddy with her."

"But—where—?" Nelia half-whispered. "Where did he go?"

"Hit were Jest Prebol," Mrs. Caope said. "You was tellin' of him, Parson."

"Hit were Prebol," Rasba nodded, "an' he shore needed shooting!"

"Yas, suh. That kind has to be shot some to make 'em behave theirselves," Mrs Caope exclaimed, sharply. "If it wa'n't fer ladies shootin' men onct in awhile, down Old Mississip', why, ladies couldn't git to live here a-tall!"

"And women, sometimes, don't do men any good," Rasba mused, aloud, "I've wondered right smart about hit. You see, a parson circuit rides around, an' he sees a sight more'n he tells. Lawse, he shore do!"

The two women glared at him, but he was studying his huge hands, first the backs and then the calloused palms. He was really wondering, so the two women glanced at each other, laughing. The idea that probably some men needed protection from women could not help but amuse while it exasperated them.

"Prebol said," Rasba continued, "hit were a pretty woman, young an' alone. 'How'd I know?' he asked. 'How'd I know she were a spit-fire an' mean, theh all alone into a lonesome bend? How'd I know?'"

"I 'low he shore found out," Mrs. Caope spoke up, tartly, and Nelia looked at her gratefully. "Hit takes a bullet to learn fellers like Jest Prebol—an' him thinkin' he's so smart an' such a lady killer. I bet he knows theh's some ladies that's men killers, too, now. Next time he meets a lady he'll wait to be invited 'fore he lands into the same eddy with her, even if hit's a three-mile eddy."

"Theh's Mrs. Minah," Jim Caope suggested.

"Mrs. Minah!" Mrs. Caope exclaimed. "Talk about riveh ladies—theh's one. She owns Mozart Bend. Seventeen mile of Mississippi River's her'n, an' nobody but knows hit, if not to start with, then by the end. She stands theh, at the breech of her rifle, and, ho law, cayn't she shoot! She's real respectable, too, cyarful an' 'cordin' to law. She's had seven husbands, four's daid an' two's divorced, an' one she's got yet, 'cordin' to the last I hearn say about it. I tell you, if a lady's got any self-respect, she'll git a divorce, an' she'll git married ag'in. That's what I say, with divorces reasonable, like they be, an' costin' on'y $17.50 to Mendova, or Memphis, er mos' anywheres."

"How long—how long does it take?" Nelia asked, eagerly.

"Why, hardly no time at all. You jes' go theh, an' the lawyer he takes all he wants to know, an' he says come ag'in, an' next day, er the next trip, why, theh's yo' papers, an' all for $17.50. Seems like they's got special reg'lations for us shanty-boaters."

"I'm glad to know about that," Nelia said. "I thought—I never knew much about—about divorces. I thought there was a lot of—of rigmarole and testimony and court business."

"Nope! I tell yo', some of them Mendova lawyers is slick an' 'commodatin'. Why, one time I was in an awful hurry, landin' in 'long of the upper ferry, an' I went up town, an' seen the lawyer, an' told him right how I was fixed. Les' see, that wa—um-m—Oh, I 'member now, Jasper Hill. I'd married him up the line, I disremember—anyhow, 'fore I'd drapped down to Cairo, I knowed he'd neveh do, nohow, so I left him up the bank between Columbus an' Hickman—law me, how he squawked! Down by Tiptonville, where I'd landed, they was a real nice feller, Mr. Dickman. Well, we kind of co'ted along down, one place an anotheh, an' he wanted to git married. I told how hit was, that I wasn't 'vorced, an' so on, but if he meant business, we'd drap into Mendova, which we done. He wanted to pay for the divorce, but I'm independent thataway. I think a lady ought to pay for her own 'vorces, so I done hit, an' I was divorced at 3 o'clock, married right next door into the Justice's, an' we drapped out an' down the riveh onto our honeymoon. Mr. Dickman was a real gentleman, but, somehow, he couldn't stand the riveh. It sort of give him the malary, an' he got to thinking about salmon fishin' so he went to the Columbia. We parted real good friends, but the Mississippi's good 'nough for me, yes, indeed. I kind of feel zif I knowed hit, an' hit's real homelike."

"It is lovely down here," Nelia remarked. "Everything is so kind of—kind of free and easy. But wasn't it dreadful—I mean the first time—the first divorce, Mamie?"

"Course, yes, course," Mrs. Caope admitted, slowly, with a frown, "I neveh will forget mine. I'd shifted my man, an' I was right down to cornmeal an' bacon. Then a real nice feller come along, Mr. Darlet. I had to take my choice between a divorce an' a new weddin' dress, an' I tell you hit were real solemocholy fer me decidin' between an' betwixt. You know how young gals are, settin' a lot by dresses an' how they look, an' so on. Young gals ain' got much but looks, anyhow. Time a lady gits experience, she don't set so much store by looks, an' she don't have to, nohow. Well, theh I was, with a nice man, an' if I didn't divorce that first scoundrel where'd I be? So I let the dress go, an' mebby you'll b'lieve hit, an' mebby yo' won't, but I had $18.97, an' I paid my $17.50 real reg'lar, an' I had jest what was left, $1.47, an' me ready to bust out crying, feelin' so mean about marryin' into an old walking skirt.

"I was all alone, an' I had a good notion to run down the back way, an' trip off down the riveh without no man, I felt so 'shamed. An' theh, right on the sidewalk, was a wad of bills, $99 to a penny. My lan'! I wropped my hand around hit, an' yo' should of seen Mr. Darlet when he seen me come walking down, new hat, new dress, new shoes, new silk stockings—the whole business new. I wa'n't such a bad-lookin' gal, afteh all. That taught me a lesson. I've always be'n real savin' sinct then, an' I ain't be'n ketched sinct with the choice to make of a 'vorce er a weddin' dress. No, indeed, not me!"

Parson Rasba looked at her, and Nelia, her eyes twinkling, looked at the Parson. Nelia could understand the feelings in all their minds. She had her own viewpoint, too, which was exceedingly different from those of the others. The strain of weeks of questioning, weeks of mental suffering, was relieved by the river woman's serious statement and Parson Rasba's look of bewilderment at the kaleidoscopic matrimonial adventuring. At the same time, his wonder and Mrs. Caope's unconscious statement stirred up in her thoughts a new questioning.

When Nelia returned on board her boat, and sat in its cabin, a freed woman, she very calmly reckoned up the advantages of Mrs. Caope's standards. Then seeing that it was after midnight, and that only the stars shone in that narrow, wooded chute, she felt she wanted to go out into the wide river again, to go where she was not shut in. She cast off her lines and noiselessly floated out and down the slow current.

She saw Parson Rasba's boat move out into the current behind her and drift along in the soft, autumn night. Her first thought was one of indignation, but when a little later they emerged into the broad river current and she felt the solitude of the interminable surface, her mood changed.

What the big, quizzical mountain parson had in mind she did not know. It was possible that he was a very bad man, indeed. She could not help but laugh under her breath at his bewilderment regarding Mrs. Caope, which she felt was a genuine expression of his real feelings. At the same time, whatever his motive in following her, whether it was to protect her—which she could almost believe—or to court her, which was not at all unlikely, or whether he had a baser design, she did not know, but she felt neither worry nor fear.

"I don't care," she shook her head, defiantly, "I like him!"

CHAPTER XIV

Carline recovered his equilibrium after a time. His nerves, long on the ragged edge, had given way, and he was ashamed of his display of emotion.

"Seems as though some things are about all a man can stand," he said to Terabon, the newspaper man. "You know how it is!"

"Oh, yes! I've had my troubles, too," Terabon admitted.

"It isn't fair!" Carline exclaimed. "Why can't a man enjoy himself and have a good time, and not—and not—"

"Have a headache the next day?" Terabon finished the sentence with a grave face.

"That's it. I'm not what you'd call a hard drinker; I like to take a cocktail, or a whiskey, the same as any man. I like to go out around and see folks, talk to 'em, dance—you know, have a good time!"

"Everybody does," Terabon admitted.

"And my wife, she wouldn't go around and she was—she was—"

"Jealous because you wanted to use your talents to entertain?"

"That's it, that's it. You understand! I'm a good fellow; I like to joke around and have a good time. Take a man that don't go around, and he's a dead one. It ain't as though she couldn't be a good sport—Lord! Why, I'd just found out she was the best sport that ever lived. I thought everything was all right. Next day she was gone—tricky as the devil! Why, she got me to sign up a lot of papers, got all my spare cash, stocks, bonds—everything handy. Oh, she's slick! Bright, too—bright's anybody. Why, she could talk about books, or flowers, or birds—about anything. I never took much interest in them."

"And brought up in that shack on Distiller's Island?"

"Stillhouse Island, yes, sir. What do you know about that?"

"A remarkable woman!"

"Yes, sir—I—I've got some photographs," and Carline turned to a writing desk built into the motorboat. He brought out fifteen or twenty photographs. Terabon looked at them eagerly. He could not associate the girl of the pictures with the island shack, with this weakling man, nor yet with the Mississippi River—at least not at that moment.

"She's beautiful," he exclaimed, sincerely.

"Yes, sir." Carline packed the pictures away.

He started the motor, straightened the boat out and steered into mid-stream, looking uncertainly from side to side.

"There's no telling," he said, "not about anything."

"On the river no one can tell much about anything!" Terabon assented.

"You're just coming down, I suppose, looking for hist'ries to write?"

"That's about it. I just sit in the skiff, there, and I write what I see, on the machine: A big sandbar, a flock of geese, a big oak tree just on the brink of the bank half the roots exposed and going to fall in a minute or a day—everything like that!"

"I bet some of these shanty-boaters could tell you histories," Carline said. "I tell you, some of them are bad. Why, they'd murder a man for ten dollars—those river pirates would."

"No doubt about it!"

"But they wouldn't talk, 'course. It must be awful hard to make up them stories in the magazines."

"Oh, if a man gets an idea, he can work it up into a story. It takes work, of course, and time."

"I don't see how anybody can do it." Carline shook his head. "There's a man up to Gage. He wants to write a book, but he ain't never been able to find anything to write about. You see, Gage ain't much but a little landing, you might say."

"Chester, and the big penitentiary is just below there, isn't it?"

"Oh, yes!"

"I'd think there might be at least one story for him to write there."

"Oh, he don't want to write about crooks; he wants to write about nice people, society people, and that kind, and big cities. He says it's awful hard to find anybody to write about."

"You've got to look to find heroes," Terabon admitted. "I came more than a thousand miles to see a shanty-boat."

"You di-i-d? Just to see a shanty-boat!" Carline stared at Terabon in amazement.

In spite of Terabon being such a queer duck he made a good companion. He was a good cook, for one thing, and when they landed in below Hickman Bend, he went ashore and killed three squirrels and two black ducks in the woods and marsh beyond the new levee.

When he returned, he found a skiff landed near by on the sandbar. Carline was talking to the man, who had just handed over a gallon jug. The man pulled away swiftly and disappeared down the chute. Carline explained:

"He's a whiskey pedlar; a man always needs to have whiskey on board; malaria is bad down here, and a fellow might catch cold. You see how it is if a man don't have some whiskey on board."

"I understand," Terabon admitted.

After supper Carline decided that there was a lot of night air around, and that a man couldn't take too many precautions against that deadly river miasma whose insidious menace so many people have ignored to their great cost. As for himself, Carline didn't propose to be taken bad when he had so universal a specific, to take or leave alone, just as he wanted.

Terabon, having put up the hoops of his skiff and stretched the canvas over them, retired to his own boat and spent two hours writing.

In the morning, when he stirred out, he found Carline lying in the engine pit, oblivious to the night air that had fallen upon him, protected as he was by his absorption of the sure preventive of night air getting him first. The jug was on the floor, and Terabon, after a little thought, poured out about two and a half quarts which he replaced with distilled water from the motorboat's drinking bottle. Then he dropped down the chute into the main river to resume his search for really interesting "histories."

The river had never been more glorious than that morning. The sun shone from a white, misty sky. It was warm, with the slight tang of autumn, and the yellow leaves were fluttering down; squirrels were barking, and a flock of geese, so high in the air that they sparkled, in the sunshine, were gossiping, and the music of their voices rained upon the river surface as upon a sounding board.

Terabon was approaching Donaldson's Point, Winchester Chute, Island No. 10, and New Madrid. An asterisk on his map showed that Slough Neck was interesting, and sure enough, he found a 60-foot boat just above Upper Slough Landing, anchored off the sandbar. This was a notorious whiskey boat, and just below it was a flight of steps up the steep bank. No plantation darky ever used those steps. He would rather scramble in the loose silt and risk his neck than climb that easy stairway—yes, indeed!

Terabon, drifting by, close at hand, gazed at the scene. From that craft Negroes had gone forth to commit crime; white men had gone out to do murder, and one of them had rolled down those steps, shot dead. On the other side of Slough Neck, just outside of Tiptonville, there was a tree on which seven men had been lynched.

He pulled across to the foot of Island No. 10 sandbar, to walk up over that historic ground, and to visit the remnants of Winchester Chute where General Grant had moored barges carrying huge mortars with which to drop shells into the Confederate works on Island No. 10.

He hailed a shanty-boat just below where he landed, and as the window opened and he saw someone within, he asked:

"Will you kindly watch my skiff? I'm going up over the island."

"Yes, glad to!"

"Thank you." He bowed, and went upon his exploration.

It was hard to believe that this sandbar, grown to switch willows which increased to poles six or seven inches in diameter, had once been a big island covered with stalwart trees, with earthworks, cannon, and desperate soldiers. Its serene quiet, undulating sands and casual weed-trees, showing the stain of floods that had filled the bark with sediment, proved the indifference of the river to fleeting human affairs—the trifling work of human hands had been washed away in a spring tide or two, and Island No. 10 was half way to the Gulf by this time.

Terabon returned to his skiff three or four hours later, and taking up his typewriter, began to write down what he had seen, elaborating the pencil notes which he had made. As he wrote he became conscious of an observer, and of the approach of someone who was diffident and curious—a familiar enough sensation of late.

He looked up, started, and reached for his hat. It was a woman, a young woman, with bright eyes, grace, dignity—and much curiosity.

"I didn't mean to disturb you," she apologized. "I was just wondering what on earth you could be doing!"

"Oh, I'm writing—making notes—"

"Yes. But—here!"

"I'm a newspaper writer," he made his familiar statement. "My name is Lester Terabon. I'm from New York. I came down here from St. Louis to see the Mississippi."

"You write for newspapers?" she repeated.

She came and sat down on the bow deck of his skiff, frankly curious and interested.

"My name's Nelia Crele," she smiled. "I'm a shanty-boater. That's my boat."

"I'm sure I'm glad to meet you," he bowed, "Mrs. Crele."

"You find lots to write about?"

"I can't write fast enough," he replied, enthusiastically, "I've been coming six weeks—from St. Louis. I've made more than 60,000 words in notes already, and the more I make the more I despair of getting it all down. Why, right here—New Madrid, Island 10, and—and—"

"And me?" she asked. "Did you stop at Gage?"

"At Stillhouse Island," he admitted, circumspectly. "Mr. Crele there said I should be sure and tell his daughter, if I happened to meet her, that her mother wanted her to be sure and write and let her know how she is getting along."

"Oh, I'll do that," she assured him. "I was just writing home when you landed in. Isn't it strange how everybody knows everybody down here, and how you keep meeting people you know—that you've heard about? You knew me when you saw me!"

"Yes—I'd seen your pictures."

"Mammy hadn't but one picture of me!" She stared at him.

"That's so," he thought, unused to such quick thought.

"Isn't it beautiful?" she asked him, looking around her. "Do you try to write all that, too—I mean this sandbar, and those willows, and that woods down there, and—the caving bank?"

"Everything," he admitted. "See?"

He handed her the page which he had just written. Holding it in one hand—there was hardly a breath of air stirring—she read it word for word.

"Yes, that's it!" She nodded her head. "How do you do it? I've just been reading—let me see, '... the best romance becomes dangerous if by its excitement it renders the ordinary course of life uninteresting, and—and–

–' I've forgotten the rest of it. Could anything make this life down here—anything written, I mean—seem uninteresting?"

He looked at her without answering. What was this she was saying? What was this shanty-boat woman, this runaway wife, talking about? He was dazed at being transported so suddenly from his observations to such reflections.

"That's right," he replied, inanely. "I remember reading that—somewhere!"

"You've read Ruskin?" she cried. "Really, have you?"

"Sesame and Lilies—there's where it was!"

"Oh, you know?" she exclaimed, looking at him. He caught the full flash of her delight, as well as surprise, at finding someone who had read what she quoted, and could place the phrase.

"The sun's bright," she continued. "Won't you come down on my boat in the shade? I've lots of books, and I'm hungry—I'm starving to talk to somebody about them!"

It was a pretty little boat, sweet and clean; the sitting room was draped with curtains along the walls, and there was a bookcase against the partition. She drew a rocking chair up for him, drew her own little sewing chair up before the shelves, and began to take out books.

He had but to sit there and show his sympathy with her excitement over those books. He could not help but remember where he had first heard her name, seen the depressed woman who was her mother. And the bent old hunter who was her father. It was useless for him to try to explain her.

Just that morning, too, he had left Nelia Crele's husband in an alcoholic stupor—a man almost incredibly stupid!

"I know you don't mind listening to me prattle!" she laughed, archly. "You're used to it. You're amused, too, and you're thinking what a story I will make, aren't you, now?"

"If—if a man could only write you!" he said, with such sincerity that she laughed aloud with glee.

"Oh, I've read books!" she declared. "I know—I've been miserable, and I've been unhappy, but I've turned to the books, and they've told me. They kept me alive—they kept me above those horrid little things which a woman—which I have. You've never been in jail, I suppose?"

"What—in jail? I've been there, but not a prisoner. To see prisoners."

"You couldn't know, then, the way prisoners feel. I know. I reckon most women know. But now I'm out of jail. I'm free."

He could not answer; her eyes flashed as they narrowed, and she fairly glared at him in the intensity of her declaration.

"Oh, you couldn't know," she laughed, "but that's the way I feel. I'm free! Isn't the river beautiful to-day? I'm like the river—"

"Which is kept between two banks?" he suggested.

"I was wrong," she shook her head. "I'm a bird—"

"I can well admit that," he laughed.

"Oh," she cried, in mock rebuke, "the idea!"

"It's your own—and a very brilliant one," he retorted, and they laughed together.

There was no resisting the gale of Nelia Crete's effervescent spirits. It was clear that she had burst through bonds of restraint that had imprisoned her soul for years. Terabon was too acute an observer to frighten the sensitive exhilaration. It would pass—he was only too sure of that. What would follow?

The sandbar was miles long, miles wide; six or seven miles of caving bend was visible below them, part of it over another sandbar that extended out into the river. There was not a boat, house, human being, or even fence in sight in any direction. Across the river there was a cotton field, but so far away it was that the stalks were but a purple haze under the afternoon sun.

"You think I'm queer?" she suddenly demanded.

"No, but I would be if—"

"If what?"

"If I didn't think you were the dandiest river tripper in the world," he exclaimed.

"You're a dear boy," she laughed. "You don't know how much good you've done me already. Now we'll get supper."

"I've two black ducks," he said. "I'll bet they'll make a good—"

"Roast," she took his word. "I'll show you I'm a dandy cook, too!"

CHAPTER XV

The Mississippi River brings people from the most distant places to close proximity; Pittsburg and even Salamanca meet Fort Benton and St. Paul at the Forks of the Ohio. On the other hand, with uncanny certainty, those most eager to meet are kept apart and thrown to the ends of the world.

Parson Rasba saw Nelia Crele's boat drift out into the current and drop down the Chute of Wolf Island, and impelled by solitude and imagination he followed her. She had awakened sensations in his heart which he had never before known, so he acted with primitive directness and moved out into the Mississippi.

The river carried him swiftly toward a town whose electric lights sparkled on a high bluff, Hickman, and he saw the cabin-boat of the young and venturesome woman clearly outlined between him and the town. For nearly an hour he was conscious of the assistance of the river in carrying him along at an even pace, permitting him to remain as guardian of the woman. He felt that she needed him, that he must help her, and there grew in his heart an emotion which strangely made him desire to sing and to shout.

He watched the cabin-boat drift down right into the pathway of reflections that fell from the lights on Hickman bluffs. His eyes were apparently fixed upon the boat, and he could not lose sight of it. The river carried him right into the same glare, and for a few minutes he looked up at the arcs, and shaded his eyes to get some view of the town whose sounds consisted of the mournful howling of a dog.

Rasba looked back at the town, and felt the awe which a sleeping village inspires in the thoughts of a passer-by. He thought perhaps he would never again see that town. He wondered if there was a lost soul there whose slumberings he could disturb and bring it to salvation. He looked down the river, and the next instant his boat was seized as by a strong hand and whirled around and around, and flung far from its course. He remembered the phenomenon at the Forks of the Ohio, and again at Columbus bluff's. With difficulty he found his bearings.

He looked around and saw to his surprise that he was drifting up stream. He looked about him in amazement. He searched the blackness of the river, and stared at the blinding lights of the town. He began to row with his sweeps, and look down stream whither had disappeared the cabin-boat whose occupant he had felt called upon to guard and protect.

That boat was gone. In the few minutes it had disappeared from his view. He surmised, at last, that he had been thrust into an eddy, for the current was carrying him up stream, and he rowed against it in vain. Only when he had floated hundreds of yards in the leisurely reverse current below the great bar of Island No. 6 and had drifted out into the main current again, almost under the Hickman lights once more, was he able in his ignorance to escape from the time-trap into which he had fallen.

Standing at his oars, and rowing down stream, he tried to overtake the young woman whose good looks, bright eyes, sympathetic understanding, and need of his spiritual tutoring had caught his mind and made it captive.

Dawn, following false dawn, saw him passing New Madrid, still rowing impatiently, his eyes staring down the wild current, past a graveyard poised ready to plunge on the left bank, and then down the baffling crossing at Point Pleasant and through the sunny breadths up to Tiptonville, half sunk in the river, only to fall away toward Little Cypress—and still no sight of the lost cabin-boat.

In mid-afternoon, weary and worn by sleeplessness and expectancy, he pulled his boat into the deadwater at the foot of an eddy and having thrown over his stone anchor, sadly entered his cabin and, without prayer, subsided into sleep.

If he dreamed he was not awakened to consciousness by his visions. He slept on in the deep weariness which followed the wakefulness that had continued through a night of undiminished anxiety into a day of doubt and increasing despair. It had not occurred to him, in his simplicity, that the young woman would escape from him. The shadow and the gloom next to the bank on either side had not suggested his passing by the object of his intention. His thought was that she must have gone right on down stream, though he might have divined from his own condition that she, too, long since must have been weary.

He awakened some time in the morning, after twelve hours or so of uninterrupted slumber. He turned out into the fascinating darkness of early morning on the Mississippi. A gust of chill wind swept down out of the sky, rippling the surface and roaring through the woods up the bank. The gust was followed by a raw calm and further blanketing of the few stars that penetrated the veil of mist.

He had in mind the further pursuit of Nelia, and hauling in his anchor he pulled out into mid-current and then by lamp-light prepared his breakfast. While he worked, he discovered that dawn was near, and at lengthening intervals he went out to look ahead, hoping to see the object of his pursuit. Perhaps he would have gone on down to New Orleans, only it is not written in Mississippi weather prophecies that the tenor of one's way shall be even.

He heard wind blowing, and felt his boat bobbing about inexplicably. He went out to look about him, and in the morning twilight he discovered that the whole aspect of the Mississippi had changed. With the invisible sunrise had come an awe-inspiring spectacle which excited in his mind forebodings and dismay.

First, there was the cold wind which penetrated his clothes and shrivelled the very meat of his bones. The river's surface, which he had come to regard as a shimmering, polished floor, was now rumpled and broken into lumpy waves, like mud on a road, and the waves broke into dull yellow foam caps. There was not a light gleam on the whole surface, and dark shadows seemed to crawl and twist about in the very substance of the heavy and turgid waters.

Rasba stared. Born and trained in mountains, where he remembered clear streams of pale, beautiful green, catching reflections of white clouds and clean foliage, with only occasional patches of sullen clay-bank wash, he refused to acknowledge the great tawny Mississippi at its best, as a relation of the streams he knew. Certainly this menacing dawn reminded him of nothing he had ever witnessed. Waves slapped against his boat, waves which did not conceal, but rather accentuated, the sullen and relentless rush of the vast body of the water. While the surface leaped and struggled, wind-racked, the deeps moved steadily on. Elijah saw that his boat was being driven into a river chute, and seizing his sweeps, he began to row toward a sandbar which promised shoal water and a landing.

He managed to strike the foot of the bar, and threw out his anchor rock. He let go enough line to let the boat swing, and went in to breakfast. While he was eating, he noticed that the table turned gray and that a yellowish tinge settled upon everything. When he went out to look around, he found that the air was full of a cloud that filled his eyes with dust, and that a little drift of sand had already formed on the deck of his boat, gritting under his feet. The cloud was so thick that he could hardly see the river shores; a gale was blowing, and a whole sandbar, miles long, was coming down upon him from the air. The sandbar, when he looked at it, seemed fairly to be running, like water.

Parson Rasba remembered the storms of biblical times, and better understood the wrath that was visited upon the Children of Israel.

He dwelt in that storm all that day. He shut the door to keep the sand out, but it spurted through the cracks. He could see the puffing gusts as they burst through the keyhole, and he could hear the heavier grains rattling upon the thin, painted boards of his roof. His clothes grayed, his hands gritted, his teeth crunched fine stone; he pondered upon the question of what sin he had committed to bring on him this ancient punishment.

For a long time his finite mind was without inspiration, without understanding, and then he choked with terror and regret. He had beguiled himself into believing that it was his duty to take care of Nelia Crele, the fair woman of the river. He had believed only too readily that his duty lay where his heart's desire had been most eager. He sat there in dumb horror at the sin which had blinded him.

"I come down yeah to find Jock Drones for his mother!" He reminded himself by speaking his mission aloud, adding, "And hyar I've be'n floating down looking for a woman, looking for a pretty woman!"

And because he could remember her shoes, the smooth leather over those exquisite ankles, Parson Rasba knew that his sin was mortal, and that no other son of man had ever strayed so far as he.

No wonder he was caught in a desert blizzard where no one had ever said there was a desert!

"Lord God," he cried out, "he'p this yeah po'r sinner! He'p! He'p!"

CHAPTER XVI

Jock, *alias* "Slip," Drones, was discovering how small the world really is. Like many another man, he had figured that no one would know him, no one could possibly find him, down the Mississippi River, more than a thousand miles from home. Having killed, or at least fought his man in a deadly feud war, he had escaped into the far places. His many months of isolation had given him confidence and taken the natural uneasiness of flight from his mind.

Now someone was coming down the Mississippi inquiring for Jock Drones! A detective, as relentless, as sure as a bullet in the heart, was coming. He might even then be lurking in the brush up the bank, waiting to get a sure drop. He might be dropping down that very night. He might step in among the players, unnoticed, unseen, and wait there for the moment of surprise and action.

Slip's mind ransacked the far places of which he had heard: Oklahoma, the Missouri River, California, the Mexican border, Texas. Far havens seemed safest, but against their lure he felt the balance of Buck's comradeship.

Caruthersville had a sporting crowd with money, lots of money. The people there were liberal spenders, and they liked a square game better than any other sport in the world. The boat was making good money, big money. The two partners had only to break even in their own play to make a big living out of the kitty in the poker tables, and there was always a big percentage in favour of the boat, because Buck and Slip understood each other so well. Slip's share often amounted to more in a week than he had earned in two years up there in the mountains felling trees, rafting them in eddies, and tripping them down painfully to the sawmills. These never did pay the price they were advertised to pay for timber, and one had to watch the sealers to see that they didn't short the measure in the under water and goose-egg good logs.

He remembered Jest Prebol, who was lying shot through in the boat alongside, and he went over to the boat, lighted the lamp, and sat down by the wounded man. Prebol was a little delirious, and Slip went over on his own boat, and called Buck out.

"We got a sick man on our hands," he whispered. "Ain't Doc Grell come oveh yet?"

"Come the last boat," Buck said, and called the doctor out.

"Say, Doc, that sick feller out here, will you look't him?"

Doctor Grell went over to the boat. He looked at the wounded man, and frowned as he took the limp wrist. He tried the temperature, too, and then shook his head.

"He's a sick man, Slip," he said. "Thought he was coming all right last night. Now—"

He looked at the wound, and gazed at the great, blue plate around the bullet hole.

"He's bad?" Slip said, in alarm. "Poison's workin', Doc?"

"Mighty bad!"

There was nothing for it. Doctor Grell's night of pleasure had turned into one of life-saving and effort. He sent Slip over to drag away one of the young men from his game, and they rigged up two square trunks and a waterproof tarpaulin into an operating table. Then, as Slip was faint and sick, the two drove him back to the gambling boat, while they, the graduate and the student, entered upon a gamble with a human life the stake.

Of that night's efforts, fighting the "poison" with the few sharp weapons at their command—later reinforced by a hasty trip across the river to get others—the two need never tell. While they worked, they could hear at intervals the shout of a winner in the other boat. In moments of perfect quiet they heard the quick rustling of shuffled cards; they heard the rattling of dice in hard, muffled boxes; they heard, at intervals, the rattling of stove lids and smelt the soft-coal smoke which blew down on them from the kitchen chimney. Slip, not forgetful of them, brought over pots of black coffee and inquired after the patient. He found the two men paler on each visit, and stripped down more and more, till they were merely in their sweaty undershirts.

Toward morning the wind began to blow; it began to grow cold. The noises on the neighbouring boat grew fainter in the low rumble of a stormy wind out of the northwest, and the shanty-boat lifted at intervals on a wave that rolled out of the main current and across the eddy, making their operating room even more unstable.

Under their onslaught the death which was taking hold of Jest Prebol was checked, and the river rat whose life had been forfeited for his sly crimes became the object of a doctor's sentiment and belief in his own training.

Long after midnight, when some few of the patrons of the games had already taken their departure, the doors opened oftener and oftener, letting the geometrical shaft of the yellow light flare out across the waters, and the grotesque shadows of those who departed stood out against the night and waters as the men shivered in the wind and bent to feel their way into the boats.

After dawn Doctor Grell and his assistant, peaked and white, limp with their tremendous effort, and shivering with exhaustion of mind and body, walked out of the little shanty-boat, up to the big one, sat down with Buck and Slip to breakfast, and then took their own course across the ruffled and tumble-surfaced river.

"I 'low he'll pull through," Doctor Grell admitted, almost reluctantly. "He's in bad shape, though, with the things the bullet carried into him, but we sure swabbed him out. How'd the game go to-night, boys?"

"Purty good." Buck shook his head. "Tammer sure had luck his way—won a seventy-dollar pot onct."

"I sure wanted to play," Grell shook his head, "but in my profession you aren't your own, and you cayn't quit."

"We owe you for it," Buck said. "He's our friend—"

"And he's ourn, too," Grell declared, "so we'll split the difference. I expect it was worth a hundred dollars what we two did to-night. That'll be fifty, boys, if it's all right."

"Yes, suh," Slip said, handing over five ten-dollar bills, and Grell handed two of them to his companion, who shook his head, saying:

"Nope, Doc! Ten only to-night. My first fee!"

"And you'll never have a more interesting case," Grell declared. "No, indeed! You'll see cases, come you go to college, but none more interesting, and if we've pulled him through, you'll never have better reason for satisfaction."

The two got into a little motorboat and went bounding and rocking in the wind and waves toward the town behind the levee on the far bank. The two gamblers watched the little boat rocking along till it was but a black fleck in the midst of the weltering brown waters.

"I don't reckon any one'll drap down to-day," Slip muttered, looking up the river.

"We'll keep our eyes open," Buck replied. "You needn't to worry, you're plumb worn out, Slip. Git to bed, now, an' I'll slick up around."

It was a cold, dry gale. From sharp gusts with near calms between the wind grew till it was a steady, driving storm that flattened against the shanty-boat sides, and whistled and roared through the trees up the bank. And instead of dying down at dusk, it increased so much that the big acetylene light was not hung out, and if any one came down to the opposite shore he saw that there would be no game that night.

Buck went in and sat down by the wounded man's bed, giving him the medicines Doctor Grell had left. For the attentions Prebol, in lucid intervals, showed wondering looks of gratitude, like an ugly dog which has been trapped and then set free. What he had suffered during the night even he could hardly recall in the enfeebled condition of his mind, but the spoonfuls of broth, the medicine that thrilled his body, the man's very companionship, lending strength, took away the feeling of despair which a man in the extremities of anguish and alone in the world finds hardest to resist.

Buck, sitting there, gazed at the wan countenance, studying it. Prebol had forgotten, but when Buck first arrived on the river, the pirate, a much younger man then, had carelessly and perhaps for display told the stranger and softpaw many things about the river which were useful. It occurred to Buck that he was now paying back a debt of gratitude.

Something boiled up in his thoughts, and he swore to himself that he owed nothing, that the world owed him, and he bridged the years of his disappointment and desolation back to the hour when he had stormed out of the life he had known, to come down the Mississippi to be a gambler. Prebol, in his lapses into delirium, called a woman's name, Sadie—always Sadie! And if he would have cursed that name in his consciousness, out of the depths of his soul it came with softness and gentleness of affection.

Buck wondered what Jest Prebol had done to Sadie that she had driven him down there, and he cursed with his own lips, while he stifled in the depths of his own soul another name. His years, his life, had been wasted, just as this man Prebol's life was wasted, just as Slip's life was being wasted. Buck gave himself over to the exquisite torture of memories and reflections. He wondered what had become of the woman for love of whom he had let go all holds and degenerated to this heartless occupation of common gambler?

True to Slip, he had watched the river for the stranger whose inquiries had been carried down in fair warning to all the river people—and Buck, suddenly conscious of his own part in that river system, laughed in surprise.

"Why," he said to himself, "humans are faithful to one another! It's what they live for, to be faithful to one another!"

It was an incredible, but undeniable theory. In spite of his own wilful disbelief in the faith of mankind, here he was sitting by one poor devil's bed while he kept his weather eye out upon the rough river in the interests of another—a murderer! He pondered on the question of whether any one kept faith with him. His mind cried out angrily, "No!" but on second thought, in spite of himself, he realized distinctly that he had let one person's faithlessness overcome his trust of all others.

No day on the Mississippi is longer than the cold, bleak monotone of a dry gale out of the north. There is an undertone to the voices which depresses the soul as the rank wind shrivels the body. On whistling wings great flocks of wild fowl come driving down before the wintry gales, or they turn back from the prospect of an early spring. Steamboats are driven into the refuge of landing or eddy, and if the power craft cannot stand the buffetings, much less are the exposed little houseboats, toys of current and breeze, able to escape the resistless blasts. So the wind possesses itself of the whole river breadth and living creatures are driven to shelter.

Prebol, shot through and conscious of the reward of his manner of living; Slip, a fugitive under the menace of a murderer's fate; and Buck, given over to melancholy, were but types on the lengths and tributaries of the indifferent flood.

Nothing happened, nothing could happen. The arrival of Slip from his restless bunk relieved Buck of his vigil, and he went to bed and slept into the dawn of another day—a day like the previous one, and fit to drive him up the bank, into the woods, and among the fallen branches of rotten trees seeking in physical activity to check the mourning and tauntings of a mind over which he found, as often before, that he had no control.

And yet, when the storm suddenly blew itself out with a light puff and a sudden flood of sunshine, just as the sun went down, Prebol's condition took a sudden turn for the better, Slip forgot his fears, and Buck burst into a gay little whistled tune, which he could never whistle except when he was absurdly and inexplicably merry.

CHAPTER XVII

Terabon's notebooks held tens of thousands of words describing the Mississippi River and the people he had met. He had drifted down long, lonely bends, and he had surprised a flock of wild geese under a little bluff on an island sandbar just above Kaskaskia, in the big cut-off there. Until this day the Mississippi had been growing more and more into his consciousness; not people, not industries, not corn, wheat, or cotton had become interesting and important, but the yellow flood itself.

His thought had been, when he left St. Louis, to stop in towns and gather those things which minds not of the newspaper profession lump under the term of "histories," but now, after his hundreds of miles of association with the river, his thought took but brief note of those trifling and inconspicuous appearances known as "river towns." He had passed by many places with hardly a glance, so entrancing had been the prospect of endless miles of earth-bound flood!—bound but wearing away its bonds.

Now, in one of the most picturesque of all the scenes he had witnessed, in the historic double bend above New Madrid, he found himself with a young and attractive woman. He realized that, in some way, the Mississippi River "spirit"—as he always quoted it in his calm and dispassionate remarks and dissertations and descriptions—had encompassed him about, and, without giving him any choice, had tied him down to what in all the societies he had ever known would have been called a "compromising position."

That morning he had left the husband of this pretty girl lying in a drunken stupor, and now in the late evening the fugitive wife was taking it for granted that he would dine with her on her boat—and he had himself entered upon a partnership with her for that meal which could not by any possibility be called prosaic or commonplace. He had a vivid recollection of having visited a girl back home—he thought the phrase with difficulty—and he remembered the word "chaperon" as from a foreign language, or at least from an obsolete and forgotten age.

His familiarity with newspaper work did not relieve him of a feeling of uncertainty. In fact, it emphasized the questionableness of the occasion. "I'll show you I'm a dandy cook," she had said, and while he followed her on board the boat, with the two big black ducks to help prepare, he wondered and remembered and, in spite of his life-long avoidance of all appearance of evil, submitted to this irresistible circumstance, wherever it might lead.

So he built the fire in her kitchen stove. She mixed up dressing and seasoned the birds, made biscuit batter for hot-bread, brought out stacks and stores of things to eat, or to eat with, and they set the table, ground the coffee, and got the oven hot for the roasting and baking.

One thing took the curse off their position: They had to have all the windows and doors wide open so that they seemed fairly to be cooking on an open sandbar at the edge of the river. Terabon took an inward satisfaction in that fact. It is not possible to feel exceedingly wicked or depraved when there is a mile-wide Mississippi on the one hand and a mile-wide sandbar on the other side, and the sun is shining calmly upon the bright and innocent waters.

As the ducks were young and tender, their cooking took but an hour, or a little more, and the interim was occupied in the countless things that must be done to prepare even a shanty-boat feast. He stirred some cranberry sauce, and she had to baste the ducks, get the flour stirred with water, and condensed cream for gravy, besides setting the table and raising the biscuits, to have them ready for the ducks. She must needs wonder if she'd forgotten the salt, and for ten minutes she was almost in a panic at the thought, while he watched her in breathless wonderment, and took covert glances up the Mississippi River, fearful of, and yet almost wishing to see, that pursuing motorboat come into view.

When at last the smoking viands were on the ample table and they sat with their knees under it, and he began to carve the ducks and dish out the unblessed meal, he glanced up stream through the cabin window on his right. He caught a glimpse of a window pane flashing miles distant in the light of the setting sun—the whiskey boat without doubt. He saw a flock of ducks coming like a great serpent just above the river surface, then a shadow lifted as out of the river, swept up the trees in the lost section of Kentucky opposite, and from spattering gold the scene turned to blue which rapidly became purple, darkening visibly.

Through the open doors and windows swept the chill of twilight, and while she lighted the big lamp he did her bidding and closed the doors and windows. Those shelves of books, classics and famous, time-tried fiction, leered at him from their racks. The gold of titles, the blues and reds and greens of covers fairly mocked him, and he saw himself struggling with the menace of sin; he saw an honourable career and carefully nurtured ambition fading from view, for did not all those master minds warn the young against evil?

But they talked over the ducks of what a pity it was that all towns could not engage themselves in thought the way Athens used to do, and they wondered to each other when the hurrying passion of greed and its varying phenomena would become reconciled to a modest competence and the simplicity which they, for example, were enjoying down the Mississippi.

When he looked up from his meat sometimes he caught her eyes looking at him. He recognized her superiority of experience and position; she made him feel like a boy, but a boy of whom she was really quite fond, or at least in whom she was interested. For that feeling he was grateful, though there was something in her smile which led him to doubt his own success in veiling or hiding the doubts or qualms which had, unbidden, risen in his thoughts at the equivocal nature of their position.

Having dined on the best meal he had had since leaving home, they talked a little while over the remains of the sumptuous repast. But their mood grew silent, and they kept up the conversation with difficulty.

"I think I'd better put up my canvas top," he blurted out, and she assented.

"And then you must come back and help me wash this awful pile of dishes," she added.

"Oh, of course!" he exclaimed.

"I'll help with the canvas," she said, and he dared not look at her.

By the light of his lantern they put up the canvas to protect the boat from dew. Then they looked around at the night; stars overhead, the strange haze from the countless grains of sand which wavered over the bar, and the river in the dark, running by.

They looked at the river together, and they felt its majesty, its power, its resistlessness.

"It's overwhelming," he whispered. "When you can't see it you hear it, or you feel it!"

"And it makes everything else seem so small, so unimportant, so perfectly negligible," she added, consciously, and then with vivacity: "I'll not make you wipe those dishes, after all. But you must take me for a walk up this sandbar!"

"Gladly," he laughed, "but I'll help with the dishes as well!"

She put on a jacket, pinned on a cap, and together, in merry mood, they romped up the sandbar. It was all sand; there was not a log of timber, not a drift barrel, not a stick of wood anywhere as far as they could see. But as they walked along every foot of the sandbar was different, wind-rifts, covering long, water-shaped reefs; or rising knolls, like hills, and long depressions which held shadows darker by far than the gloom of the night. They walked along, sometimes yards apart, sometimes side by side. They forgot Ruskin and Carlyle—they remembered Thoreau's "Cape Cod" and talked of the musical sands which they could hear now under their own feet. In the silence they heard river voices; murmurings and tones and rhythms and harmonies; and Terabon, who had accumulated a vast store of information from the shanty-boaters, told her some of the simple superstitions with which the river people beguile themselves and add to the interest and difficulties of their lives.

"An old river man can look at the river and tell when a headrise is coming," he told her. "He knows by the looks of the water when the river is due to fall again. When he dreams, he says he knows what is going to happen, and where to find buried treasure, and if there is going to be an earthquake or a bad storm."

"They get queer living alone!" she said, thoughtfully. "Lots of them used to stop in at our slough on Kaw River. I was afraid of them!"

"You afraid of anything!" he exclaimed. "Of any one!"

"Oh, that was a long time ago—ages ago!" She laughed, and then gave voice to that most tragic riverside thought. "But now—nothing at all matters now!"

She said it with an intonation which was almost relief and laughing, that Terabon, whose mind had grappled for years with one of Ruskin's most touching phrases, understood how it could be that the heart of a human being could become so used to sorrows that no misery could bring tears.

He knew in that very moment, as by revelation, that he had caught from her lips one of the bitterest phrases which the human mind is capable of forming. He was glad of the favour which fate had bestowed upon him, and he thrilled, while he regretted, that in that hour he could not forget that he was a seeker of facts, a gatherer of information.

To match her mood was beyond his own power. By a simple statement of fact she had given herself a place in his thought comparable to—he went at making ideas again, despite himself—comparable to one of those wonderful widows which are the delight, while they rend to tatters the ambitions of delvers into the mysteries of Olympian lore. This bright, pretty, vivacious young woman had suffered till she had arrived at a Helen's recklessness—nothing mattered!

There was a pause.

"I think you are in a fair way to become unforgetable in connection with the Mississippi River," he suggested, with even voice.

"What do you mean?" she demanded, quickly.

"Well, I'll tell you," with the semblance of perfect frankness. "I've been wondering which one of the Grecian goddesses you would have been if you had lived, say, in Homer's time."

"Which one of them I resemble?" she asked, amused.

"Exactly that," he declared.

"Oh, that's such a pretty compliment," she cried. "It fits so well into the things I've been thinking. The river grows and grows on me, and I feel as though I grew with it! You don't know—you could never know—you're a man—masculine! For the first time in my life I'm free—and—and I don't—I don't care a damn!"

"But the future!" he protested, feebly.

"That's it!" she retorted. "For a river goddess there is no future. It's all in the present for her, because she is eternal."

They had walked clear up to the southernmost tip of the sandbar point. They could hear someone, perhaps a chorus of voices, singing on the whiskey boat at the Upper Landing. They could see the light of the boat's windows. There they turned and started back down the sandbar, reaching the two boats moored side by side in the deadwater.

"Shall I help with those dishes to-night?" he asked.

"No, we'll do them in the morning," she replied without emphasis and as a matter of course, which left him unassisted in his obvious predicament.

"Well," he drawled, after a time, "it's about midnight. I must say a river goddess is—is beyond my most vivid dreams. I wonder—"

"What do you wonder?"

"If you'll let me kiss you good-night now?"

"Yes," she answered.

The stars twinkled as he put his arm around her and took the kiss which her lips gave—smiling.

"I'll help with those dishes in the morning," he said, helping her up the gang plank of her boat. "Good-night!"

"Good-night," she answered, and entered the cabin, the dim light of her turned-down lamp flashing across the sandbar and revealing his face for a moment. Then the door closed between them.

He went to his skiff, raised the cover, and crawled into his canvas hammock which was swung from both sides of his boat. Before going to sleep he looked under the canvas at the river, at the stars, at the dark cabin-boat forty feet distant in the eddy.

At the same moment he saw a face against a window pane in the cabin.

"What does it mean?" he asked himself, but there was no answer. The river, when asked, seldom answers. Just as he was about to go to sleep, he started up, wide awake.

For the first time on the river, he had forgotten to post up his notes. He felt that he had come that day, as never before, to the forks in the road—when he must choose between the present and the future. He lighted his lantern, sat up in his cot, and reached for his typewriter.

He wrote steadily, at full speed, for an hour. When he had those wonderful and fleeting thoughts and observations nailed down and safe, he again put out his lantern, and turned in once more.

Then he heard a light, gay laugh, clear and distinct-a river voice beyond question—full of raillery, and yet beneath the mocking note was something else which he could neither identify nor analyze, which he hoped was not scorn or mere derision, which he wished might be understanding and sympathy—till he thought of his making those notes.

Then he despised himself, which was really good for his soul. His conscience, instead of rejoicing, rebuked him as a cad. He swore under his breath.

CHAPTER XVIII

Augustus Carline was a long time recovering even his consciousness. A thousand dreams, a thousand nightmares tormented his thoughts while the mangling grip of unnumbered vises and ropes sank deep into his flesh; ploughs and harrows dragged through his twisted muscles.

Yet he did rise at last out of his pit and, leaning against the cabin of his boat, look about him to see what hell he had escaped into. The sun was shining somewhere, blinding his eyes, which were already seared. A river coiled by, every ripple a blistering white flame. He heard birds and other music which sounded like an anvil chorus performing in the narrow confines of a head as large as a cabin.

He remembered something. It was even worse than what he was undergoing, but he could not quite call the horror to the surface of the weltering sea of his feelings; he did not even know his name, nor his place, nor any detail except the present pain—and he didn't want to know. He fought against knowing, till the thing pressed exuberantly forward, and then he knew that the beautiful girl, the woman he loved and to whom he was married, had left him. That was the exquisite calamity of his soul, and he flinched from the fact as from a blow. He was always flinching, he remembered. He was always turning from the uncomfortable and the bothering to seek what was easy and unengaging. Now, for the moment, he could not undertake any relief from his present misery.

Acres and lakes of water were flowing by, but his thirst was worse than oceans could quench. He wanted to drink, but the thought of drinking disgusted him beyond measure. It seemed to him that a drop of water would flame up in his throat like gasolene on a bed of coals, and at that moment his eyes fell upon the jug which stood by the misty engine against the intangible locker. The jug was a monument of comfort and substantiality.

At the odour which filled the air when he had taken out the cork his very soul was filled with horror.

"But I got to drink it!" he whimpered. "It's the only thing that'll cure me, the only thing I can stand. If I don't I'll die!"

Not to drink was suicide, and to drink was living death! He could not choose between the suggestions; he never had been trained to face fate manfully. His years' long dissipation had unfitted him for every squarely made decision, and now with horror on one side and terror on the other, he could not procrastinate and wonder what folly had brought him to this state.

"Why couldn't it smell good!" he choked. "The taste'll kill me!"

Taste he must, or perish! The taste was all that he had anticipated, and melted iron could hardly have been more painful than that first torture of cold, fusil acid. Gulping it down, he was willing to congratulate himself on his endurance and wisdom, his very heroism in undertaking that deadly specific.

After it was over with, however, the raw chill, which the heat of the sun did not help, began to yield to a glow of warmth. He straightened his twisted muscles and after a hasty look around retreated into his cabin and flung himself on his bunk.

What length of time he spent in his recovery from the attacks of his enemy, or rather enemies of a misspent youth, he could not surmise. He did at last stir from his place and look with subdued melancholy into a world of woe. He recalled the visitor, the man who wrote for newspapers, and in a panic he searched for his money.

The money was gone; $250, at least, had disappeared from his pockets. An empty wallet on the cabin floor showed with what contemptuous calm the funds had been abstracted from his pockets. He turned, however, to a cunning little hiding place, and found there his main supply of currency—a thousand dollars or more.

No man likes to be robbed, and Carline, fixing upon his visitor Terabon as his assailant, worked himself into a fine frenzy of indignation. The fellow had purposely encouraged him to drink immoderately—Carline's memory was clear and unmistaken on that point—and then, taking advantage of his unconsciousness, the pseudo writer had committed piracy.

"I'd ought to be glad he didn't kill me!" Carline sneered to himself, looking around to conjure up the things that might have been.

The prospect was far from pleasing. The sky was dark, although it was clearly sometime near the middle of a day—what day, he could but guess. The wind was raw and penetrating, howling through the trees, and skipping down the chute with a quick rustling of low, breaking waves. The birds and animals which he had heard were gone with the sunshine.

When Carline took another look over his boat, he found that it had been looted of many things, including a good blanket, his shot gun and rifle, ammunition, and most of his food supply—though he could not recall that he had had much food on board.

He lighted the coal-oil heater to warm the cabin, for he was chilled to the bone. He threw the jug overboard, bound now never again to touch another drop of liquor as long as he lived—that is, unless he happened to want a drink.

Wearily he set about cleaning up his boat. He was naturally rather inclined to neatness and orderliness. He picked up, folded, swept out, and put into shape. He appeased his delicate appetite with odds and ends of things from a locker full of canned goods which had escaped the looter.

As long as he could, Carline had not engaged his thoughts with the subject of his runaway wife. Now, his mind clearing and his body numb, his soul took up the burden again, and he felt his helplessness thrice confounded. He did not mind anything now compared to the one fact that he had lost and deserved to lose the respect of the pretty girl who had become his wife. He took out the photographs which he had of her, and looked at them, one by one. What a fool he had been, and what a scoundrel he was!

He could not give over the pursuit, however; he felt that he must save her from herself; he must seek and rescue her. He hoisted in his anchor and starting the motor, turned into the chute and ran down before the wind into the river. Never had he seen the Mississippi in such a dark and repellent mood.

When he had cleared the partial shelter of Island No. 8, he felt the wind and current at the stern of his boat, driving it first one way then the other. Steering was difficult, and fear began to clutch at his heart. He felt his helplessness and the hopelessness of his search down that wide river with its hundred thousand hiding places. He knew nothing of the gossiping river people except that he despised them. He could not dream that his ignorance of things five or ten miles from his home was not typical of th shanty-boaters; he could not know that where he was a stranger in the ne township to his own home, a shanty-boater would know the landing pl of his friends a thousand miles or so down stream.

Without maps, without knowledge, without instinct, he might a' as well have been blind. His careless, ignorant glance swept the eight (miles of shoreline of sandbar from above Island No. 10 clear dow' fresh sloughing above Hotchkiss's Landing, opposite the dry Wi Chute—in which deep-draft gun-barges had been moored fifty y before. He did not even know it was Island No. 10, Donaldson'

didn't know that he was leaving Kentucky to skirt Tennessee; much less did he dream that he was passing Kentucky again. He looked at a shanty-boat moored at the foot of a mile-long sandbar; saw, without observing, a skiff against the bar just above the cabined scow. His gaze discovered smoke, houses, signs of settlement miles below, and he quickened the beat of his motor to get down there.

He longed for people, for humanity, for towns and cities; and that was a big sawmill and cotton-gin town ahead of him, silhouetted along the top of a high bank. He headed straight for it, and found his boat inexplicably slowed up and rebuffed. Strangers on the river always do find themselves baffled by the big New Madrid eddy, which even power boats engage with difficulty of management. He landed at last against a floating dock, and found that it was a fish market.

Having made fast, he went up town and spent hours, till long after dark, buying supplies, talking to people, getting the lonesomeness out of his system, and making veiled inquiries to learn if anything had been heard about a woman coming down the Mississippi. He succeeded in giving the impression that he was a detective. In the restaurant he talked with a cocky little bald-headed man all spruced up and dandyish.

"I'm from Pittsburgh," the man said. "My name's Doss, Ronald Doss; I'm a sportsman, but every winter I drop down here, hunting and fishing; sometimes on the river, sometimes back in the bottoms. I suppose, Mr. Carline, that you're a stranger on the river?"

"Why, yes-s, down this way; I live near it, up at Gage."

"I see, your first trip down. Got a nice gasolene boat, though!"

"Oh, yes! You're stopping here?"

"Just arrived this morning; trying to make up my mind whether I'll go over on St. Francis, turkey-and deer-hunting, or get a boat and drop down the Mississippi. Been wondering about that."

"Well, say, now—why can't you drop down with me?"

"Oh, I'd be in the way—"

"Not a bit—"

"Costs a lot to run a motorboat, and I'd have to—"

"No, you wouldn't! Not a cent! Your experience and my boat—"

"Well, of course, if you put it that way. If it'd be any accommodation to you to have an old river man—I mean I've always tripped the river, off and on, for sport."

"It'd be an education for me, a great help!"

"Yes, I expect it would be an education, if you don't know the river." Doss smiled.

They walked over to the river bank. An arc light cast its rays upon the end of the street, down the sloping bank, and in a light circle upon the rocking, muddy waters where the fish dock and several shanty-boats rested against the bank.

Doss whistled a little tune as he rested on his cane.

The front door of the third houseboat up the eddy opened and closed. A man climbed the bank and passed the two with a basket on his arm.

"Come on down," Carline urged.

"Not to-night," Doss said. "I've got my room up at the hotel, and I'll have to get my stuff out of the railroad baggage room. But I'll come down about 10 or 11 o'clock in the morning. Then we'll fit up and drop down the river. Good-night!"

Doss watched Carline go down to the dock and on to his boat. Then he went up the street and held earnest confab with a man who had a basket on his arm. They whispered ten minutes or so, then the man with the basket returned to his shanty-boat, and within half an hour was back up town, carrying two suitcases, a gun case, and a duffle bag.

Doss went to the smaller hotel with these things and registered. He walked down to the river in the morning and noticed that the third shanty-boat had dropped out into the river during the night, in spite of the storm that was blowing up. He went down and ate breakfast with Carline, and the two went up and got Doss's outfit at the hotel. They returned to the motorboat, and, having laid in a supply of groceries, cast off their lines and steered away down the river.

"Yes, sir, we'll find that girl if it takes all winter!" the fish-market man heard Doss tell Carline in a loud voice.

That afternoon a man in a skiff came down the river and turned into the dock. As he landed, the fish-market man said to him:

Yes.

"If you see any lady coming down, tell her a detector is below, lookin' fo' her. He's a cheap skate, into a motorboat—but I don't expect he'll be into hit long, 'count of some river fellers bein' with him. But he mout be bad, that detector. If you should see a nice lady, tell her."

"You bet!" the skiff man, who was Lester Terabon, exclaimed.

CHAPTER XIX

For long hours Parson Rasba endured the drifting sand and the biting wind which penetrated the weather-cracks in his poplar shanty-boat. It was not until near nightfall that it dawned on him that he need not remain there, that it was the simplest thing in the world to let go his hold and blow before the wind till he was clear of the sandblast.

He did haul in his anchor and float away. As he rode the waves and danced before the wind the clouds of sand were flung swiftly down upon the water, where the surface was covered with a film and a sheet of dust.

Standing at his sweeps, he saw that he was approaching the head of another sandbar, and as he felt the water shoaling under the boat he cast over the anchor and rode in clear air again. He was not quite without a sense of humour.

Shaking the dust out of his long hair and combing it out of his whiskers, he laughed at his ignorance and lack of resource. He swept the decks and floor of his cabin, and scooped the sand up with an ash shovel to throw overboard. A lesson learned on the Mississippi is part of the education of the future—if there is anything in the pupil's head to hold a memory of a fact or experience.

Even though he knew it was his own ignorance that had kept him a prisoner in that storm, Parson Rasba did not fail to realize that his ignorance had been sin, and that his punishment was due to his absorption in the fate of a pretty woman.

Certainly after such a sharp rebuke he could not fail to return to his original task, imposed upon him because of his fault in bringing the feud fighters of his home mountains together, untrained and unrepentant, to hear the voice of his pride declare the Word for the edification of sinners. Parson Rasba did not mince his words as he contemplated the joy he had felt in being eloquent and a "power" of a speaker from the pulpits of the mountain churches. The murdering by the feud fighters had taught him what he would never forget, and his frank acknowledgment of each rebuke gave him greater understanding.

While the gale lasted he watched the river and the sky. The wild fowl flying low, and dropping into woods behind him led to forays seeking game, and in a bayou a mile distant he drew down with deadly aim on one of a flock of geese. He killed that bird, and then as its startled and lumbering mates sought flight, he got two more of them, missing another shot or two in the excitement.

The three great birds made a load for him, and he returned to his boat with a heart lighter than he had known in many a day because it seemed to him a "sign" that he need not hate himself overmuch. The river consoled him, and its constancy and integrity were an example which he could not help but take to heart.

Gales might blow, fair weather might tempt, islands might interpose themselves in its way, banks and sandbars might stand against the flood, but come what might, the river poured on through its destined course like a human life.

He entertained the whimsical fancy, as his smallest goose was roasting, that perhaps the Mississippi might sin. In so many ways the river reminded him of humankind. He had stood beside a branch of the Mississippi which was so small and narrow that he could dam it with his ample foot, or scoop it up with a bucket—and yet here it was a mile wide! In its youth it was subject to the control of trifling things, a stone or a log, or the careless handiwork of a man. Down here all the little threads of its being had united in a full tide of life still subject to the influences of its normal course, but wearing and tearing along beyond any power to stop till its appointed course was run.

Insensibly Parson Rasba felt the resources of his own mind flocking to help him. Just being there beside that mighty torrent helped him to get a perspective on things. Tiny things seemed so useless in the front of that overwhelming power. What were the big things of his own life? What were the important affairs of his existence?

He could not tell. He had always meant to do the right thing. He could see now, looking back on his life, that his good intentions had not prevented his ignorance from precipitating a feud fight.

"I should have taken them, family by family, and brought them to their own knees fustest," he thought, grimly. "Then I could have helt 'em all together in mutual repentance!"

Having arrived at that idea, he shrugged his shoulders almost self-contemptuously. "I'm a learnin'. That's one consolation, I'm a learnin'!"

And then Rasba heard the Call!

It was Old Mississip's voice; the river was heaping duties upon him more and more. So far, he had been rather looking out for himself, now he recalled the houseboats which he had seen moored down the reaches and in the bends. Those river people, dropping down incessantly with the river current, must sometimes need help, comfort, and perhaps advice. His humility would not permit him to think that he could preach to them or exhort them.

"Man to man, likely I could he'p some po'r sinner see as much as I can see. If I could kind of get 'em to see what this big, old riveh is like! Hit's carryin' a leaf er a duck, an' steamboats an' shanty-bo'ts; hit carries the livin' an' hit carries the daid; hit begrudges no man it's he'p if he comes to it to float down a log raft er a million bushels of coal. If Ole Mississip'll do that fo' anybody, suttin'ly hit's clear an' plain that God won't deny a sinner His he'p! Yas, suh! Now I've shore found a handle to keep hold of my religion!"

Peace of mind had come to him, but not the peace of indolence and neglect. Far from that! He saw years of endless endeavour opening before him, but not with multitudes looking up to him as he stood, grand and noble, in the bright light of a thousand pulpits, circuit riding the earth. Instead, he would go to a sinning man here, a sorrowing woman there, and perhaps sit down with a little child, to give it comfort and instruction.

People were too scattered down the Mississippi to think of congregations. All days were Sunday, and for him there could be no day of rest. If he could not do big work, at least he could meet men and women, and he could get to know little children, to understand their needs. He knew it was a good thought, and when he looked across the Mississippi, he saw night coming on, but between him and the dark was sunset.

The cold white glare changed to brilliant colours; clouds whose gray-blue had oppressed the soul of the mountain man flashed red and purple, growing thinner and thinner, and when he had gazed for a minute at the glow of a fixed government light he was astonished by the darkness of night—only the night was filled with stars.

Thus the river, the weather, the climate, the sky, the sandbars, and the wooded banks revealed themselves in changing moods and varying lights to the mountain man whose life had always been pent in and narrowed, without viewpoint or a sense of the future. The monster size of the river dwarfed the little affairs of his own life and humbled the pride which had so often been humbled before. At last he began to look down on himself, seeing something of the true relation of his importance to the immeasurable efforts of thousands and millions of men.

The sand clouds carried by the north wind must ever remain an epoch in his experience. Definitely he was rid of a great deal of nonsense, ignorance, and pride; at the same time it seemed, somehow, to have grounded him on something much firmer and broader than the vanities of his youth.

His eyes searched the river in the dark for some place to begin his work, and as they did so, he discovered a bright, glaring light a few miles below him across the sandbar at the head of which he had anchored. He saw other lights down that way, a regular settlement of lights across the river, and several darting firefly gleams in the middle of the stream which he recognized were boats, probably small gasolene craft.

In forty minutes he was dipping his sweep blades to work his way into the eddy where several small passenger craft were on line-ends from a large, substantial craft which was brightly lighted by lanterns and a big carbide light. Its windows were aglow with cheeriness, and the occupants engaged in strange pastimes.

"Come, now, come on, now!" someone was crying in a sing-song. "Come along like I said! Come along, now—Seven—Seven—Seven!"

Parson Rasba's oar pins needed wetting, for the strain he put on the sweeps made them squeak. The splash of oars down the current was heard by people on board and several walked out on the deck.

"Whoe-e-e!" one hailed. "Who all mout yo' be?"

"Rasba!" the newcomer replied. "Parson Elijah Rasba, suh. Out of the Ohio!"

"Hi-i-i!" a listener cried out, gleefully, "hyar comes the Riveh Prophet after yo sinners. Hi-i i!"

There was a laugh through the crowd. Others strolled out to see the phenomenon. A man who had been playing with fortune at one of the poker tables swore aloud.

"I cayn't neveh git started, I don't shift down on my luck!" he whined. "Las' time, jes' when I was coming home, I see a piebald mewl, an' now hyar comes a parson. Dad drat this yeah ole riveh! I'm goin' to quit. I'm gwine to go to Hot Springs!"

These casual asides were as nothing, however, to the tumult that stirred in the soul of Jock Drones, who had been cutting bread to make boiled-ham sandwiches for their patrons that night. His acute hearing had picked up the sound of the coming shanty-boat, and he had felt the menace of a stranger dropping in after dark. Few men not on mischief bent, or determined to run all night, run into shanty-boat eddies.

He even turned down the light a little, and looked toward the door to see if the way was clear. The hail relieved the tension of his mind strain, but only for a minute. Then he heard that answer.

"Rasba!" he heard. "Parson Elijah Rasba, suh. Out of the Ohio!"

In a flash he knew the truth! Old Rasba, whose preaching he had listened to that bloody night away up in the mountains, had come down the rivers. A parson, none else, was camping on the mountain fugitive's trail. That meant tribulation, that meant the inescapableness of sin's punishment—not in jails, not in trial courts, not on the gallows, but worse than that!

"Come abo'd, Parson!" someone shouted, and the boats bumped. There was a scramble to make a line fast, and then the trampling of many feet, as the Prophet was introduced to that particular river hell, amid stifled cries of expectancy and murmurs of warning. Next to being raided by the sheriff of an adjacent county, having a river prophet come on board is the greatest excitement and the smartest amusement of the bravados down the river.

"Hyar's the Prophet!" a voice shouted. "Now git ready fo' yo' eternal damnation. See 'im gather hisse'f!"

Rasba gathering himself! Jock could not help but take a peep. It was Rasba, gaunt, tall, his head up close to the shanty-boat roof and his shoulders nearly a head higher than the collars of most of those men who stood by with insolence and doubtful good humour.

"Which'd yo' rather git to play, Parson?" someone asked, slyly. "Cyards er bones er pull-sticks?"

"I've a friend down yeah, gentlemen." The Prophet ignored the insult. "His mother wants him. She's afeared likely he mout forget, since he was jes' a boy friendly and needing friends. He's no runt, no triflin' no-'count, puppy man, like this thing," in the direction whence the invitation had come, "but tall an' square, an' honourable, near six foot, an' likely 160 pounds. Not like this little runt thing yeah, but a real man!"

There was a yell of approval and delight.

"Who all mout yo' friend be?" Buck asked, respectfully, seeing that this was not a raid, but a visit.

"Jock, suh, Jock Drones, his mammy wants him, suh!"

Buck eyed the visitor keenly for a minute. Someone said they never had heard of him. Buck, who saw that the visitor was in mind to turn back, suggested:

"Won't yo' have a cup of coffee, suh? Hit's raw outside to-night, fresh and mean. Give him a chair, boys! I'm friendly with any man who takes a message from a mother to her wandering son."

A dozen chairs were snatched out to the stove, and when Parson Rasba had accepted one, Buck stepped into the kitchen. He found Slip, *alias* Jock Drones, standing with beads of sweat on his forehead. No need to ask the first question; Buck poured out a cup of coffee and said:

"What'll I tell him, Slip?"

"I cayn't go back, Buck!" Slip whimpered. "Hit's a hanging crime!"

"Something may have changed," Buck suggested.

"No, suh, I've heard. Hit were my bullet—I've heard. Hit's a trial, an' hit's—hit's hanging!"

"Sh-h! Not so loud!" Buck warned. "If it's lawyer money you need?"

"I got 'leven hundred, an' a trial lawyer'll cost only a thousand, Buck! Yo's a friend—Lawse! I'd shore like to talk to him. He's no detector, Parson Rasba yain't. Why, he's be'n right into a stillhouse, drunk the moonshine—an' no revenue hearn of hit, the way some feared. My sister wrote me. I want to talk to him, Buck, but—but not let them outside know."

"I'll fix it," Buck promised, carrying out steaming coffee, a plate of sandwiches, and two big oranges for the parson.

He returned, filled up the trays for the others, and took them out. Soon the crowd were sitting around, or leaning against the heavy crap table, talking and listening.

"Yo' come way down from the mountangs to find a mammy's boy?" someone asked, his tone showing better than his words how well he understood the sacrifice of that journey.

"Hit's seo," Rasba nodded. "I'm partly to blame, myse'f, for his coming down. I was a mountain preacher, exhorter, and I 'lowed I knowed hit all.

One candlelight I had a congregation an' I hit 'er up loud that night, an' I 'lowed I'd done right smart with those people's souls. But—but hit were no such thing. This boy, Jock, he runned away that night, 'count of my foolishness, an' we know he's down thisaway; if I could git to find him, his mammy'd shore be comforted. She's a heap more faith in me'n I have, but I come down yeah. Likely I couldn't do much for that boy, but I kin show I'd like to."

"Trippin' a thousand miles shows some intrust!" somebody said.

"I lived all my life up theh in the mountangs, an' hit's God's country, gem'men! This yeah—" he glanced around him till his glance fell upon the card cabinet on the wall between two windows, full of decks of cards and packets of dice and shaker boxes—"this yeah, sho! Hit ain't God's country, gem'men! Hit's shore the Devil's, an' he's shore ketched a right smart haul to-night! But I live yeah now!"

Buck, who had been coming and going, had stopped at the parson's voice. He did not laugh, he did not even smile. The point was not missed, however. Far from it! He went out, bowed by the truth of it, and in the kitchen he looked at Slip, who was sitting in black and silent consideration of that cry, carried far in the echoes.

"You're one of us, Parson!" a voice exclaimed in disbelief.

"Yas, suh," Rasba smiled as he looked into the man's eyes, "I'm one of you. I 'low we uns'll git thar together, 'cordin' as we die. Look! This gem'men gives me bread an' meat; he quenches my thirst, too. An' I take hit out'n his hands. 'Peahs like he owns this boat!"

"Yas, suh," someone affirmed.

"Then I shall not shake hit's dust off my feet when I go," Rasba declared, sharply. Buck stared; Rasba did not look at even his shoes; Buck caught his breath. Whatever Rasba meant, whatever the other listeners understood, Buck felt and broke beneath those statements which brought to him things that he never had known before.

"He'll not shake the dust of this gambling dive from his feet!" Buck choked under his breath. "And this is how far down I've got!"

Rasba, conscious only of his own shortcomings, had no idea that he had fired shot after shot, let alone landed shell after shell. He knew only that the men sat in respectful, drawn-faced silence. He wondered if they were not sorry for him, a preacher, who had fallen so far from his circuit riding and feastings and meetings in churches. It did not occur to him that these men knew they were wicked, and that they were suffering from his unintentional but overwhelming rebuke.

They turned away impatiently, and went in their boats to the village landing across the river; a night's sport spoiled for them by the coming of a luck-breaking parson. Others waited to hear more of what they knew they needed, partly in amusement, partly in curiosity, and partly because they liked the whiskery fellow who was so interesting. At the same time, what he said was stinging however inoffensive.

"Game's closed for the night!" Buck announced, and the gamesters took their departure. They made no protest, for it was not feasible to continue gambling when everyone knows a parson brings bad luck to a player.

The outside lights were extinguished, and Buck brought Slip from the kitchen inside to Rasba.

"This is Slip," Buck explained, and the two shook hands, the fugitive staring anxiously at the other's face, expecting recognition.

"Don't yo' know me, Parson?" Slip exclaimed. "Jock Drones. Don't yo' know me?"

"Jock Drones?" Rasba cried, staring. "Why, Sho! Hit is! Lawse—an' I found yo' right yeah—thisaway!"

"Yassuh," Jock turned away under that bright gaze, "but I'm goin' back, Parson! I'm goin' back to stand trial, suh! I neveh knowed any man, not a blood relation would think so much of me, as to come way down yeah to tell me my mammy, my good ole mammy, wanted me to be safe—"

"An' good, Jock!" Rasba cried.

"An' good, suh," the young man added, obediently.

"I'd better go over and see our sick man," Buck turned to Slip.

"A sick man?" Rasba asked. "Where mout he be?"

"In that other shanty-boat, that little boat," Slip exclaimed. "We'll all go!"

When they entered the little boat, which sagged under their combined weights, Slip held the light so it would shine on the cot.

"Sho!" Rasba exclaimed. "Hyar's my friend who got shot by a lady!"

"Yes, suh, Parson!" Prebol grinned, feebly. "Seems like I cayn't get shut of yo' nohow, but I'm shore glad to see yo'. These yeah boys have took cyar of me great. Same's you done, Parson, but I wa'nt your kind, swearin' around, so I pulled out. Yo' cayn't he'p me much, but likely—likely theh's some yo' kin."

"I'd shore like to find them," Rasba declared, smoothing the man's pillow. "But there's not so many I can he'p. Yo' boys are tired; I'll give him his medicine till to'd mornin'. Yo'd jes' soon, Prebol?"

"Hit'd be friendly," Prebol admitted. "Yo' needn't to sit right yeah—"

"I 'low I shall," Rasba nodded. "I got some readin' to do. I'll git my book, an' come back an' set yeah!"

He brought his Bible, and looking up to bid the two good-night, he smiled.

"Hit's considerable wrestle, readin' this yeah Book! I neveh did git to understand hit, but likely I can git to know some more now. I've had right smart of experiences, lately, to he'p me git to know."

CHAPTER XX

Terabon possessed a newspaper man's feeling of aloofness and detachment. When he went afloat on the Mississippi at St. Louis he had no intention of becoming a part of the river phenomena, and it did not occur to his mind that his position might become that of a participator rather than an observer.

The great river was interesting. It had come to his attention several years before, when he read Parkman's "La Salle," and a little later he had read almost a column account of a flood down the Mississippi. The A. P. had collected items from St. Louis, Cincinnati, Memphis, Cairo, Natchez, Vicksburg, Baton Rouge, and New Orleans, and fired them into the aloof East. New York, Boston, Bangor, Utica, Albany, and other important centres had learned for the first time that a "levee"—whatever that might be—had suffered a cravasse; a steamboat and some towbarges had been wrecked, that Cairo was registering 63.3 on the gauge; that some Negroes had been drowned; that cattle thieves were operating in the Overflow, and so on and so forth.

The combination of La Salle's last adventure and the Mississippi flood caught the fancy of the newspaper man.

"Shall I ever get out there?" Terabon asked himself.

His dream was not of reporting wars, not of exploring Africa, not of interviewing kings and making presidents in a national convention. Far from it! His mind caught at the suggestion of singing birds in their native trees, and he could without regret think of spending days with a magnifying glass, considering the ant, or worshipping at the stalk of the flowering lily.

He was astonished, one day, to discover that he had several hundred dollars in the Chambers Street Savings Bank. It happened that the city editor called him to the desk a few minutes later and said:

"Go see about this conference."

"You go to hell!" the reporter replied, smilingly, gently replacing the slip on the greenish desk.

"T-t-t-t-t—" Mr. Dekod sputtered. There *is* something new under the sun!

Lester Terabon strolled forth with easy nonchalance, and three days later he was in the office of the secretary of the Mississippi River Commission, at St. Louis, calmly inquiring into the duties and performance thereof, involving the efforts of 100,000 Negroes, 40,000 mules, 500 contractors, 10,000 government officials, a few hundred pieces of floating plant, and sundry other things which Terabon had conceived were of importance.

He had approached the Mississippi River from the human angle. He knew of no other way of approach. His first view of the river, as he crossed the Merchants Bridge, had not disturbed his equilibrium in the least, and he had floated out of an eddy in a 16-foot skiff still with the human-viewpoint approach.

Then had begun a combat in his mind between all his preconceived ideas and information and the river realities. Faithfully, in the notebooks which he carried, he put down the details of his mental disturbances.

By the time he reached Island No. 10 sandbar he had about resigned himself to the whimsicalities of river living. He had, however, preserved his attitude of aloofness and extraneousness. He regarded himself as a visiting observer who would record the events in which others had a part. It still pleased his fancy to say that he was interviewing the Mississippi River as he might interview the President of the United States.

But as Lester Terabon rowed his skiff back up the eddy above New Madrid, and breasted the current in the sweep of the reach to that little cabin-boat half a mile above the Island No. 10 light, his attitude was undergoing a conscious change. While he had been reporting the Mississippi River in its varying moods something had encircled him and grasped him, and was holding him.

For some time he had felt the change in his position; glimmerings of its importance had appeared in his notes; his mind had fought against it as a corruption, lest it ruin the career which he had mapped out for himself.

When the New Madrid fish-dock man told him to carry the warning that a "detector" was hunting for a certain woman, and that the detective had gone on down with some river fellows, his place as a river man was assured. River folks trusted and used him as they used themselves. Moreover, he was possessed of a vital river secret.

Nelia Crele, *alias* Nelia Carline, was the woman, and they were both stopping over at the Island No. 10 sandbar. He knew, what the fish-dock man probably did not know, that the pursuer was the woman's husband.

"What'll I tell her?" Terabon asked himself.

With that question he uncovered an unsuspected depth to his feelings. It was a dark, dull day. The waves rolled and fell back, sometimes the wind seeming the stronger and then the current asserting its weight. With the wind's help over the stern, Terabon swiftly passed the caving bend and landed in the lee above the young woman's boat.

He carried some things he had bought for her into the kitchen and they sat in the cabin to read newspapers and magazines which he had obtained.

"I heard some news, too," he told her.

"Yes? What news?"

"The fish-dock man at New Madrid told me to tell the people along that a detective has gone on down, looking for a woman."

"A detective looking for a woman?" she repeated.

"A man the name of Carline—"

"Oh!" she shrugged her shoulders. "Why didn't you tell me!"

He flushed. Almost an hour had elapsed since he had returned. He had found it difficult to mention the subject.

"I did not tell you either," he apologized, "that I happened to meet Mr. Carline up at Island No. 8, when I had no idea the good fortune would come to me of meeting you, whose—whose pictures he showed me. I could not—I saw—There was—"

"And you didn't tell me," she accused him.

"It seemed to me none of my affair. I'm a newspaper man—I—"

"And did that excuse you from letting me know of his—of that pursuit of me?"

His newspaper impartiality had failed him, and he hung his head in doubt and shame. She claimed, and she deserved, his friendship; the last vestige of his pretence of mere observation was torn from him. He was a human among humans—and he had a fervid if unexpected thought about the influence and exasperation of the river out yonder.

"I could not tell you!" he cried. "I didn't think—it seemed—"

"You know, then, you saw why I had left him?"

"Liquor!" he grasped at the excuse. "Oh, that was plain enough."

"Perhaps a woman could forgive liquor," she suggested, thoughtfully, "but not—not stupidity and indifference. He never disturbed the dust on any of the books of his library. Oh, what they meant my books mean to me!"

She turned and stared at her book shelves.

"Suppose you hadn't found books?" he asked, glad of the opportunity for a diversion.

"I'd be dead, I think," she surmised, "and one day, I did deliberately choose."

"How was that?"

"Get your notebook!" she jeered. "I thought if he was going to rely on the specious joys of liquor I would, and tried it. It was a blizzard day last winter. He had gone over to see the widow, and there was a bottle of rum in the cupboard. I took some hot milk, nutmeg, sugar, and rum. I've never felt so happy in my life, except—"

"With what exception?" he asked.

"Yesterday," she answered, laughing, "and last night and to-day! You see, I'm free now. I say and do what I please. I don't care any more. I'm perfectly brazen. I don't love you, but I like you very much. You're good company. I hope I am, too—"

"You are—splendid!" he cried, almost involuntarily, and she shivered.

"Let's go walking again, will you?" she said. "I want to get out in the wind; I want to have the sky overhead, a sandbar under my feet, and all outdoors at my command. You don't mind, you'd like to go?"

"To the earth's end!" he replied, recklessly, and her gay laugh showed how well he had pleased her mood.

They kept close up to the north side of the bar because down the wind the sand was lifting and rolling up in yellow clouds. They went to Winchester Chute, and followed its winding course through the wood patch. There was a slough of green water, with a flock of ducks which left precipitately on their approach. They returned down to the sandbar, and pressed their way through the thick clump of small willows into the switch willows and along the edge of the unbroken desert of sand. They could see the very surface of the bar rolling along before the wind, and as they walked along they found their feet submerged in the blast.

But when they arrived at the boat night was near at hand, and the enveloping cold became more biting and the gloom more depressing.

Just when they had eaten their supper together, and had seated themselves before the fire, and when the whirl and whistle of the wind was heard in the mad music of a river storm, a motorboat with its cut-out open ploughed up the river through the dead eddy and stopped to hail.

Jim Talum, a fisherman whose line of hoop nets filled the reach of Island No. 9 for eight or ten miles, was on his way to his tent which he had pitched at the head of Winchester Chute.

He tramped aboard, and welcomed a seat by the fire.

"'Lowed I'd drap in a minute," he declared. "Powerful lonesome up on the chute where I got my tent. Be'n runnin' my traps down the bank, yeah, an' along of the chute, gettin' rats. Yo' trappin'?"

"No, just tripping," Terabon replied. "I was down to New Madrid this morning."

"I'm just up from there. Ho law! Theh's one man I'd hate to be down below. I expect yo've hearn tell of them Despard riveh pirates? No! Well, they've come drappin' down ag'in, an' they landed into New Madrid yestehd'y evenin'. Likely they 'lowed to raid some commissary down b'low—cayn't tell what they did 'low to do. But they picked good pickin's down theh! Feller come down lookin' fo' a woman, hisn's I expect. Anyhow, he's a strangeh on the riveh. He's got a nice power boat, an' likely he's got money. If he has, good-bye! Them Despards'd kill a man for $10. One of 'em, Hilt Despard's onto the bo't with him, pretendin' to be a sport, an' they've drapped out. The rest the gang's jes' waitin' fo' the wind to lay, down b'low, an' down by Plum P'int, some'rs, Mr. Man'll sudden come daid."

The fisherman had been alone so much that the pent-up conversation of weeks flowed uninterruptedly. He told details; he described the motorboat; he laughed at the astonishment the man would feel when the pirates disclosed their intentions with a bullet or knife; and he expected, by and by, to hear the story of the tragedy through the medium of some whiskey boater, some river gossip coming up in a power boat.

For an hour he babbled and then, as precipitately as he had arrived, he took his departure. When he was gone, Nelia Crele turned to Terabon with helpless dismay. Augustus Carline was worthless; he had been faithless to her; he had inflicted sufferings beyond her power of punishment or forgiveness.

"But he's looking for me!" she recapitulated, "and he doesn't know. He's a fool, and they'll kill him like a rat! What can I do?"

Obviously there was nothing that she could do, but Lester Terabon rose instantly.

"I'd better drop down and see if I can't help him—do something. I know that crew."

"You'll do that for me!" her voice lifted in a cry of thankfulness. "Oh, if you would, if you would. I couldn't think of his being—his being killed, trying to find me. Get him; send him home!"

"I'd better start right down," Terabon said, "it's sixty or seventy miles, anyhow. They'll not hurry. They can't, for the gang's in a shanty-boat."

She walked up to him with her arms raised.

"How can I thank you?" she demanded. "You do this for me—a stranger!"

"Why not, if I can help?" he asked.

"Where shall I see you again?"

He brought in his book of river maps, and together they looked down the tortuous stream; he rested the tip of his pencil on Yankee Bar below Plum Point.

"It's a famous pirate resort, this twenty miles of river!" he said. "I'll wait at Fort Pillow Landing. Or if you are ahead?"

"We'll meet there!" she cried. "I'll surely find you there. Or at Mendova—surely at Mendova."

She followed him out on the bow deck.

"Just a minute," she whispered, "while I get used to the thought of being alone again. I did not know there were men like you who would rather do a favour than ask for kisses."

"It isn't that we don't like them!" he blurted out. "It's—it's just that we'd rather deserve them and not have them than have them and not deserve them!"

She laughed. "Good-bye—and don't forget, Fort Pillow!"

"Does a man forget his meals?" he demanded, lightly, and with his duffle packed low in his skiff he rowed out into the gray river and the black night.

Having found a lee along the caving bank above New Madrid he gain-speeded down the current behind the sandbar, but when he turned the New Madrid bend he pulled out into mid-river and with current and wind both behind him, followed the government lights that showed the channel.

He had expected to linger long down this historic stretch of river with its Sunk Lands of the New Madrid earthquakes, with its first glimpse of the cotton country, and with its countless river phenomena.

"But Old Mississip' has other ideas," he said to himself, and miles below he was wondering if and when he would meet the girl of Island No. 10 again.

CHAPTER XXI

Pirates have infested the Mississippi from the earliest days. The stranger on the river cannot possibly know a pirate when he sees one, and even shanty-boaters of long experience and sharp eyes penetrate their disguises with difficulty. How could Gus Carline suspect the loquacious, ingratiating, and helpful Renald Doss?

Lonely; pursued by doubts, ignorance, and a lurking timidity, Carline was only too glad to take on a companion who discoursed about all the river towns, called river commissioners by their first names, knew all the makes of motors, and called the depth of the water in Point Pleasant crossing by reading the New Madrid gauge.

He relinquished the wheel of his boat to the dapper little man, and fed the motor more gas, or slowed down to half speed, while he listened to volumes of river lore.

"You've been landing along down?" Doss asked.

"All along," Carline replied, "everywhere."

"Seen anybody?"

"I should say so; there was a fellow come down pretending to be a reporter. He stopped over with me, got me full's a tick, and then robbed me."

"Eh—*he* robbed you?"

"Yes, sir! He got me to drinking heavy. I like my stew a little, but he fixed me. Then he just went through me, but he didn't get all I had, you bet!"

This was rich!

"Lucky he didn't hit you on the head, and take the boat, too!" Doss grinned.

"I suppose so."

"Yes, sir! Lots of mean men on this river, they play any old game. They say they're preachers, or umbrella menders, or anything. Every once in a while some feller comes down, saying he's off'n some magazine. They come down in skiffs, mostly. It's a great game they play. Everybody tells 'em everything. If I was going to be a crook, I bet I'd say I was a hist'ry writer. I'd snoop around, and then I'd land—same's that feller landed on you. Get much?"

"Two—three hundred dollars!"

The little man laughed in his throat. He handled the boat like a river pilot. His eyes turned to the banks, swept the sandbars, gazed into the coiling waters alongside, and he whispered names of places as he passed them—landings, bars, crossings, bends, and even the plantations and log cuttings. He named the three cotton gins in Tiptonville, and stared at the ferry below town with a sidelong leer.

Carline would have been the most astonished man on the Mississippi had he known that nearly all his money was in the pockets of his guest. He babbled on, and before he knew it, he was telling all about his wife running away down the Mississippi.

"What kind of a boat's she in?" Doss asked.

"I don't know."

"How do you expect to find her if you don't know the boat?"

"Why—why, somebody might know her; a woman alone!"

"She's alone?"

"Why—yes, sir. I heard so."

"Good looker?"

Without a word Carline handed the fellow a photograph. Doss made no sign. For two minutes he stared at that fine face.

"I bet she's got an awful temper," he half whispered.

"She's quick," Carline admitted, fervently.

"She'd just soon shoot a man as look at him," Doss added, with a touch of asperity.

"Why—she—" Carline hesitated. He recalled a day in his own experience when she took his own shot gun from him, and stood a fury, flaming with anger.

"Yes, sir, she would," Doss declared, with finality.

Doss had seen her. By that time a thousand shanty-boaters had heard about that girl's one shot of deadly accuracy. The woman folks on a thousand miles of reach and bend had had a bad example set before them. Doss himself felt an anger which was impotent against the woman who had shot Jest Prebold down. Probably other women would take to shooting, right off the bat, the same way. He despised that idea.

Carline, doubtful as to whether his wife was being insulted, congratulated, or described, gazed at the photograph. The more he looked, the more exasperated he felt. She was a woman—what right had she to run away and leave him with his honour impugned? He felt as though he hadn't taught her her place. At the same time, when he looked at the picture, he discovered a remembrance of his feeling that she was a very difficult person to teach anything to. Her learning always had insulted his own meagreness of information and aptness in repartee. Next to not finding her, his big worry had become finding her.

They steered down the river without great haste. Doss studied the shanty-boats which he saw moored in the various eddies, large and small. Some he spoke of casually, as store-boats, fishermen, market hunters, or, as they passed between Caruthersville and the opposite shore, a gambling boat. Even the river pirate, gloating over his prey, and puzzled only as to the method of making the most of his victim, could not penetrate the veil which it happened the Mississippi River interposed between them and the river gambling den—for the moment. There is no use seeking the method of the river, nor endeavouring to discover the processes by which the lives of thousands who go afloat down the Mississippi are woven as woof and warp in the fabric of river life and river mysteries. The more faithful an effort to select one of the commonest and simplest of river complications, the more improbable and fanciful it must seem.

Doss, in intervals when he was not consciously registering the smile of good humour, the generosity of an experienced man toward the chance visitor, and the willingness to defer to the gentleman from Up the Bank, brought his expression unconsciously to the cold, rough woodenness of blank insensitiveness—the malignance of a snapping turtle, to mention a medium reptilian face. A whim, and the necessity of delay, led Doss to suggest that they take a look up the Obion River as a likely hiding place. Of course, Doss knew best, and they quit the tumbling Mississippi for the quiet wooded aisle of the little river.

When they emerged, two days later, Augustus Carline could well thank his stars, though he did not know it, that he was still on the boat. All unconscious of the real nature and habits of river rats he had given the little wretch a thousand opportunities to commit one of the many crimes he had in mind. But he developed a reluctance to choose the easiest one, when from hint after hint he understood that a mere river piracy and murder would be folly in view of the opportunity for a more profitable stake which a man of means offered.

As he steered by the government boat which was surveying Plum Point bars, Doss showed his teeth like an indignant cat. Five or six miles below he offered the supine and helpless Carline the information:

"There's Yankee Bar. We'll swing wide and land in below, so's not to scare up any geese or ducks that may be roosting there."

Eagerly Doss searched through the switch willows for a glimpse of the setback of the water beyond the bar. Away down in the old eddy he discovered a shanty-boat, and to cover his involuntary exclamation of satisfaction he said:

"Shucks! There's somebody theh. I hoped we'd have it to ourselves but they may be sports, too. If they are, we'll sure have a good time. Some of these shanty-boaters are great sports. We'll soon find out!"

He steered into the eddy and the two men stepped out on the flat boat's deck to greet them.

"Seems like I've seen them before," Doss said in a low voice; "I believe they're old timers. Hello, boys! Hunting?"

"Yes, suh! Lots of game. Sho, ain' yo' Doss, Ren Doss?"

"You bet. I knew you! I told Mr. Carline, here, that I knew you, that I'd seen you before! I'm glad to see you boys again. Catch a line there."

No doubt about it, they were old friends. In a minute they were shaking hands all around, then went into the shanty-boat, and they sat down in assorted chairs, and Doss, Jet, and Cope exchanged the gossip of a river year.

Carline's eyes searched about him with interest, and the three men watched him more and more openly. When he walked toward the bow of the boat, where the slope of the yellow sand led up to the woods of Flower Island, one of them casually left his seat and followed.

Carline looked at the stand of guns in the cabin corner and started with surprise. He reached and picked up one of them to look at it.

"Why," he shouted, "this is my shot gu—"

No more. His light went out on the instant and he felt that he was suspended in mid-air, poised between the abyss and the heavens.

CHAPTER XXII

Fortune, or rather the Father of Waters, had favoured Parson Elijah Rasba in the accomplishment of his errand. It might not have happened in a decade that he locate a fugitive within a hundred miles of Cairo, where the Forks of the Ohio is the jumping-off place of the stream of people from a million square miles.

Rasba knew it. The fervour of the prophets was in his heart, and the light of understanding was brightening in his mind. Something seemed to have caught the doors of his intelligence and thrown them wide open.

In the pent-up valleys of the mountains, with their little streams, their little trails, their dull and hopeless inhabitants, their wars begun in disputes over pigs and abandoned peach orchards, their moonshine and hate of government revenues, there had been no chance for Parson Rasba to get things together in his mind.

The days and nights on the rivers had opened his eyes. When he asked himself: "If this is the Mississippi, what must the Jordan be?" he found a perspective.

Sitting there beside the wounded Jest Prebol, by the light of a big table lamp, he "wrestled" with his Bible the obscurities of which had long tormented his ignorance and baffled his mental bondage.

The noises of the witches' hours were in the air. Wavelets splashed along the side and under the bow of the Prebol shanty-boat. The mooring ropes stretched audibly, and the timber heads to which they were fastened squeaked and strained; the wind slapped and hissed and whined on all sides, crackling through the heavy timber up the bank. The great river pouring by seemed to have a low, deep growl while the wind in the skies rumbled among the clouds.

No wonder Rasba could understand! He could imagine anything if he did not hold fast to that great Book which rested on his knees, but holding fast to it, the whisperings and chucklings and hissings which filled the river wilderness, and the deep tone of the flood, the hollow roar of the passing storm, were but signs of the necessity of faith in the presence of the mysteries.

So Rasba wrestled; so he grappled with the things he must know, in the light of the things he did know. And a kind of understanding which was also peace comforted him. He closed the Book at last, and let his mind drift whither it would.

Panoramas of the river, like pictures, unfolded before his eyes; he remembered flashes taken of men, women, and children; he dwelt for a time on the ruin of the church up there in the valley, standing vainly against a mountain slide; his face warmed, his eyes moistened. His mind seized eagerly upon a vision of the memory, the pretty woman, whose pistol had shot down the deluded and now stricken wretch there in the cabin.

The anomaly of the fact that he was caring for her victim was not lost on his shrewd understanding. He was gathering up and helping patch the wreckage she was making. It was a curious conceit, and Elijah Rasba, while he smiled at the humour of it, was at the same time conscious of its sad truth.

Her presence on the river meant no good for any one; Prebol was but one of her victims; perhaps he was the least unfortunate of them all! Others might perish through her, while it was not too much to hope that Prebol, through his sufferings, might be willing to profit by their lesson. Rasba was glad that he had not overtaken her that night of inexplicable pursuit. Her brightness, her prettiness, her appeal had been irresistible to him, and he could but acknowledge, while he trembled at the fact, that for the time he had been possessed by her enchantment.

Thus he meditated and puzzled about the things which, in his words, had come to pass. Before he knew it, daylight had arrived, and Jock Drones came over to greet him with "Good mo'nin', Parson!" Prebol was sleeping and there was colour in his cheeks, enough to make them look more natural. When Doctor Grell arrived, just as the three sat down to breakfast, he cheered them with the information that Prebol was coming through though the shadow had rested close to him.

None of them admitted, even to himself, the strain the wounded man had been and was on their nerves. Under his seeming indifference Buck was near the breaking point; Jock, victim of a thousand worries, was bent under his burdens. Grell, having fought the all-night fight for a human life, was still weak with weariness from the effort. Rasba, a newcomer, brought welcome reserves of endurance, assistance, and confidence.

"Yo' men shore have done yo' duty by a man in need," he told them, and none of them could understand why that truthful statement should make them feel so very comfortable.

They left the sick man to go on board the gaming boat, and they sat on the stern deck, where they looked across the river and the levee to the roofs of Caruthersville. If they looked at the horizon, their attention was attracted and their gaze held by the swirling of the river current. Their eyes could not be drawn away from that tremendous motion, the rush of a thousand acres of surface; the senses were appalled by the magnitude of its suggestion.

"Going to play to-night?" Grell asked, uneasily.

"No," Buck replied, instantly.

"So!" the doctor exclaimed.

"Slip's going up on the steamboat."

"For good?"

"So'm I!" Buck continued, breathlessly; "I'm quitting the riveh, too! I've been down here a good many years. I've been thinking. I'm going back. I'm going up the bank again."

"What'll you do with the boat?" Grell continued.

"Slip and I've been talking it all over. We're through with it. We guessed the Prophet, here, could use it. We're going to give it to him."

"Going to give hit to me!" Rasba started up and stared at the man.

"Yes, Parson; that poplar boat of yours isn't what you need down here." Buck smiled. "This big pine boat's better; you could preach in this boat."

Tears started in Rasba's eyes and dripped through his dark whiskers. Buck and Jock had acted with the impulsiveness of gambling men. Something in the fact that Rasba had come down those strange miles had touched them, had given Drones courage to go back and face the music, and to Buck the desire to return into his old life.

"We're going up on the *Kate* to-morrow morning," Buck explained. "Slip'd better show you how to run the gasolene boat if you don't know how, Parson!"

Dazed by the access of fortune, Rasba spent the mid-afternoon learning to run the 28-foot gasolene launch which was used to tow the big houseboat which would make such a wonderful floating church. It was a big boat only a little more than two years old. Buck had made it himself, on the Upper Mississippi, for a gambling boat. The frame was light, and the cabin was built with double boards, with building paper between, to keep out the cold wintry winds.

"Gentlemen," Rasba choked, looking at the two donors of the gift, "I'm going to be the best kind of a man I know how—"

"It's your job to be a parson," Buck laughed. "If it wasn't for men like us, that need reforming, you'd be up against it for something to look out for. You aren't much used to the river, and I'll suggest that when you drop down you land in eddies sheltered from the west and south winds. They sure do tear things up sometimes. I've had the roof tore off a boat I was in, and I saw sixty-three boats sunk at Cairo's Kentucky shanty-boat town one morning after a big wind."

"I'll keep a-lookin'," Rasba assured him, "but I've kind-a lost the which-way down heah. One day I had the sun ahead, behind, and both sides—"

"There's maps in that pile of stuff in the corner," Buck said, going to the duffle. "You're on Sheet 4 now. Here's Caruthersville."

"Yas, suh. Those red lines?"

"The new survey. You see, that sandbar up in Little Prairie Bend has cut loose from Island No. 15, and moved down three miles, and we're at the foot of this bar, here. That's moved down, too, and that big bar down there was made between the surveys. You see, they had to move the levee back, and Caruthersville moved over the new levee—"

"Sho!" Rasba gasped. "What ails this old riveh?"

"She jes' wriggles, same's water into a muddy road downhill," Kippy laughed. "Up there in Little Prairie Bend hit's caved right through the old levee, and they had to loop around. Now they've reveted it."

"Reveted?"

"They've woven a willow mattress and weighted it down with broken rock from up the river—more than a mile of it, now, and they'll have to put down another mile before they can head the river off there."

"Put a carpet down. How wide?"

"Four hundred feet probably—"

"An' a mile long!" Rasba whispered, awed. "Every thing's big on the riveh!"

"Yes, sir—that's it—big!" Buck laughed.

Thus the four gossiped, and when Doctor Grell had taken his departure the three talked together about the river and its wonders. At intervals they went over to look after Prebol whose chief requirement was quiet, meat broths, and his medicines.

As night drew down Drones turned to Buck:

"It's goin' to be hard leaving the riveh! I neveh will forget, Buck. If I'm sent to jail for all my life, I'll have something to remember. If they hang me, I shore will come back to walk with those that walk in the middle of the river."

"What's that?" Rasba turned and demanded.

"Riveh folks believe that thousands of people who died down thisaway, sunk in snagged steamers, caught in burned-up boats, blown to kingdom come in boiler explosions, those that have been murdered, and who died along the banks, keep a-goin' up and down."

"Sho!" Rasba exclaimed. "Yo' b'lieve that?"

"A man believes a heap more after he's tripped the riveh once or twice, than he ever believed in all his borned days, eh, Buck?"

"It's so!" Buck cried out. "Last night I was thinking that I'd wasted my life down here; years and years I've been a shanty-boater, drifter, fisherman, trapper, market hunter, and late years, I've gambled. I've been getting in bad, worse all the while. The Prophet here, coming along, seemed to wake me up—the man I used to be—I mean. It wasn't so much what you said, Parson, but your being here. Then I've been thinking all over again. I've an idea, boys, that when I go back up to-morrow I won't be so sorry for what I've been, as glad that I didn't grow worse than I did. It won't be easy, boys—going back. I'm taking the old river with me, though. I've framed its bends and islands, its chutes and reaches, like pictures in my mind. Old Parson here, too, coming in on us the way he did, saying that this was hell, but he'd come here to live in it. That's what waked me up, Parson! I could see how you felt. You'd never seen such a place before, but you said in your heart and your eyes showed it, Parson, that you would leave God's country to help us poor devils. It's just a point of view, though. I'm going right up to my particular hell, and I'll look back here to this thousand miles of river as heaven. Yes, sir! But my job is up there—in that hell!"

So they talked, and always their thoughts were on the river channel, and their minds groping into the future.

When the *Kate* whistled way down at Bell's Landing, Rasba took the two across to Caruthersville and bade them good-bye at the landing.

The *Kate* pulled out and Parson Rasba crossed to the three houseboats, two of them his own. He went in to see Prebol, who was lonesome and wanted to talk a little.

"What you going to do, Parson?" Prebol asked.

It was all a new experience, and its novelty compelled him at times
 pause in his efforts to jot down a few hasty words by light of a little
ectric flash to preserve in his memory the sequence of the constantly
rying features of the night, beginning with the curtain of the shanty-
at which flicked its good luck after him, passing the bright, clear lights
New Madrid. After leaving far behind their glow against the thin haze
the night he "made" the scattered shoals of Point Pleasant, and hugged
wn vanishing Ruddles Point, taking a glimpse of Tiptonville—which
thdraws year by year from the fatal caving brink of its site—wishing as
passed that he might return to that strange place and visit Reelfoot Lake
e or four miles beyond, where the New Madrid earthquakes drowned a
st whose dead stubs rise as monuments to the tragedy.

In Little Cypress Bend, twenty-five miles below where he had left the
ng woman, he heard the splash and thud of a caving bank, and felt the
ollers from the falling earth twisting and tumbling him about for a third
mile.

t was after 1 o'clock when he looked at his watch. He was beginning to
he pull on his shoulders, and the crick which constantly looking over
houlder to see the lights ahead caused him. The dulness of his vision,
o inevitable fatigue, compelled him constantly to sit more alert and
away the fine spray which whipped up from the waves. A feeling of
sness overpowered him. He could not row on forever, without resting
Taking advantage of a moment of calm in the wind, he pulled the bow
d and drifted down stern first.

e had lost track of his position; he had not counted the lights, and
or many miles there was no town distinguishable. He had felt the
ess of a mile-breadth; now he wondered whether he was in Missouri
ansas, whether he had come forty miles or eighty, and after a little he
o worry for fear he might have gone more than a hundred.

h the wind astern or nearly astern, he knew that he had pulled four
miles an hour, and he did not know how fast the current of the river
ight be four miles or eight miles. In ten hours he might leave more
undred miles of river bank behind him.

ew sensation began to possess him: the feeling that he was no
e looked around, while he rested trying to find what proximity thu
him. The wind? Those dull banks, seemingly so distant? Perhap
ow traveller? It was none of those things.

s the river! The "feel" of the flood was that of a person. He could nc
the sensation, which seemed absurd. He shook his head resolutel
searched through the gloom to discover what eyes might b

"I'd kind-a like to get to see shanty-boaters, and talk to them," the man answered. "I wonder couldn't yo' sort of he'p me; tell me where I mout begin and where it'd he'p the most, an' hurt people's feelin's the least? I'd jes' kind-a like to be useful. Course, I got to get you cured up an' took cyar of first."

"I cayn't say much about being pious on Old Mississip'," Prebol grinned, "but theh's two ways of findin' trouble. One's to set still long enough, and then, again, you can go lookin' fo' hit. Course, yo' know me! I've hunted trouble pretty fresh, an' I've found hit, an' I've lived onto hit. I cayn't he'p much about doin' good, an' missionaryin', an' River Prophetin'."

When Prebol's voice showed the strain of talking Rasba bade him rest. Then he went over to the big boat, a gift that would have sold for $1,000. He looked at the crap table, the little poker tables with the brass-slot kitties; he stared at the cabinet of cards and dice.

"All mine!" he said.

He walked out on the deck where he could commune with the river, using his eyes, his ears, and the feeling that the warm afternoon gave him. The sun shone upon him, and made a narrow pathway across the rushing torrent. The sky was blue and cloudless. Of the cold, the wind, the sea of liquid mud, not one trace remained.

He looked down and up the river, and his eyes caught a flicker which became a flutter, like the agitation of a duck preening its feathers on a smooth surface.

He watched it for a long time. He did not know what it was. As a river man, his curiosity was excited, but there was something more than mere curiosity; the river instinct that the inexplicable and unknown should be watched and inquired into moved him almost unconsciously to watch that distant agitation which became a dot afloat in a mirage of light. A little later a sudden flash along the river surface disclosed that the thing was a shanty-boat turning in the coiling currents at the bend.

The sun drew nearer the tree tops. The little cabin-boat was seeking a place to land or anchor for the night. If it was an old river man, the boat would drop into some little eddy at Caruthersville or down below; but a stranger on the river would likely shoot across into the gamblers' eddy tempted, perhaps, by the three boats already there.

The boat drew swiftly near, and as it ran down, the navigator rowed to make the shanty-boat eddy. Parson Rasba discovered that it was a woman at the sweeps, and a few strokes later he knew that it was a slim, young woman. When she coasted down outside the eddy, to swing in at the foot, and arrived opposite him, he recognized her.

"God he'p me!" he choked, "hit's Missy Nelia. Hit's Missy Nelia! An' she's a runned away married woman—an' theh's the man she shot!"

"Hello-o, Parson!" she hailed him, "did you see a skiff with a reporter man drop by?"

"No, missy!" he shook his head, his heart giving a painful thump

"I'm a-landing in, Parson!" she cried. "I want to talk with you!"

With that she leaned forward, drove the sweeps deep, and her boat started in like a skiff. It seemed to Parson Rasba that he had never seen a more beautiful picture in all his days.

CHAPTER XXIII

Lester Terabon rowed down the rolling river waters in the
He had, of course, looked out into the Mississippi shades from
of landing, anchorage, and sandbar; he knew the looks of the
the activities of currents and bends when a gale is sweeping
is, by turns, penetrated by the hissing of darting whitecaps a
the blustering winds.

He would not from choice have selected a night of gale
the Mississippi, and his first sensation as he sought a stor
was one of doubt. What dangers might engulf him was n
waves, for his skiff bobbed and rocked over them; not ri
on plunder, for they could not see him; perhaps a snag in
crossing; perhaps the leap of a sawyer, a great tree trunk
in the mud and the roots bounding up and down in the
collision with some other craft.

He had salt-water rowlocks on his boat, open-toppe
the oars he used were cased with a foot of black leather a
strips; the tips were covered with copper sheets whicl
and balance. At first he pulled awkwardly, catching
and backing into the heft of the waves, but after a time
they came, and the oars feathered and caught. While h
searched the black horizon for the distant sparkle of
fell into the swing of his stroke before he knew it, and
surprised to observe that he swayed to the side-wash
rhythm of the waves.

The government lights guided him. He had no
them before; he had seen their white post standar
day after day, but his skiff, drawing only five inch
the shallowest crossings and along the most gra
Now he must keep to the deep water, follow the m
of the meandering channel, lest he collide with a b
line of sunken trees, or climb the point of a towh

shining in it. He saw the inevitable government lights between which was deep water and a safe channel. He had but to keep on the line between the lights, cutting across when he spied another one far ahead. The lights but accentuated the certainty that on all sides, but a little way from him, a host of invisible beings speculated on his presence and influenced his course.

A newspaper man of much experience could not help but protest in his practical mind against such a determination of the invisible and the unknown to give him such nonsensical ideas. He had in play, in intellectual persiflage, and with some show of traditional reasonableness, called Nelia Crele "a river goddess." She was very well placed in his mind—a reckless woman, pretty, with a fine character for a masterpiece of fiction (should he ever get to the story-writing stage) and a delight to think about; commanding, too, mysterious and exacting; and now he thought it might be the laughter of her voice that carried in the wind, not a mocking laugh, nor a jeering one, but one of sweet encouragement which neither distance nor circumstances could dismiss from a distressed and reluctant heart, let alone a heart so willing to receive as his.

Lester Terabon accepted the possibility of river lore and proclaimed beliefs. Fishermen, store-boaters, trippers, pirates, and all sorts of the shanty-boaters whom he had interviewed on his way down had solemnly assured him that there were spirits who promenaded down mid-stream, and who sometimes could be seen.

Terabon was sorry when his cool, calculating mind refused to believe his eyes, which saw shapes; his flesh, which felt creeps; his ears, which heard voices; and his nostrils, which caught a whiff of a faint, sweet perfume more exquisite than any which he remembered. He knew that when he had kissed the river goddess whose eyes were blue, whose flesh was fair, whose grace was lovely, he had tasted that nectar and sniffed that ambrosia. He wondered if she were near him, watching to see whether he performed well the task which she had set for him, the rescue of the husband who had forfeited her love, and yet who still was under her protection since in his indignant sorrow he had supposed himself capable of finding and retaining her.

Terabon would have liked nothing better than to believe what the Grecians used to believe, that goddesses and gods do come down to the earth to mingle among mankind. He fought the impossibility with his reason, and night winds laughed at him, while the voices of the waves chuckled at his predicament. They assailed him with their presence like living things, and then roared away to give room to new voices and new presences.

"Anyhow," Terabon laughed, in spite of himself, "you're good company, Old Mississip'!"

Yet he felt the chilling and depressing possibility that he might never again see that woman who would remain as a "river goddess" in his imagination. He had been heart-free, a bystander in the world's affairs. Now he knew what it was to see the memory of a woman rise unbidden to disturb his calculations; more than that, too, he was a part of the affairs of the River People.

As a reporter "back home" he had never been able quite to reconcile himself to his constant position as a spectator, a neutral observer, obliged to write news without feeling and impartially. A politician could look him in the eye and tell him any smooth lie, and he could not, with white heat, deny the statement. He could not rise with his own strength to champion the cause of what he knew to be right against wrong; he could not elaborate on the details of things that he felt most interested in, but must consult the fancies of a not-particularly discriminating public, whose average intelligence, according to some learned students, must be placed at seventeen-years plus. As he was twenty-four plus, Terabon was immensely discouraged with the public when he had set forth down the Mississippi.

Now he was on the way from a river goddess to interfere with the infamous plans of river pirates, through a dry gale out of the north, on the winding course of the Mississippi, a transition which troubled the self-possession while it awakened the spirit of the young man.

Dawn broke on the troubled river, and the prospect was enchanting to the heroic in the mind of the skiff-tripper. He could not be sure which was east or west, for the gray light appeared on all sides, in spots and patches of varying size. No gleam reflected from the yellow clay of the tumbling and tortured waters. As far as he could see there was light, but not a bright light. Dull purples, muddy waters, gray tree trunks, black limbs against dark clouds; Terabon felt the weariness of a desert, the melancholy of a wet, dripping-tree wilderness, and of a tumbling waste of waters; and yet never had the solid body of the stream been so awe-inspiring as in that hour of creeping and insinuating dawn.

He ran out into the main river again, and a wonderful prospect opened before his eyes. Sandbars spread out for miles across the river and lengthwise of the river; the bulk of the stream seemed broken up into channels and chutes and wandering waterways. He saw column after column of lines of spiles, like black teeth, through which the water broke with protesting foam.

When he thought to reckon up, as he passed Osceola Bar, he found that he had come ninety-five miles. Yankee Bar was only five or six miles below him, and he eagerly pulled down to inspect the long beaches, the chutes and channels, which the river pirates had used for not less than 150 years; where they still had their rendezvous.

Wild ducks and geese were there in many flocks. There were waters sheltered from the wind by willow patches. The woods of Plum Point Peninsula were heavy and dark. The river main current slashed down the miles upon miles of Craighead Point, and shot across to impinge upon Chickasaw Bluffs No. 1, where a made dirt bank was silhouetted against the sky.

Not until his binoculars rested upon the bar at the foot of Fort Pillow Bluff did Terabon's eyes discover any human beings, and then he saw a white houseboat with a red hull. He headed toward it to ask the familiar river question.

"No, suh!" the lank, sharp-eyed fisherman shook his head. "Theh's no motorboat landed up theh, not this week. Who all mout you be?"

"Lester Terabon; I'm a newspaper writer; I live in New York; I came down the Mississippi looking for things to tell about in the newspapers. You see, lots of people hardly know there's a Mississippi River, and it's the most interesting place I ever heard of."

"Terabon? I expect you all's the feller Whiskey Williams was tellin' about; yo'n a feller name of Carline was up by No. 8. He said yo' had one of them writin' machines right into a skift. Sho! An' yo' have! The woman an' me'd jes' love to see yo' all use hit."

"You'll see me," Terabon laughed, "if you'll let me sit by your stove. I've some writing I could do. Here's a goose for dinner, too."

"Sho! The woman shore will love to cook that goose! I'm a fisherman but no hunter. 'Tain't of'en we git a roast bird!"

So Terabon sat by the stove, writing. He wrote for more than an hour—everything he could remember, with the aid of his pencilled midnight notes, about that long run down. With his maps before him he recognized the bends and reaches, the sandbars and islands which had loomed up in the dark. Of all the parts of the river, the hundred miles from Island No. 10 down to Fort Pillow became the most familiar to his thoughts, black though the night had been. Even each government light began to have characteristics, and the sky-line of levee, wilderness, sandbar, and caving bank grew more and more defined.

Having written his notes, and Jeff Slamey having fingered the nine loose-leaf sheets with exclamatory interest and delight, Terabon said he must go rest awhile.

"Yas, suh," the fisherman cried, "when a man's pulled a hundred mile he shore needs sleep. When the woman's got that goose cooked, I bet yo'll be ready to eat, too."

So Terabon turned in to sleep. He was awakened at last by the sizzling of a goose getting its final basting. He started up, and Slamey said:

"Hit's ready. I bet yo' feel betteh, now; six hours asleep!"

It didn't seem like six minutes of dreamless recreation.

With night the wind fell. The flood of sunset brilliance spread down the radiant sandbars and the bright waterways. The trees were plated with silver and gold, and the sweep of the caving bend was a dark shadow against which the river current swept with ceaseless attack.

For hours that night Terabon amused his host with his adventures, except that he made but most casual mention of the woman whom Carline was seeking. He was cautious, too, about the motorboat and the companion who had taken Carline down the river, till Slamey burst out:

"I know that feller. He's a bad man; he's a river rat. If he don't kill Gus Carline, I don't know these yeah riveh fellers. They use down thisaway every winter. I know; I know them all. I leave them alone, an' they leave me alone. I knew they was comin'. They got three four boats now. One feller, name of Prebol—he's bad, too—was shot by a lady above Cairo. He's with a coupla gamblers to Caruthersville now. Everybody stops yeah; I know everybody; everybody knows me."

The next day was calm all day long, and Terabon went up the bank to shoot squirrels or other woods game; he went almost up to the Plum Point, killed several head of game, and rejoiced in the bayous and sloughs and chutes of a changing land.

The following morning he was hailed by Slamey:

"Hi—i, Terabon! Theh's a shanty-boat up the head of Flower Island Bar jes' drappin' in. They've floated down all night!"

Through his glasses Terabon saw two men walking a shanty-boat across the dead water below Yankee Lower Bar to the mainland.

They were too far away for him to distinguish their personalities, but one was a tall, active man, the other obviously chunky, and when they ran their lines out and made fast to half-buried snags, it was with the quick decision of men used to work against currents and to unison of effort. There was something suggestive in their bearing, their scrutiny up and down the river, their standing close to each other as they talked. If Terabon had not suspected them of being pirates, their attitude and actions would have betrayed them.

Terabon, after a little while, pulled up the eddy toward them; he was willing to take a long chance. Few men resent a newspaper man's presence. The worst of them like to put themselves, their ideas, right with the world. Terabon risked their knavery to win their approbation. Come what might, he would seek to save Augustus Carline from the consequences of his ignorance, money, folly, and remorse.

CHAPTER XXIV

The flow of the Mississippi River is down stream—a perfectly absurd and trite statement at first thought. On second thought, one reverts to the people who are always trying to fight their way up that adverse current, with the thrust of two miles perpendicular descent and the body of a thousand storms in its rush.

There are steamers which endeavour to stem the current, but they make scant headway; sometimes a fugitive afraid of the rails will pull up stream; the birds do fly with the spring winds against the retreat of winter; but all these things are trifles, and merely accentuate the fact that everything goes down.

The sandbars are not fixed, they are literally rivers of sand flowing down, tormenting the current, and keeping human beings speculating on their probable course and the effect, when after a few years on a point, they disappear under the water. Later they will lunge up and out into the wind again, gallumphing along, some coarse gravel bars, some yellow sand, some white sand, some fine quicksand, some gritty mud, and others of mud almost fit to use in polishing silver.

Thousands of people in shanty-boats, skiff's, fancy little yachts, and jon-boats, rag-shacks on rafts, and serviceable cruisers drift down with the flood, and are a part of it.

Autumn was passing; most of the birds had speeded south when the wild geese brought the alarm that a cold norther was coming. When the storm had gone by, shanty-boaters, having shivered with the cold, determined not to be caught again. The sunshine of the evening, when the wind died, saw boats drifting out for the all-night run. Dawn, calm and serene, found boats moving out into mid-channel more or less in haste.

So they floated down, sometimes within a few hundred feet of other boats, sometimes in merry fleets tied together by ropes and common joyousness, sometimes alone in the midst of the vacant waters. The migration of the shanty-boaters was watched with mingled hate, envy, and admiration by Up-the-Bank folks, who pretend to despise those who live as they please.

And Nelia Carline pulled out into the current and followed her river friend, Lester Terabon, who had gone on ahead to save her husband from the river pirates. She despised her husband more as she let her mind dwell on the man who had shown no common frailties while he did enjoy a comradeship which included the charm of a pretty woman, recognizing her equality, and not permitting her to forget for a moment that he knew she was lovely, as well as intelligent.

She had not noticed that fact so much at the time, as afterward, when she subjected him to the merciless scrutiny of a woman who has heretofore discovered in men only depravity, ignorance, selfishness, or brutality. Her first thought had been to use Terabon, play with him, and, if she could, hurt him. She knew that there were men who go about plaguing women, and as she subjected herself to grim analysis, she realized that in her disappointment and humiliation she would have hurt, while she hated, men.

The long hours down the river, in pleasant sunshine, with only an occasional stroke of the oar to set the boat around broadside to the current, enabled her to sit on the bow of her boat and have it out with herself. She had never had time to think. Things crowded her Up-the-Bank. Now she had all the time in the world, and she used that time. She brought out her familiar books and compared the masters with her own mind. She could do it—there.

"Ruskin, Carlyle, Old Mississip', Plato, Plutarch, Thoreau, the Bible, Shelley, Byron, and I, all together, dropping down," she chuckled, catching her breath. "I'm tripping down in that company. And there's Terabon. He's a good sport, too, and he'll be better when I've—when I've caught him."

Terabon was just a raw young man as regards women. He might flatter himself that he knew her sex, and that he could maintain a pose of writing her into his notebooks, but she knew. She had seen stunned and helpless youth as she brought into play those subtle arts which had wrenched from his reluctant and fearful soul the kiss which he thought he had asked for, and the phrase of the river goddess, which he thought he had invented. She laughed, for she had realized, as she acted, that he would put into words the subtle name for which she had played.

It all seemed so easy now that she considered the sequence of her inspired moves. Drifting near another shanty-boat, she passed the time of day with a runaway couple who had come down the Ohio. They had dinner together on their boat. A solitaire and an unscarred wedding ring attested to the respectability of the association.

"Larry's a river drifter," the girl explained, "and Daddy's one of those set old fellows who hate the river. But Mamma knew it was all right. Larry's saved $7,000 in three years. He'd never tell me that till I married him, but I knew. We're going clear down to N'Orleans. Are you?"

"Probably."

"And all alone—aren't you afraid?"

"Oh, I'll be all right, won't I?" She looked at the stern-featured youth.

"If you can shoot and don't care," Larry replied without a smile.

"I can shoot," Nelia said, showing her pistol.

"That's river Law!" Larry cried, smiling. "That's Law. You came out the Upper River?"

"Yes," she nodded.

"Then I bet—" the girl-wife started to speak, but stopped, blushing.

"Yes," Nelia smiled a hard smile. "I'm the woman who shot Prebol above Buffalo Island—I had to."

"You did right; men always respect a lady if she don't care who she shoots," Larry cried, enthusiastically. "Wish you'd get my wife to learn how to shoot. She's gun shy!"

So Nelia coaxed the little wife to shoot, first the 22-calibre repeating rifle and then the pistol. When Nelia had to go down they parted good friends and Larry thanked her, saying that probably they would meet down below somewhere.

"You'll make Caruthersville," Larry told her. "There's a good eddy on the east side across from the town. There's likely some boats in there. They'll know, perhaps, if the folks you are looking for are around. There's an old river man there now, name of Buck. He's a gambler, but he's all right, and he'll treat you all right. He's from up in our country, on the Ohio. Hardly anybody knows about him. He was always a dandy fellow, but he married a woman that wasn't fit to drink his coffee. She bothered the life out of him, and—well, he squared up. He gave her to the other fellow with a double-barrelled shotgun."

When Nelia ran down to the gambling boat and found Parson Rasba there, she enjoyed the idea. Certainly the River Prophet and the river gambler were an interesting combination. She was not prepared to find that Buck had taken his departure and that Parson Rasba was converting the gambling hell into a mission boat. Least of all was she prepared when Parson Rasba said with an unsteady voice:

"Theh's a man sick in that other boat, and likely he'd like to see somebody."

"Oh, if there's anything I can do!" she exclaimed, as a woman does.

He led the way to the brick-red little boat, the like of which could be found in a thousand river eddies. She followed him on board and over to the bed. There she looked into the wan countenance and startled eyes of Jest Prebol.

"Hit's Mister Prebol," Rasba said. "I know you have no hard feelings against him, and I know he has none against you, Missy Carline!"

An introduction to a contrite river pirate, whom she had shot, for the moment rendered the young woman speechless. Prebol was less at loss for words.

"I'm glad to git to see yo'," he said, feebly. "If I'd knowed yo', I shore would have minded my own business. I'm bad, Missy Carline, but I ain' mean—not much. Leastwise, not about women. I reckon the boys shore will let yo' be now. I made a mistake, an' I 'low to 'pologise to yo'."

"I was—I was scairt to death," she cried, sitting in a chair. "I was all alone. I was afraid—the river was so big that night. I was so far away. I should have given you fair warning. I'm sorry, too, Jest."

"Lawse!" Prebol choked. "Say hit thataway ag'in—"

"I'm sorry, too, Jest!"

"I cayn't thank yo' all enough," the man-whispered. "I've got friends along down the riveh. I'll send word along to them, they'll shore treat yo' nice. Treat friends of yourn nice, too. Huh! 'Pologizin' to me afteh what I 'lowed to do!"

"We'll be good friends, Jest. The Prophet here and I are good friends, too. Aren't we, Parson?"

"I hearn say, Missy," the Prophet said, slowly, picking his words, "I hearn say you've a power and a heap of book learning! Books on yo' boat, all kinds. What favoured yo' thataway?"

"Oh, I read lots!" she exclaimed, surprised by the sudden shift of thought. "Somehow, I've read lots!"

"In my house I had a Bible, an almanac, and the 'Resources of Tennessee,' Yo' have that many books?"

"Why, I've a hundred—more than a hundred books!" she answered.

"A Bible?"

"Yes."

"Would you mind, Missy, comin' on board this boat to-night, an' tellin' us about these books you have? I'm not educated; my daddy an' I read the Bible, an' tried to understand hit. Seems like we neveh did git to know the biggest and bestest of the words."

"You had a dictionary?"

"A which?"

"A dictionary, a book that explains the meaning of all the words!"

"Ho law! A book that tells what words mean, Missy. Where all kin a man git to find one of them books?"

"Why, I've got—I'm hungry, Mr. Rasba, I must get something to eat. After supper we'll bring some books over here and talk about them!"

"My supper is all ready, keeping warm in the oven," Rasba said. "I always cook enough for one more than there is. Yo' know, a vacant chair at the table for the Stranger."

"And I came?" she laughed.

"An' yo' came, Missy!" he replied.

"Parson," Prebol pleaded, "I'm alone mos' the time. Mout yo' two eat hyar on my bo't? The table—hit'd be comp'ny."

"Certainly we'll come," Nelia promised, "if he'd just soon."

"I'd rather," Rasba assented, and at his tone Nelia felt a curious sensation of pity and mischievousness. At the same time, she recovered her self-possession. She demanded that Rasba let her help him bring over the supper, add a feminine relish, and set the table with a daintiness which was an addition to the fascination of her presence. Gaily she fed Prebol the delicate things which he was permitted to eat, then sat down with Rasba, her face to the light, and Prebol could watch her bantering, teasing, teaching Parson Rasba things he had never known he lacked.

After supper she brought over a basket full of books, twenty volumes. She dumped them onto the table, leather, cloth, and board covers, of red, blue, gray, brown, and other gay colours. Parson Rasba had seen government documents and even some magazines with picture covers, but in the mountains where he had ridden his Big Circuit with such a disastrous end he had never seen such books. He hesitated to touch one; he cried out when three or four slipped off the pile onto the floor.

"Missy, won't they git muddied up!"

"They're to read!" she told him. "Listen," and she began to read—poetry, prose at random.

The Prophet did not know, he had never been trained to know—as few men ever are trained—how to combat feminine malice and spoiled power. He listened, but not with averted eyes. Prebol, himself a spectator at a scene different from any he had ever witnessed, was still enough more sophisticated to know what she was doing, and he was delighted.

By and by the injured man drifted into slumber, but Rasba gave no sign of flagging interest, no traces of a mind astray from the subject at hand. He felt that he must make the most of this revelation, which came after the countless revelations which he had had since arriving down the river. There was a fear clutching at his heart that it might end; that in a moment this woman might depart and leave him unenlightened, and unable ever to find for himself the unimaginable world of words which she plucked out of those books and pinned into the great vacant spaces of his mind which he had kept empty all these years—not knowing that he was waiting for this night, when he should have the Mississippi bring into his eddy, alongside his own mission boat, what he most needed.

He sat there, a great, pathetic figure, shaggy, his heart thumping, taking from this trim, neat, beautiful woman the riches which she so casually, almost wantonly, threw to him in passing.

The corridors of his mind echoed to the tread of hosts; he heard the rumblings of history, the songs of poets whose words are pitched to the music of the skies, and he hung word pictures which Ruskin had painted in his imagination.

Fate had waited long to give him this night. It had waited till the man was ready, then with a lavish hand the storehouses of the master intellects of the world were opened to him, for him to help himself. Nelia suddenly started up from her chair and looked around, herself the victim of her own raillery, which had grown to be an understanding of the pathetic hunger of the man for these things.

It was daylight, and the flood of the sunrise was at hand.

"Parson," she said, "do you like these things—these books?"

"Missy," he whispered, "I could near repeat, word for word, all those things you've said and read to me to-night."

"There are lots more," she laughed. "I want to do something for your mission boat, will you let me?"

"Lawse! Yo've he'ped me now more'n yo' know!"

She smiled the smile that women have had from all the ages, for she knew a thousand times more than even the Prophet.

"I'll give you a set of all these books!" she said; "all the books that I have. Not these, my old pals—yes, these books, Mr. Rasba. If you'll take them? I'll get another lot down below."

"Lawd God! Give me yo' books!"

"Oh, they're not expensive—they're—"

"They're yours. Cayn't yo' see? It's your own books, an' hit's fo' my work. I neveh knowed how good men could be, an' they give me that boat fo' a mission boat. Now—now—missy—I cayn't tell yo'—I've no words—"

And with gratitude, with the simplicity of a mountain parson, he dropped on his knees and thanked God. As he told his humility, Prebol wakened from a deep and restful sleep to listen in amazement.

When at last Rasba looked up Nelia was gone. The books were on the table and he found another stack heaped up on the deck of the mission boat. But the woman was gone, and when he looked down the river he saw something flicker and vanish in the distance.

He stared, hurt; he choked, for a minute, in protest, then carried that immeasurable treasure into his cabin.

CHAPTER XXV

Renn Doss, the false friend, saw the danger of the recognition of the firearms by Carline. The savage swing of a half pound of fine shot braided up in a rawhide bag, and a good aim, reduced Carline to an inert figure of a man. "Renn Doss" was Hilt Despard, pirate captain, whose instantaneous action always had served him well in moments of peril.

The three men carried Carline to a bunk and dropped him on it. They covered him up and emptied a cupful of whiskey on his pillow and clothes. They even poured a few spoonfuls down his throat. They thus changed him to what might be called a "natural condition."

Then, sitting around the stove, they whispered among themselves, discussing what they had better do. Half a hundred possibilities occurred to their fertile fancies and replete memories. Men and women who have always led sheltered lives can little understand or know what a pirate must understand and know even to live let alone be successful.

"What's Terabon up to?" Despard demanded. "Here he is, drappin' down by Fort Pillow Landing, running around. Where's that girl he had up above New Madrid? What's his game? Coming up here and talking to us? Asking us all about the river and things—writin' it for the newspapers?"

"That woman's this Carline's wife!" Jet sneered.

"Sure! An' here's Terabon an' here's Carline. Terabon don't talk none about that woman—nor about Carline," Dock grumbled.

"I bet Terabon would be sorry none if Carline hyar dropped out. Y' know she's Old Crele's gal," Jet said. "Crele's a good feller. Sent word down to have us take cyar of her, an' Prebol, the fool, didn't know 'er, hadn't heard. Look what she give him, bang in the shoulder! That old Prophet'll take cyar of him, course. See how hit works out. She shined up to Terabon, all right."

"I 'low I better talk to him," Despard suggested. "Terabon's a good sport. He said, you' know, that graftin' and whiskey boatin', an' robbin' the bank wa'n't none of his business. He said, course, he could write it down in his notes, but without names, 'count of somebody might read somethin' in them an' get some good friend of his in Dutch. He said it wouldn't be right for him to know about somebody robbin' a commissary, or a bank, or killin' somebody, because if somebody like a sheriff or detective got onto it, they might blame him, or somethin'."

"I like that Terabon!" Jet declared. "Y'see how he is. He says he's satisfied, makin' a fair living, gettin' notes so's he can write them magazine stories, an' if he was to try to rob the banks, he'd have to learn how, same's writin' for newspapers. An' probably he wouldn't have the nerve to do it really, 'count of his maw and paw bein' the kind they was. He told me hisself that they made him go to Sunday school when he was a kid, an' things like that spoil a man for graftin'. Stands to reason, all right, the way he talks. I like him; he knows enough to mind his own business."

"He's comin' up to-night to go after geese on the bar. We'll talk to him. He'll look that business over, level-headed. That motorboat any good?"

"Nothin' extra. He's got ready money, though, I forgot that," Despard grinned, walking over to the hapless victim of his black-jack skill.

The three divided nearly thirteen hundred dollars among them. The money made them good humoured and they had some compassion for their prisoner. One of them noticed that a skiff was coming up from Fort Pillow Landing, and fifteen minutes later Terabon was talking to Despard on the snag to one prong of which was fastened the line of Carline's motorboat.

"I was wondering where I'd see you again," Terabon said. "Didn't have a chance at New Madrid, saw you was in business, so I didn't follow up none."

"I was wondering if you had a line on that," Despard said, doubtfully. "Y'know that woman you was staying with up on Island Ten Bar? Well, we got her man in here full's a fish. Lookin' for his woman, an' he's no good. Fell off the cabin, hit a spark in the back of the head when the water sucked when that steamboat went by this morning. He'd ought to go down to Memphis hospital, but—Well, we can't take 'im. You know how that is."

"Be glad to help you boys out any way I can," Terabon said. "I'll run him down."

"Say, would you? We don't want him on our hands," the pirate explained. "We'd get to see you down b'low some'rs."

"Sure, I would," Terabon exclaimed. "Fact is, the woman said it'd be a favour to her, too, if I'd get him home. She'll be dropping down likely. Darn nice girl, but quick tempered."

"That's right; quick ain't no name for it. She plugged a friend of mine up by Buffalo Island—"

"Prebol? I heard about him. She was scairt."

"She needn't be, never again!" Despard grinned. "When a lady can handle a river Law like she does, us bad uns are real nice!"

Terabon laughed, and the two went into the cabin-boat where Carline lay on the bunk. Terabon ran his hand around the man's head and neck, found the lump near the base of the skull, found that the neck wasn't broken, and made sure that the heart was beating—things a reporter naturally learns to do in police-station and hospital experience.

Jet brought the motorboat down to the stern of the cabin-boat, and the four carried Carline on board. They put him in his bunk, and Terabon, his skiff towing astern, steered out into the main current and soon faded down by Craighead Point Bar.

"I knowed he'd be all right," Despard declared. "He'll take him down to Memphis, and out of our way. I'd 'a' hated to kill him; it ain't no use killin' a man less'n it's necessary. We got what we was after. Course, if we'd rewarded him, likely we'd got a lot, but it ain't safe, holdin' a man for rewards ain't."

"That boat'd been a good one to travel in," Jet suggested.

"Everybody'd knowed it was Carline's, an' it wa'n't worth fixing over. Hull not much good, and the motor's been abused some. We'll do better'n that."

They had rid themselves of an incumbrance. They had made an acquaintance who was making himself useful. They were considerably richer than they had been for some time.

"I'd like to drap into Mendova," Jet mused. "We ain't had what you'd call a time—"

"Let's kill some birds first," Gaspard suggested. "I got a hunch that Yankee Bar's a good bet for us for a little while. We dassn't look into Memphis, 'count of last trip down. Mendova's all right, but wait'll we've hunted Yankee Bar."

The money burned in their pockets, but as they stood looking out at the long, beautiful Yankee Bar its appeal went home. For more than a hundred years generations of pirates had used there, and no one knows how many tragedies have left their stain in the great band around from Gold Dust Landing to Chickasaw Bluffs No. 1.

After dark they rowed over to the point and put out their decoys, dug their pits, screened them, and brushed over their tracks in the sand. Then they played cards till midnight, turned in for a little sleep, and turned out again in the black morning to go to their places with repeating shotguns and cripple-killer rifles in their hands.

When they were in their places, and the river silence prevailed, they saw the stars overhead, the reflections on sand and water around them, and the quivering change as air currents moved in the dark—the things that walk in the night. They heard, at intervals, many voices. Some they knew as the fluent music of migrant geese flying over on long laps of their fall flight, but some they did not know, except that they were river voices.

Ducks flew by no higher than the tops of the willow trees up the bar, their wings whistling and their voices eager in the dark. The lurkers saw these birds darting by like black streaks, tempting vain shots, but they were old hunters, and knew they wanted at least a little light. Over on the mainland they heard the noises of wilderness animals, and away off yonder a mule's "he-haw" reverberated through the bottoms and over bars and river.

For these things, if the pirates had only known it, they found the world endurable. Each in his own pit, given over to his own thoughts, they thrilled to the joy of living. All they wanted, really, was this kind of thing; hunting in fall and winter, fishing in the summer, and occasional visits to town for another kind of thrill, another sort of excitement. But their boyhood had been passed in privation, their youth amid temptations of appetite and vice, and now they were hopelessly mixed as to what they liked, what they didn't like, what the world would do for them, and what they would do to the world. Weaklings, uneducated, without balance; habit-ridden, yet with all that miserable inheritance from the world, they waited there rigid, motionless, their hearts thrilling to the increasing music of the march of dawn across the bottoms of the Mississippi.

False dawn flushed and faded almost like a deliberate lightning flash. Then dawn appeared, marking down the gray lines of the wilderness trees with one stroke, sweeping out all the stars with another brush, revealing the flocks of birds glistening against the sky while yet the earth was in shade. The watchers spied a score of birds, great geese far to the northward, coming right in line with them. They waited for a few seconds—ages long. Then one of the men cried:

"They're stoopin', boys! They're comin'!"

The wild geese, coming down a magnificent slant from a mile height, headed straight for Yankee Bar. Will birds never learn? They ploughed down with their wings folding, and poised. Their voices grew louder and louder as they approached.

With a hissing roar of their wings they pounded down out of the great, safe heights and circled around and inward. With a shout the three men started up through their masks and with levelled guns opened fire.

Too late the old gander at the point of the "V" began to climb; too late the older birds in the point screamed and gathered their strength. The river men turned their black muzzles against the necks of the young tail birds of the feathered procession and brought them tumbling down out of the line to the ground, where on the hard sand two of them split their breasts and exposed thick layers of fat dripping with oil.

The cries of the fleeing birds, the echoes of the barking guns, died away. The men shouted their joy in their success, gathered up their victims, scurried pack to cover, brushing over their tracks, and crouched down again, to await another flock.

Hunger drove them to their cabin-boat within an hour. They had thought they wanted to get some more birds, but in fact they knew they had enough. They went over to their boat, cooked up a big breakfast, and sat around the fire smoking and talking it over. They chattered like boys. They were gleeful, innocent, harmless! But only for a time. Then the hunted feeling returned to them. Once more they had a back track to watch and ambushes to be wary of. They wanted to go to Mendova, but again they didn't want to go there. They didn't know but what Mendova might be watching for them, the same as Memphis was. Certainly, they determined, they must go to Mendova after dark, and see a friend who would put them wise to actual conditions around town.

They took catnaps, having had too little sleep, and yet they could not sleep deeply. They watched the shanty-boats which dropped down the river at intervals, most of them in the main current close to the far bank, and often hardly visible against the mottled background of caving earth, fallen trees, and flickering mirage. Their restlessness was silent, morose, and one of them was always on the lookout.

Despard himself was on watch in the afternoon. He sat just inside the kitchen door, out of the sunshine, in a comfortable rocking chair. Two windows and the stern door gave him a wide view of the river, sandbars and eddy. It seemed but a minute, but he had fallen into a doze, when the splash of a shanty-boat sweeps awakened all the crew with a sudden, frightened start. Whispers, hardly audible, hailed in alarm. The three, crouching in involuntary doubt and dismay, glared at the newcomer.

It was a woman drifting in. Apparently she intended to land there, and the three men stared at her.

"His wife!" Despard said with soundless lips. The others nodded their recognition.

Mrs. Carline had run into the great dead eddy at the foot of Yankee Lower Bar, turned up in the slow reverse eddy of the chute, and was coming by their boat at the slowest possible speed.

Despard pulled his soft shirt collar, straightened his tie, hitched his suspenders, put on his coat, walked out on the stern deck, and, after a glance around, seemed suddenly to discover the stranger.

"Howdy!" he nodded, touching his cap respectfully, and gazing with flickering eyes at the woman whose marksmanship entitled her to the greatest respect.

"Howdy!" she nodded, scrutinizing him with level eyes. "Where am I?"

"Yankee Bar. Them's Chickasaw Bluffs No. 1."

"Do you know Jest Prebol?"

"Yessum." Despard's head bobbed in alarmed, unwilling assent.

"I thought perhaps you'd like to know that he's getting along all right."

"I bet he learnt his lesson," Despard grimaced.

"What? I don't just understand."

"About bein' impudent to a lady that can shoot—straight!"

A flicker moved the woman's countenance, and she smiled, oddly.

"Oh, any one is likely to make mistakes!"

"Darn fools is, Miss Crele. And you Old Crele's girl! He might of knowed!"

The other two stepped out to help enjoy the conversation and the scenery.

"You know me?" she demanded.

"Yessum, we shore do. My name's Despard—Jet here and Cope."

She acknowledged the introductions.

"I've friends down here," she said, with a little catch of her breath. "I was wondering if you—any of you gentlemen had seen them?"

"Your man, Gus Carline an' that writin' feller, Terabon?" Jet asked, without delicacy. Her cheeks flamed.

"Yes!" she whispered.

"Terabon took him down to Mendova or Memphis," Despard said. "Carline was—was on the cabin and the boat lurched when the steamboat passing drawed. He drapped over and hit a spark plug on the head!"

"Was he badly hurt?"

"Not much—kind of a lump, that's all."

She looked down at Fort Pillow Bluff. The pirates awaited her pleasure, staring at her to their heart's content. They envied her husband and Terabon; they felt the strangeness of the situation. She was following those two men down. She was part of the river tide, drifting by; she had shot Prebol, their pal, and had cleverly ascertained their knowledge of him while insuring that they had fair warning.

Her boat drifted down till it was opposite them, and then, with quick decision, she caught up a handy line, and said:

"I'm going to tie in a little while. I've been alone clear down from Caruthersville; I want to talk to somebody!"

She threw the rope, and they caught and made it fast. They swung her boat in, ran a plank from stern to bow, and Despard gave her his hand. She came on board, and they sat on the stern deck to talk. Only one kind of woman could have done that with safety, but she was that kind. She had shot a man down for a look.

The three pirates took one of the fat young geese, plucked and dressed it, and baked it in a hot oven, with dressing, sweet potatoes, hot-bread, and a pudding which she mixed up herself.

For three hours they gossiped, and before she knew it, she had told them about Prebol, about Parson Rasba introducing them. The pirates shouted when she told of Jest's apology. With river frankness, they said they thought a heap of Terabon, who minded his own business so cleverly.

"I like him, too," she admitted. "I was afraid you boys might make trouble for Carline, though. He don't know much about people, treating them right."

"He's one of those ignorant Up-the-Bankers," Despard said.

"Oh, I know him." She shrugged her shoulders a little bitterly.

As they ate the goose in camaraderie, the pirates took to warning and advising her about the Lower River; they told her who would treat her right, and who wouldn't. They especially warned her against stopping anywhere near Island 37.

"They're bad there—and mean." Despard shook his head, gravely.

"I won't stop in there," Nelia promised. "River folks anybody can get along with, but those Up-the-Bankers!"

"Hit's seo," Jet cried. "They don't have no feelings for nobody."

"You'll be dropping on down?" Nelia asked.

"D'rectly!" Cope admitted. "We 'lowed we'd stop into Mendova. You stop in there an' see Palura; he'll treat you right. He was in the riveh hisse'f once. You talk to him—"

"What did Terabon and Mr. Carline go on in? What kind of a boat?"

"A gasolene cruiser."

"Did he say where he'd be?"

"Terabon? No. Ask into Mendova or into Memphis. They can likely tell."

"Thank you, boys! I'm awful glad you've no hard feelings on account of my shooting your partner; I couldn't know what good fellows you are. We'll see you later."

Her smile bewitched them; she went aboard her boat, pulled over into the main current, and floated away in the sunset—her favourite river hour.

After hours of argument, debate, doubts, they, too, pulled out and floated past Fort Pillow.

CHAPTER XXVI

Parson Rasba piled the books on the crap table in his cabin and stood them in rows with their lettered backs up. He read their titles, which were fascinating: "Arabian Nights," "Representative Men," "Plutarch's Lives," "Modern Painters," "Romany Rye"—a name that made him shudder, for it meant some terrible kind of whiskey to his mind—"Lavengro," a foreign thing, "Thesaurus of English Words and Phrases," "The Stem Dictionary," "Working Principles of Rhetoric"—he wondered what rhetoric meant—"The Fur Buyers' Guide," "Stones of Venice," "The French Revolution," "Sartor Resartus," "Poe's Works," "Balzac's Tales," and scores of other titles.

All at once the Mississippi had brought down to him these treasures and a fair woman with blue eyes and a smile of understanding and sympathy, who had handed them to him, saying:

"I want to do something for your mission boat; will you let me?"

No fairyland, no enchantment, no translation from poverty and sorrow to a realm of wealth and happiness could have caught the soul of the Prophet Rasba as this revelation of unimagined, undreamed-of riches as he plucked the fruits of learning and enjoyed their luxuries. He had descended in his humility to the last, least task for which he felt himself worthy. He had humbly been grateful for even that one thing left for him to do: find Jock Drones for his mother.

He had found Jock, and there had been no wrestling with an obdurate spirit to send him back home, like a man, to face the law and accept the penalty. There had been nothing to it. Jock had seen the light instantly, and with relief. His partner had also turned back after a decade of doubt and misery, to live a man's part "back home." The two of them had handed him a floating Bethel, turning their gambling hell over to him as though it were a night's lodging, or a snack, or a handful of hickory nuts. The temple of his fathers had been no better for its purpose than this beautiful, floating boat.

Then a woman had come floating down, a beautiful strange woman whose voice had clutched at his heart, whose smile had deprived him of reason, whose eyes had searched his soul. With tears on her lashes she had flung to him that treasure-store of learning, and gone on her way, leaving him strength and consolation.

He left his treasure and went out to look at the river. Everybody leaves everything to look at the river! There is nothing in the world that will prevent it. He saw, in the bright morning, that Prebol had raised his curtain, and was looking at the river, too, though the effort must have caused excruciating pain in his wounded shoulder. Day was growing; from end to end of that vast, flowing sheet of water thousands upon thousands of old river people were taking a look at the Mississippi.

Rasba carried a good broth over to Prebol for breakfast, and then returned to his cabin, having made Prebol comfortable and put a dozen of the wonderful books within his reach. Then the River Prophet sat down to read his treasures, any and all of them, his lap piled up, three or four books in one hand and trying to turn the pages of another in his other hand by unskilful manipulation of his thumb. He was literally starving for the contents of those books.

He was afraid that his treasure would escape from him; he kept glancing from his printed page to the serried ranks on the crap table, and his hands unconsciously felt around to make sure that the weight on his lap and in his grasp was substantial and real, and not a dream or vision of delight.

He forgot to eat; he forgot that he had not slept; he sat oblivious of time and river, the past or the future; he grappled with pages of print, with broadsides of pictures, with new and thrilling words, with sentences like hammer blows, with paragraphs that marched like music, with thoughts that had the gay abandon of a bird in song. And the things he learned!

When night fell he was dismayed by his weariness, and could not understand it. For a little while he ransacked his dulled wits to find the explanation, and when he had fixed Prebol for the night, with medicine, water, and a lamp handy to matches, he told the patient:

"Seems like the gimp's kind of took out of me. My eyes are sore, an' I doubt am I quite well."

"Likely yo' didn't sleep well," Prebol suggested. "A man cayn't sleep days if he ain't used to hit."

"Sleep days?" Rasba looked wildly about him.

"Sho! When did I git to sleep, why, I ain't slept—I—Lawse!"

Prebol laughed aloud.

"Yo' see, Parson, yo' all cayn't set up all night with a pretty gal an' not sleep hit off. Yo' shore'll git tired, sportin' aroun'."

"Sho!" Rasba snapped, and then a smile broke across his countenance. He cried out with laughter, and admitted: "Hit's seo, Prebol! I neveh set up with a gal befo' I come down the riveh. Lawse! I plumb forgot."

"I don't wonder," Prebol replied, gravely. "She'd make any man forget. She sung me to sleep, an' I slept like I neveh slept befo'."

Rasba went on board his boat and, after a light supper, turned in. For a minute he saw in retrospect the most wonderful day in his life, a day which a kindly Providence had drawn through thirty or forty hours of unforgettable exaltation. Then he settled into the blank, deep sleep of a soul at peace and at rest.

When in the full tide of the sunshine he awakened, he went about his menial tasks, attending Prebol, cleaning out the boats, shaking up the beds, hanging the bedclothes to air in the sun, and getting breakfast. On Prebol's suggestion he moved the fleet of boats out into the eddy, for the river was falling and they might ground. He went over to Caruthersville and bought some supplies, brought Doctor Grell over to examine the patient to make sure all was well, killed several squirrels and three ducks back in the brakes, and, all the while, thought what duties he should enter upon.

Doctor Grell advised that Prebol go down to Memphis, to the hospital, so as to have an X-ray examination, and any special treatment which might be necessary. The wound was healing nicely, but it would be better to make sure.

Rasba took counsel of Prebol. The river man knew the needs of the occasion, and he agreed that he had better drop down to Memphis or Mendova, preferring the latter place, for he knew people there. He told Rasba to line the two small shanty-boats beside the big mission boat, and fend them off with wood chunks. The skiffs could float on lines alongside or at the stern. The power boat could tow the fleet out into the current, and hold it off sandbars or flank the bends.

Rasba did as he was bid, and lashed the boats together with mooring lines, pin-head to towing bits, and side to side. Then he floated the boats all on one anchor line, and ran the launch up to the bow. He hoisted in the anchor, rowed in a skiff out to the motorboat, and swung wide in the eddy to run out to the river current. There was a good deal of work to the task, and it was afternoon before the fleet reached the main stream.

Then Rasba cast off his tow lines, ran the launch back to the fleet, and made it fast to the port bow of the big boat, so that it was part of the fleet, with its power available to shove ahead or astern. A big oar on the mission boat's bow and another one out from Prebol's boat insured a short turn if it should be necessary to swing the boats around either way.

Rasba carried Prebol on his cot up to the bow of the big boat, and put him down where he could help watch the river, and they cast off. Prebol knew the bends and reaches, and named most of the landings; they gossiped about the people and the places. Prebol told how river rats sometimes stole hogs or cattle for food, and Rasba learned for the first time of organized piracy, of river men who were banded together for stealing what they could, raiding river towns, attacking "sports," tripping the river, and even more desperate enterprises.

While he talked, Prebol slyly watched his listener and thought for a long time that Rasba was merely dumbfounded by the atrocities, but at last the Prophet grinned:

"An' yo's a riveh rat. Ho law!"

"Why, I didn't say—" Prebol began, but his words faltered.

"Yo' know right smart about such things," Rasba reminded him. "I 'low hit were about time somebody shot yo' easy, so's to give yo' repentance a chance to catch up with yo' wickedness. Don't yo'?"

Prebol glared at the accusation, but Rasba pretended not to notice.

"Yo' see, Prebol, this world is jes' the hounds a-chasin' the rabbits, er the rabbits a-gittin' out the way. The good that's into a man keeps a-runnin', to git shut of the sin that's in him, an' theh's a heap of wrestlin' when one an' tother catches holt an' fights."

"Hit's seo!" Prebol admitted, reluctantly. He didn't have much use for religious arguments. "I wisht yo'd read them books to me, Parson. I ain't neveh had much eddycation. I'll watch the riveh, an' warn ye, 'gin we make the crossin's."

Nothing suited them better. Rasba read aloud, stabbing each word with his finger while he sought the range and rhythm of the sentences, and, as they happened to strike a book of fables, their minds could grasp the stories and the morals at least sufficiently to entertain and hold their attention.

Prebol said, warningly, after a time:

"Betteh hit that sweep a lick, Parson, she's a-swingin' in onto that bar p'int."

A few leisurely strokes, the boats drifted away into deep water, and Rasba expressed his admiration.

"Sho, Prebol! Yo' seen that bar a mile up. We'd run down onto hit."

"Yas, suh," the wounded man grinned. "Three-four licks on the oars up theh, and down yeah yo' save pullin' yo' livin' daylights out, to keep from goin' onto a sandbar or into a dryin'-up chute."

"How's that?" Rasba cocked his ear. "Say hit oveh—slow!"

"Why, if yo's into the set of the current up theh, hit ain't strong; yo' jes' give two-three licks an' yo' send out clear. Down theh on the bar she draws yo' right into shallow water, an' yo' hang up."

Rasba looked up the river; he looked down at the nearing sandbar, and as they passed the rippling head in safety he turned a grave face toward the pilot.

"Up theh, theh wasn't much suck to hit, but down yeah, afteh yo've drawed into the current, theh's a strong drag an' bad shoals?"

"Jes' so!"

"Hit's easy to git shut of sin, away long in the beginnin'," Rasba bit his words out, "but when yo' git a long ways down into hit—Ho law!"

Prebol started, caught by surprise. Then both laughed together. They could understand each other better and if Prebol felt himself being drawn in spite of his own reluctance by a new current in his life, Rasba did not fail to gratify the river man's pride by turning always to him for advice about the river, its currents and its jeopardies.

"I've tripped down with all kinds," Prebol grinned as he spoke, "but this yeah's the firstest time I eveh did get to pilot a mission boat."

"If you take it through in safety, do yo' reckon God will forget?" Rasba asked, and Prebol's jaw dropped. He didn't want to be reformed; he had no use for religion. He was very well satisfied with his own way of living. He objected to being prayed over and the good of his soul inquired into—but this Parson Rasba was making the idea interesting.

They anchored for the night in the eddy at the head of Needham's Cut-Off Bar, and Prebol was soon asleep, but Rasba sat under the big lamp and read. He could read with continuity now; dread that the dream would vanish no longer afflicted him. He could read a book without having more than two or three other books in his lap.

Sometimes it was almost as though Nelia were speaking the very words he read; sometimes he seemed to catch her frown of disapproval. The books, more precious than any other treasure could have been, seemed living things because she had owned them, because her pencil had marked them, and because she had given them all to his service, to fill the barren and hungry places in the long-empty halls of his mind.

He would stop his reading to think, and thinking, he would take up a book to discover better how to think. He found that his reading and thinking worked together for his own information.

He was musing, his mind enjoying the novelty of so many different images and ideas and facts, when something trickled among his senses and stirred his consciousness into alert expectancy. For a little he was curious, and then touched by dismay, for it was music which had roused him—music out of the black river night. People about to die sometimes hear music, and Parson Rasba unconsciously braced himself for the shock.

It grew louder, however, more distinct, and the sound was too gay and lively to fit in with his dreams of a heavenly choir. He caught the shout of a human voice and he knew that dancers were somewhere, perhaps dancers damned to eternal mirth. He went out on the deck and closed the door on the light behind him; at first he could see nothing but black night. A little later he discovered boats coming down the river, eight or nine gleaming windows, and a swinging light hung on a flag staff or shanty-boat mast.

As they drew nearer, someone shouted across the night:

"Goo-o-o-d wa-a-a-ter thar?"

"Ya-s-su-uh!" Rasba called back.

"Where'll we come in?"

"Anywhere's b'low me fo' a hundred yards!"

"Thank-e-e!"

Three or four sweeps began to beat the water, and a whole fleet of shanty-boats drifted in slowly. They began to turn like a wheel as part of them ran into the eddy while the current carried the others down, but old river men were at the sweeps, and one of them called the orders:

"Raunch 'er, boys! Raunch 'er! Raunchin's what she needs!"

They floated out of the current into the slow reverse eddy, and coming up close to Rasba's fleet, talked back and forth with him till a gleam of light through a window struck him clearly out of the dark.

"Hue-e-e!" a shrill woman's voice laughed. "Hit's Rasba, the Riveh Prophet Rasba! Did yo' all git to catch Nelia Crele, Parson?"

"Did I git to catch Missy Crele!" he repeated, dazed.

"When yo' drapped out'n Wolf Island Chute, Parson, that night she pulled out alone?"

"No'm; I lost her down by the Sucks, but she drapped in by Caruthersville an' give me books an' books—all fo' my mission boat!"

"That big boat yourn?"

"Yeh."

"Where all was hit built?"

"I don' remembeh, but Buck done give hit to me, him an' Jock Drones."

"Hi-i-i! Yo' all found the man yo' come a-lookin' fo'. Ho law!"

"Hit's the Riveh Prophet," someone replied to a hail from within, the dance ending.

A crowd came tumbling out onto the deck of the big boat of the dance hall, everyone talking, laughing, catching their breaths.

"Hi-i! Likely he'll preach to-morrow," a woman cried. "To-morrow's Sunday."

"Sunday?" Rasba gasped. "Sunday—I plumb lost track of the days."

"You'll preach, won't yo', Parson? I yain't hearn a sermon in a hell of a while," a man jeered, facetiously.

"Suttingly. An' when hit's through, yo'll think of hell jes' as long," Rasba retorted, with asperity, and his wit turned the laugh into a cheer.

The fleet anchored a hundred yards up the eddy, and Rasba heard a woman say it was after midnight and she'd be blanked if she ever did or would dance on Sunday. The dance broke up, the noise of voices lessened, one by one the lights went out, and the eddy was still again. But the feeling of loneliness was changed.

"Lord God, what'll I preach to them about?" Rasba whispered. "I neveh 'lowed I'd be called to preach ag'in. Lawse! Lawse! What'll I say?"

CHAPTER XXVII

Carline ascended into the world again. It was a painful ascent, and when he looked around him, he recognized the interior of his motorboat cabin, heard and felt the throbbing of his motor, and discovered aches and pains that made his extremities tingle. He sat up, but the blackness that seemed to rise around him caused him to fall hastily back upon the stateroom bunk.

He remembered his discovery of his own firearms on the shanty-boat, and fear assailed him. He remembered his folly in crying out that those were his guns. He might have known he had fallen among thieves. He cursed himself, and dread of what might yet follow his indiscretion made him whimper with terror. A most disgusting odour of whiskey was in his nostrils, and his throat was like a corrugated iron pipe partly filled with soot.

The door of the tiny stateroom was closed, but the two ports were open to let the air in. It occurred to him that he might be a captive, and would be held for ransom. Perhaps the pirates would bleed him for $50,000; perhaps they would take all his fortune! He began to cry and sob. They might cut his throat, and not give him any chance of escape. He had heard of men having had their throats cut down the river.

He tried to sit up again, and succeeded without undue faintness. He could not wait, but must know his fate immediately. He found the door was unlocked, and when he slipped out into the cabin, he found that there was only one man on board, the steersman, who was sitting in the engine pit, and steering with the rail wheel instead of the bow-cabin one.

He peered out, and found that it was Terabon, who discovered him and hailed him, cheerily:

"How are you feeling?"

"Tough—my head!"

"You're lucky to be alive!" Terabon said. "You got in with a crew of river pirates, but they let me have you. Did they leave you anything?"

"Leave me anything!" Carline repeated, feeling in his pockets. "I've got my watch, and here's—"

He opened up his change pocketbook. There were six or seven dollars in change and two or three wadded bills. When he looked for his main supply, however, there was a difference. The money was all gone. He was stripped to the last dollar in his money belt and of his hidden resources.

"They did me!" he choked. "They got all I had!"

"They didn't kill you," Terabon said. "You're lucky. How did they bang you and knock you out?"

"Why, I found they had my guns on board—"

"And you accused them?"

"No! I just said they were mine, I was surprised!"

"Then?"

"My light went out."

"When did they get your guns?"

"I woke up, up there, and you were gone. My guns and pocket money were gone, too. I thought—"

"You thought I'd robbed you?"

"Ye—Well, I didn't know!"

"This is a devil of a river, old man!" said Terabon. "I guess you travelled with the real thing out of New Madrid—"

"Doss, Renald Doss. He said he was a sportsman—"

"Oh, he is, all right, he's a familiar type here on the river. He's the kind of a sport who hunts men, Up-the-Bankers and game of that kind. He's a very successful hunter, too—"

"He said we'd hunt wild geese. We went up Obion River, and had lots of fun, and he said he'd help—he'd help—"

"Find your wife?"

"Yes, sir."

Carline was abject. Terabon, however, was caught wordless. This man was the husband of the woman for whose sake he had ventured among the desperate river rats, and now he realized that he had succeeded in the task she had set him. Looking back, he was surprised at the ease of its accomplishment, but he was under no illusions regarding the jeopardy he had run. He had trusted to his aloofness, his place as a newspaper man, and his frankness, to rescue Carline, and he had brought him away.

"You're all righ now," Terabon suggested. "I guess you've had your lesson."

"A whole book full of them!" Carline cried. "I owe you something—an apology, and my thanks! Where are we going?"

"I was taking you down to a Memphis hospital, or to Mendova—"

"I don't need any hospital. I'm broke; I must get some money. We'll go to Mendova. I know some people there. I've heard it was a great old town, too! I always wanted to see it."

Terabon looked at him; Carline had learned nothing. For a minute remorse and comprehension had flickered in his mind, now he looked ahead to a good time in Mendova, to sight-seeing, sporting around, genial friends, and all the rest. Argument would do no good, and Terabon retreated from his position as friend and helper to that of an observer and a recorder of facts. Whatever pity he might feel, he could not help but perceive that there was no use trying to help fools.

It was just dusk when they ran into Mendova. The city lights sparkled as they turned in the eddy and ran up to the shanty-boat town. They dropped an anchor into the deep water and held the boat off the bank by the stern while they ran a line up to a six-inch willow to keep the bow to the bank. The springy, ten-foot gangplank bridged the gap to the shore.

More than thirty shanty-boats and gasolene cruisers were moored along that bank, and from nearly every one peered sharp eyes, taking a look at the newcomers.

"Hello, Terabon!" someone hailed, and the newspaper man turned, surprised. One never does get over that feeling of astonishment when, fifteen hundred miles or so from home, a familiar voice calls one's name in greeting.

"Hello!" Terabon replied, heartily, and then shook hands with a market hunter he had met for an hour's gossip in the eddy at St. Louis. "Any luck, Bill? How's Frank?"

"Averaging fine," was the answer. "Frank's up town. Going clear down after all, eh?"

"Probably."

"Any birds on Yankee Bar?"

"I saw some geese there—hunters stopped in, too. How is the flight?"

"We're near the tail of it; mostly they've all gone down. We're going to drive for it, and put out our decoys down around Big Island and below."

"Then I'll likely see you down there."

"Sure thing; here's Frank."

Terabon shook hands with the two, introduced Carline, and then the hunters cast off and steered away down the stream. They had come more than a thousand miles with the migrating ducks and geese, intercepting them at resting or feeding places. That touch and go impressed Terabon as much as anything he had ever experienced.

He went up town with Carline, who found a cotton broker, a timber merchant, and others who knew him. It was easy to draw a check, have it cashed, and Carline once more had ready money. Nothing would do but they must go around to Palura's to see Mendova's great attraction for travellers.

Palura supplied entertainment and excitement for the whole community, and this happened to be one of his nights of special effort. Personally, Palura was in a temper. Captain Dalkard, of the Mendova Police, had been caught between the Citizens' Committee and Palura's frequenters. There were 100 citizens in the committee, and Palura's frequenters were unnamed, but familiar enough in local affairs.

The cotton broker thought it was a good joke, and he explained the whole situation to Terabon and Carline for their entertainment.

"Dalkard called in Policeman Laddam and told him to stand in front of Palura's, and tell people to watch out. You see, there's been a lot of complaints about people being short changed, having their pockets picked, and getting doped there, and some people think it doesn't do the town any good. Some think we got to have Palura's for the sake of the town's business. I'm neutral, but I like to watch the fun. We'll go down there and look in to-night."

They had dinner, and about 9 o'clock they went around to Palura's. It was an old market building made over into a pleasure resort, and it filled 300 feet front on Jimpson Street and 160 feet on the flanking side streets. A bright electric sign covered the front with a flare of yellow lights and there was one entrance, under the sign.

As Terabon, Carline, and the cotton broker came along, they saw a tall, broad-shouldered, smooth-shaven policeman in uniform standing where the lights showed him up.

"Watch your pocketbooks!" the policeman called softly to the patrons. "Watch your change; pickpockets, short-changers, and card-stackers work the unwary here! Keep sober—look out for knock-out drops!"

He said it over and over again, in a purring, jeering tone, and Terabon noticed that he was poised and tense. In the shadows on both sides of the policeman Terabon detected figures lurking and he was thrilled by the evident fact that one brave policeman had been sent alone into that deadly peril to confront a desperate gang of crooks, and that the lone policeman gloried to be there.

The cotton broker, neutral that he was, whispered as they disregarded the warnings: "Laddam cleaned up Front Street in six months; the mob has all come up here, and this is their last stand. It'll hurt business if they close this joint up, because the town'll be dead, but I wish Palura'd kind of ease down a bit. He's getting rough."

Little hallways and corridors led into dark recesses on either side of the building, and faint lights of different colours showed the way to certain things. Terabon saw a wonderfully beautiful woman, in furs, with sparkling diamonds, and of inimitable grace waiting in a little half-curtained cubby hole; he heard a man ask for "Pete," and caught the word "game" twice. The sounds were muffled, and a sense of repression and expectancy permeated the whole establishment.

They entered a reception room, with little tables around the sides, music blaring and blatant, a wide dancing floor, and a scurrying throng. All kinds were there: spectators who were sight-seeing; participants who were sporting around; men, women, and scoundrels; thugs and their prospective victims; people of supposed allurement; and sports of insipid, silly pose and tricked-up conspicuousness.

Terabon's gaze swept the throng. Noise and merriment were increasing. Liquor was working on the patrons. The life of Mendova was stirring to blaring music. The big hall was bare, rough, and gaunt. Dusty flags and cobwebs dangled from the rafters and hog-chain braces. A few hard, white lights cast a blinding glare straight down on the heads of the dancers and drinkers and onlookers.

Business was brisk, and shouts of "Want the waiter!" indicated the insistence with which trade was encouraged and even insisted upon. No sooner had Terabon and his companions seated themselves than a burly flat-face with a stained white apron came and inflicted his determined gaze upon them. He sniffed when Terabon ordered plain soda.

"We got a man's drink."

"I'm on the water wagon for awhile," Terabon smiled, and the waiter nodded, sympathetically. A tip of a quarter mollified his air of surly expectancy completely, and as he put the glasses down he said:

"The Boss is sick the way he's bein' treated. They ain't goin' to git away wit' stickin' a bull in front of his door like he was a crook."

Terabon heard a woman at a near-by table making her protest against the policeman out in front. No other topic was more than mentioned, and the buzz and burr of voices vied with the sound of the band till it ended. Then there was a hush.

"Palura!" a whisper rippled in all directions.

Terabon saw a man about 5 feet 10 inches tall, compactly built, square shouldered, and just a trifle pursy at the waist line, approaching along the dancing floor. He was light on his small feet, his shoulders worked with feline grace, but his face was a face as hard as limestone and of about the same colour—bluish gray. His eyes were the colour of ice, with a greenish tinge. Smooth-shaven cheeks, close-cropped hair, wing-like ears, and a little round head were details of a figure that might have been heroic—for his jaw was square, his nose large, and his forehead straight and broad.

Everyone knew he was going out to throw the policeman, Laddam, into the street. The policeman had not hurt business a pennyworth as yet, but Palura felt the insult. Palura knew the consequences of failing to meet the challenge.

"Give 'im hell!" someone called.

Palura turned and nodded, and a little yelping cheer went up, which ceased instantly. Terabon, observing details, saw that Palura's coat sagged on the near side—in the shape of an automatic pistol. He saw, too, that the man's left sleeve sagged round and hard—a slingshot or black-jack.

There was no delay; Palura went straight through to his purpose. He disappeared in the dark and narrow entrance way and not a sound was audible except the scuffling of feet.

"Palura's killed four men," the cotton broker whispered to Terabon, under his breath.

What seemed an age passed. The lights flickered. Terabon looked about in alarm lest that gang—

A crash outside brought all to their feet, and the whole crowd fell back against the walls. Out of the corridor surged a mass of men, and among them stalked a stalwart giant of a man draped with the remnants of a policeman's uniform. He had in his right hand a club which he was swinging about him, and every six feet a man dropped upon the floor.

Terabon saw Palura writhing, twisting, and working his way among the fighting mass. He heard a sharp bark:

"Back, boys!"

Four or five men stumbled back and two rolled out of the way of the feet of the policeman. It flashed to Terabon what had been done. They had succeeded in getting the policeman into the huge den of vice, where he could not legally be without a warrant, where Palura could kill him and escape once more on the specious plea of self-defence. Terabon saw the grin of perfect hate on Palura's face as both his hands came up with automatics in them—a two-handed gunman with his prey.

This would teach the policemen of Mendova to mind their own business! Suddenly Policeman Laddam threw his night stick backhanded at the infamous scoundrel, and Palura dodged, but not quite quickly nor quite far enough. The club whacked noisily against his right elbow and Palura uttered a cry of pain as one pistol fell to the floor.

Then Laddam snatched out his own automatic, a 45-calibre gun, three pounds or more in weight, and began to shoot, calmly, deliberately, and with the artistic appreciation of doing a good job thoroughly.

His first bullet drove Palura straight up, erect; his next carried the bully back three steps; his next whirled him around in a sagging spiral, and the fourth dropped the dive keeper like a bag of loose potatoes.

Laddam looked around curiously. He had never been there before. Lined up on all sides of him were the waiters, bouncers, men of prey, their faces ghastly, and three or four of them sick. The silent throng around the walls stared at the scene from the partial shadows; no one seemed even to be breathing. Then Palura made a horrible gulping sound, and writhed as he gave up his last gasp of life.

"Now then!" Laddam looked about him, and his voice was the low roar of a man at his kill. "You men pick them up, pack them outside there, and up to headquarters. March!"

As one man, the men who had been Palura's marched. They gathered up the remains of Palura and the men with broken skulls, and carried them out into the street. The crowd followed, men and women both. But outside, the hundreds scurried away in all directions, men afraid and women choking with horror. Terabon's friend the cotton broker fled with the rest, Carline disappeared, but Terabon went to headquarters, writing in his pocket notebook the details of this rare and wonderful tragedy.

Policeman Laddam had single-handed charged and captured the last citadel of Mendova vice, and the other policemen, when they looked at him, wore expressions of wonder and bewilderment. They knew the Committee of 100 would make him their next chief and a man under whom it would be a credit to be a cop.

Terabon, just before dawn, returned toward Mousa Slough. As he did so, from a dull corner a whisper greeted him:

"Say, Terabon, is it straight, Palura killed up?"

"Sure thing!"

"Then Mendova's sure gone to hell!" Hilt Despard the river pirate cried. "Say, Terabon, there's a lady down by the slough wants to get to talk to you."

"Who—?"

"She just dropped in to-night, Nelia Crele! She's into her boat down at the head of the sandbar, facing the switch willows. There's a little gasolene sternwheeler next below her boat."

"She's dropped in? All right, boys, much obliged!"

They separated.

But when Terabon searched along the slough for Nelia's boat he did not find it, and to his amazed anger he found that the gasolene boat in which he had arrived was also gone, as well as his own skiff and all his outfit.

"Darn this river!" he choked. "But that's a great story I sent of the killing of Palura!"

CHAPTER XXVIII

Nelia Crele had laughed in her heart at Elijah Rasba as he sat there listening to her reading. She knew what she was doing to the mountain parson! She played with his feelings, touched strings of his heart that had never been touched before, teased his eyes with a picture of feminine grace, stirred his mind with the sense of a woman who was bright and who knew so much that he had never known. At the same time, there was no malice in it—just the delight in making a strong man discover a strength beyond his own, and in humbling a masculine pride by the sheer superiority of a woman who had neglected no opportunity to satisfy a hunger to know.

She knew the power of a single impression and a clear, quick getaway. She left him dazed by the fortune which heaped upon him literary classics in a dozen forms—fiction, essays, history, poetry, short stories, criticism, fable, and the like; she laughed at her own quick liking for the serious-minded, self-deprecatory, old-young man whose big innocent eyes displayed a soul enamoured by the spirited intelligence of an experienced and rather disillusioned young woman who had fled from him partly because she did know what a sting it would give him.

So with light heart and singing tongue she floated away on the river, not without a qualm at leaving those books with Rasba; she loved them too much, but the sacrifice was so necessary—for his work! The river needed him as a missionary. He could help ease the way of the old sinners, and perhaps by and by he would reform her, and paint her again with goodness where she was weather-beaten.

It is easy to go wrong on the Mississippi—just as easy, or easier, than elsewhere in the world. The student of astronomy, gazing into the vast spaces of the skies, feels his own insignificance increasing, while the magnitude of the constellations grows upon him. What can it matter what such a trifling thing, such a mere atom, as himself does when he is to the worlds of less size than the smallest of living organisms in a drop of water?

Nelia Crele looked around as she left the eddy and saw that her houseboat was but a trifle upon a surface containing hundreds of square miles. A human being opposite her on the bank was less in proportion than a fly on the cabin window pane. Then what could it matter what she did? Why shouldn't she be reckless, abandoned, and live in the gaiety of ages?

She had read thousands of pages of all kinds with no guide posts or moral landmarks. A picture of dangerous delights had come into her imagination. Having read and understood so much, she had not failed to discover the inevitable Nemesis on the trail of wrongdoing, as well as the inevitableness of reward for steadfastness in virtues—but she wondered doubtfully what virtue really was, whether she was not absolved from many rigid commandments by the failure of the world to keep faith with her and reward her for her own patience and atone for her own sufferings.

It was easy, only too easy, on the surface to feel that if she wanted to be gay and wanton, living for the hour, it was no one's affair but her own. She fought the question out in her mind. She fixed her determination on the young and, in one sense, inexperienced newspaper man whose ambitions pleased her fancy and whose innocence delighted her own mood.

He was down the river somewhere, and when she landed in at Mendova in the late twilight she saw his skiff swinging from the stern of a motorboat. Having made fast near it, she quickly learned that he had gone up town, and that someone had heard him say that he was going to Palura's.

Palura's! Nelia had heard the fascination of that den's ill-fame. She laughed to herself when she thought that Terabon would excuse his going there on the ground of its being right in his line of work, that he must see that place because otherwise he would not know how to describe it.

"If I can catch him there!" she thought to herself.

She went to Palura's, and Old Mississippi seemed to favour her. She found another woman who knew the ropes there and who was glad to help her play the game. From a distance Nelia Crele discovered that Terabon was with Carline, her own husband. She dismissed him with a shrug of her shoulders, and told her companion to take care of him.

Nelia, having plagued the soul of the River Prophet, Rasba, now with equal zest turned to seize Terabon, careless of where the game ended if only she could begin it and carry it on to her own music and in her own measure.

They had it all determined: Carline was to be wedged away with his friend, a cotton broker that Daisy—Nelia's newfound accomplice—knew, and Terabon was to be tempted to "do the Palace," and he was to be caught unaware, by Nelia, who wanted to dance with him, dine with him under bright lights, and drink dangerous drinks with him. She knew him sober and industrious, good and faithful, a decent, reputable working man—she wanted to see him waked up and boisterous, careless for her sake and because of her desires.

She just felt wicked, wanted to be wicked, and didn't care how wicked she might be. She counted, however, without the bonds which the Mississippi River seems at times to cast around its favourites—the Spirit of the river which looks after his own.

She had not even seen Policeman Laddam standing at the main entrance of the notorious resort, for Daisy had taken her through another door. She went to the exclusive "Third," and from there emerged onto the dancing floor just as Palura ostentatiously went forth to drive Laddam away, or to kill him.

Daisy checked her, for the minute or two of suspense, and then the whole scene, the tragedy, was enacted before her gaze. She was not frightened; she was not even excited; the thing was so astonishing that she did not quite grasp its full import till she saw Palura stumbling back, shot again and again. Daisy caught her arm and clutched it in dumb panic, and when the policeman calmly bent the cohorts of the dead man to his will and carried away his victims, Daisy dragged Nelia away.

Then Daisy disappeared and Nelia was left to her own devices.

She was vexed and disappointed. She knew nothing of the war in Mendova. Politics had never engaged her attention, and the significance of the artistic killing of Palura did not appear to her mind. She was simply possessed by an indignant feminine impatience to think that Terabon had escaped, and she was angry when she had only that glimpse of him, as with his notebook in hand he raced his pencil across the blank pages, jotting down the details and the hasty, essential impressions as he caught them.

She heard the exodus. She heard women sobbing and men gasping as they swore and fled. She gathered up her own cloak and left with reluctant footsteps.

She realized that she had arrived there just one day too late to "do" Palura's. The fugitives, as they scurried by, reminded her of some description which she had read of the Sack of Rome; or was it the Fall of Babylon? Their sins were being visited upon the wicked, and Nelia Crele, since she had not sinned, could not thrill with quite the same terror and despair of the wretches who had sinned in spite of their consciences, instead of through ignorance or wantonness. She took her departure not quite able to understand why there had been so much furore because one man had been killed.

She was among the last to leave the accursed place, and she saw the flight of the ones who had delayed, perhaps to loot, perhaps having just awakened to the fact of the tragedy. She turned toward Mousa Slough, and her little shanty-boat seemed very cool and bare that late evening. The bookshelves were all empty, and she was just a little too tired to sleep, just a little too stung by reaction to be happy, and rather too much out of temper to be able to think straight and clearly on the disappointment.

Mendova had been familiar in her ears since childhood; she had heard stories of its wildness, its gayeties, its recklessness. Impression had been made upon impression, so that when she had found herself nearing the place of her dreams, she was in the mood to enter into its wildest and gayest activities; she had expected to, and she had known in her own mind that when she met Terabon she would be irresistible.

At last she shuddered. She seemed to hear a voice, the river's voice, declare that this thing had happened to prevent her seeking to betray herself and Terabon, not to mention that other matter which did not affect her thought in the least, her husband's honour.

The idea of her husband's honour made the thing absurd to her. There was no such thing as that honour. She had plotted to get Carline out of the way now that she heard he was clear of the pirates. On second thought, she was sorry that she had been so hasty in returning to the boat, wishing that she had followed up Terabon.

She walked out onto the bow deck, and standing in the dark, with her door closed, looked up and down the slough. A dozen boats were in sight. She heard a number of men and women talking in near-by boats, and the few words she heard indicated that the river people had a pretty morsel of gossip in the killing of Palura.

She heard men rustling through the weeds and switch willows of the boatmen's pathway, and she hailed; she was now a true river woman, though she did not know it.

"Say, boys, do you know if Terabon and Carline landed here to-night?"

"We just landed in," one answered. "I don't know."

"Going up town?"

"Yes—"

"I want to know about them—"

"Hit's Nelia Crele!" one exclaimed.

"That's right. Hello, boys—Despard—Jet—Cope!"

"Sure! When'd you land?"

"Late this evening; I was up to Palura's when—"

"That ain't no place fo' a lady."

She laughed aloud, as she added, "I was there when Palura was killed by the policeman."

"Palura killed a policeman!" Despard said. "He's killed—"

"No, Palura was killed by a policeman. Shot him dead right on the dance-hall floor."

The pirates choked. The thing was unbelievable. They came down to the boat and she described the affair briefly, and they demanded details.

They felt that it would vitally affect Mendova. They whispered among themselves as to what it meant. They learned that a policeman had been stationed in front of the notorious resort and that that policeman had done the shooting during a fight with waiters and bouncers and with Palura himself.

"We hadn't better get to go up town," Jet whimpered. "Hit don't sound right!"

They argued and debated, and finally went on their way, having promised Nelia that they would see and tell Terabon, on the quiet, that she had come into the slough, and that she wanted to see him.

She waited for some time, hoping that Terabon would come, but finally went to sleep. She was tired, and excitement had deserted her. She slept more soundly than in some time.

Once she partly awakened, and thought that some drift log had bumped into her boat; then she felt a gentle undulation, as of the waves of a passing steamer, but she was too sleepy to contemplate that phenomenon in a rather narrow water channel around a bend from the main current.

It was not till she had slept long and well that she began to dream vividly. She was impatient with dreams; they were always full of disappointment.

Daylight came, and sunshine penetrated the window under which she slept. The bright rays fell upon her closed eyes and stung her cheeks. She awakened with difficulty, and looked around wonderingly. She saw the sunlight move along the wall and then drift back again. She felt the boat teetering and swaggering. She looked out of the window and saw a distant wood across the familiar, glassy yellow surface of the Mississippi. With a low whisper of dismay she started out to look around, and found that she was really adrift in mid-river.

On the opposite side of the boat she saw the blank side of a boat against her cabin window. As she stood there, she heard or felt a motion on the boat alongside. Someone stepped, or rather jumped heavily, onto the bow deck of her boat and flung the cabin door open.

She sprang to get her pistol, and stood ready, as the figure of a man stumbled drunkenly into her presence.

CHAPTER XXIX

Parson Elijah Rasba, the River Prophet, could not think what he would say to these river people who had determined to have a sermon for their Sabbath entertainment. Neither his Bible nor his hurried glances from book to book which Nelia Crele had given him brought any suggestion which seemed feasible. His father had always declared that a sermon, to be effective, "must have one bullet fired straight."

What bullet would reach the souls of these river people who sang ribald songs, danced to lively music, and lived clear of all laws except the one they called "The Law," a deadly, large-calibre revolver or automatic pistol?

"I 'low I just got to talk to them like folks," he decided at last, and with that comforting decision went to sleep.

The first thing, after dawn, when he looked out upon the river in all the glory of sunshine and soft atmosphere and young birds, he heard a hail:

"Eh, Prophet! What time yo' all goin' to hold the meeting?"

"Round 10 or 11 o'clock," he replied.

Rasba went to one of the boats for breakfast, and he was surprised when Mamie Caope asked him to invoke a blessing on their humble meal of hot-bread, sorghum, fried pork chops, oatmeal, fried spuds, percolator coffee, condensed cream, nine-inch perch caught that morning, and some odds and ends of what she called "leavings."

Then the women all went over on his big mission boat and cleaned things up, declaring that men folks didn't know how to keep their own faces clean, let alone houseboats. They scrubbed and mopped and re-arranged, and every time Rasba appeared they splashed so much that he was obliged to escape.

When at last he was allowed to return he found the boat all cleaned up like a honey-comb. He found that the gambling apparatus had been taken away, except the heavy crap table, which was made over into a pulpit, and that chairs and benches had been arranged into seats for a congregation. A store-boat man climbed to the boat's roof at 10:30, with a Texas steer's horn nearly three feet long, and began to blow.

The blast reverberated across the river, and echoed back from the shore opposite; it rolled through the woods and along the sandbars; and the Prophet, listening, recalled the tales of trumpets which he had read in the Bible. At intervals of ten minutes old Jodun filled his great lungs, pursed his lips, and swelled his cheeks to wind his great horn, and the summons carried for miles. People appeared up the bank, swamp angels from the timber brakes who strolled over to see what the river people were up to, and skiffs sculled over to bring them to the river meeting. The long bend opposite, and up and down stream, where no sign of life had been, suddenly disgorged skiffs and little motorboats of people whose floating homes were hidden in tiny bays, or covered by neutral colours against their backgrounds.

The women hid Rasba away, like a bridegroom, to wait the moment of his appearance, and when at last he was permitted to walk out into the pulpit he nearly broke down with emotion. There were more than a hundred men and women, with a few children, waiting eagerly for him. He was a good old fellow; he meant all right; he'd taken care of Jest Prebol, who had deserved to be shot; he was pretty ignorant of river ways, but he wanted to learn about them; he hadn't hurt their feelings, for he minded his own business, saying not a word about their good times, even if he wouldn't dance himself. They could do no better than let him know that they hadn't any hard feelings against him, even if he was a parson, for he didn't let on that they were sinners. Anyway, they wanted to hear him hit it up!

"I came down here to find a son whose mother was worrited about him," Rasba began at the beginning. "I 'lowed likely if I could find Jock it'd please his mammy, an' perhaps make her a little happier. And Jock 'lowed he'd better go back, and stand trial, even if it was a hanging matter.

"You see, I didn't expect you'd get to learn very much from me, and I haven't been disappointed. I'm the one that's learning, and when I think what you've done for me, and when I see what Old Mississip' does, friendlying for all of us, tripping us along—"

They understood. He looked at the boat, at them, and through the wide-open windows at the sun-rippled water.

"Now for religion. Seems like I'm impudent, telling you kindly souls about being good to one another, having no hard, mean feelings against anybody, and living like you ought to live. We're all sinners! Time and again hit's ag'in the grain to do what's right, and if we taste a taste of white liquor, or if hit's stained with burnt sugar to make hit red, why—"

"Sho!" someone grinned. "Parson Rasba knows!"

The preacher joined the laughter.

"Yas, suh!" he admitted, more gravely, "I know. I 'lowed, one time, that I'd git to know this yeah happiness that comes of liquor, an' I shore took one awful gulp. Three nights an' three days I neveh slept a wink, an' me settin' theh by the fireplace, waitin' to be lit up an' jubulutin', but hit didn't come. I've be'n happier, jes' a-settin' an' lookin' at that old riveh, hearin' the wild geese flocking by!

"That old riveh—Lawse! If the Mississippi brings you fish and game; if it gives you sheltered eddies to anchor in, and good banks or sandbars to tie against; if this great river out here does all that for you, what do you reckon the Father of that river, of all the world, of all the skies would do, He being so much friendlier and powerfuller?

"Hit's easy to forget the good that's done to you. Lots an' lots of times, I bet you've not even thought of the good you've had from the river, from the sunshine, from the winds, plenty to eat and warm of nights on your boats and in your cabins. It's easy to remember the little evil things, the punishments that are visited upon us for our sins or because we're ignorant and don't know; but reckon up the happiness you have, the times you are blessed with riches of comfort and pleasure, and you'll find yourself so much happier than you are sad that you'll know how well you are cared for.

"I cayn't preach no reg'lar sermon, with text-tes and singing and all that. Seems like I jes' want to talk along rambling like, and tell you how happy you are all, for I don't reckon you're much wickeder than you are friendly on the average. I keep a-hearing about murdering and stealing and whiskey boating and such things. They're signs of the world's sinfulness. We talk a heap about such things; they're real, of course, and we cayn't escape them. At the same time, look at me!

"I came down here, sorry with myse'f, and you make me glad, not asking if I'd done meanness or if I'd betrayed my friends. You 'lowed I was jes' a man, same's you. I couldn't tell you how to be good, because I wasn't no great shakes myse'f, and the worse I was the better you got. Buck an' Jock gives me this boat for a mission boat; I'm ignorant, an' a woman gives me—"

He choked up. What the woman had given him was too immeasurable and too wonderful for mere words to express his gratitude.

"I'm just one of those shoutin', ignorant mountain parsons. I could out-whoop most of them up yonder. But down yeah, Old Mississip' don't let a man shout out. When yo' play dance music, hit's softer and sweeter than some of those awful mountain hymns in which we condemn lost souls to the fire. Course, the wicked goes to hell, but somehow I cayn't git up much enthusiasm about that down yeah. What makes my heart rejoice is that there's so much goodness around that I bet 'most anybody's got a right smart chanct to get shut of slippin' down the claybanks into hell."

"Jest Prebol?" someone asked, seeing Prebol's face in the window of the little red shanty-boat moored close by, where he, too, could listen.

"Jest Prebol's been my guide down the riveh," the Prophet retorted. "I can say that I only wish I could be as good a pilot for poor souls and sinners toward heaven as Jest is a river pilot for a wandering old mountain parson on the Mississippi—"

"Hi-i-i!" a score of voices laughed, and someone shouted, "So row me down the Jordan!"

They all knew the old religious song which fitted so nicely into the conditions on the Mississippi. Somebody called to someone else, and the musicians in the congregation slipped away to return with their violins, banjos, accordions, guitars, and other familiar instruments. Before the preacher knew it, he had more music in the church than he had ever heard in a church before—and they knew what to play and what to sing.

The sermon became a jubilee, and he would talk along awhile till something he said struck a tuneful suggestion, and the singing would begin again; and when at last he brought the service to an end, he was astonished to find that he had preached and they had sung for more than two hours.

Then there was scurrying about, and from all sides the calm airs of the sunny Sabbath were permeated with the odours of roasts and fried things, coffee and sauces. A score wanted Rasba to dine out, but Mrs. Caope claimed first and personal acquaintance, and her claim was acknowledged. The people from far boats and tents returned to their own homes. Two or three boats of the fleet, in a hurry to make some place down stream, dropped out in mid-afternoon, and the little shanty-boat town was already breaking up, having lasted but a day, but one which would long be remembered and talked about. It was more interesting than murder, for murders were common, and the circumstances and place were so remarkable that even a burning steamboat would have had less attention and discussion.

The following morning Mrs. Caope offered Rasba $55 for his old poplar boat, and he accepted it gladly. She said she had a speculation in mind, and before nightfall she had sold it for $75 to two men who were going pearling up the St. Francis, and who thought that a boat a parson had tripped down in would bring them good luck.

The dancers of Saturday night, the congregation of Sunday, on Monday afternoon were scattered. Mrs. Caope's and another boat dropped off the river to visit friends, and mid-afternoon found Parson Rasba and Prebol alone again, drawing down toward Mendova.

Prebol knew that town, and he told Rasba about it. He promised that they would see something of it, but they could not make it that evening, so they landed in Sandbar Reach for the night. Just after dawn, while the rising sun was flashing through the tree tops from east to west, a motorboat driving up stream hailed as it passed.

"Ai-i-i, Prebol! Palura's killed up!"

Prebol shouted out for details, and the passer-by, slowing down, gave a few more:

"Had trouble with the police, an' they shot him daid into his own dance floor—and Mendova's no good no more!"

"Now what the boys goin' to do when they make a haul?" Prebol demanded in great disgust of Parson Rasba. "Fust the planters shot up whiskey boats; then the towns went dry, an' now they closed up Palura's an' shot him daid. Wouldn't hit make yo' sick, Parson! They ain't no fun left nowheres for good sports."

Rasba could not make any comment. He was far from sure of his understanding. He felt as though his own life had been sheltered, remote from these wild doings of murders and shanty-boat-fleet dances and a congregation assembling in a gambling boat handed to him for a mission! He could not quite get his bearings, but the books blessed him with their viewpoints, as numerous as the points of the compass. He could not turn a page or a chapter without finding something that gave him a different outlook or a novel idea.

They landed in late on Monday at Mendova bar, just above the wharf. Up the slough were many shanty-boats, and gaunt dogs and floppy buzzards fed along the bar and down the wharf.

Groups of men and women were scattered along both the slough and the river banks, talking earnestly and seriously. Rasba, bound up town to buy supplies, heard the name of Palura on many lips; the policemen on their beats waltzed their heavy sticks about in debonair skilfulness; and stooped, rat-like men passing by, touched their hats nervously to the august bluecoats.

When Rasba returned to the boat, he found a man waiting for him.

"My name is Lester Terabon," the man said. "I landed in Saturday, and went up town. When I returned, my skiff and outfit were all gone—somebody stole them."

"Sho!" Rasba exclaimed. "I've heard of you. You write for newspapers?"

"Yes, sir, and I'm some chump, being caught that way."

"They meant to rob you?" Rasba asked.

"Why, of—I don't know!" Terabon saw a new outlook on the question.

"Did they go down?"

"Yes, sir, I heard so. I don't care about my boat, typewriter, and duffle; what bothers me is my notebooks. Months of work are in them. If I could get them back!"

"What can I do for you?"

"I don't know—I'm going down stream; it's down below, somewhere."

"I need someone to help me," Rasba said. "I've a wounded man here who has a doctor with him. If he goes up to the hospital or stays with us, I'll be glad to have you for your help and company."

"I'm in luck." Terabon laughed with relief.

Just that way the Mississippi River's narrow channel brought the River Prophet and the river reporter together. Terabon went up town and bought some clothes, some writing paper, a big blank notebook, and a bottle of fountain-pen ink. With that outfit he returned on board, and a delivery car brought down his share of things to eat.

The doctor said Prebol ought to go into the hospital for at least a week, and Terabon found Prebol's pirate friends, hidden up the slough on their boat, not venturing to go out except at night. They took the little red shanty-boat up the slough, and Prebol went to the hospital.

Rasba, frankly curious about the man who wrote for newspapers for a living, listened to accounts of an odd and entertaining occupation. He asked about the Palura shooting which everyone was talking about, and when Terabon described it as he had witnessed it, Rasba shook his head.

"Now they'll close up that big market of sin?" he asked. "They've all scattered around."

"Yes, and they scattered with my skiff, too, and probably robbed Carline of his boat—"

"Carline! You know him?"

"I came down with him from Yankee Bar, and we went up to Palura's together. I lost him in the shuffle, when the big cop killed Palura."

"And Mrs. Carline, Nelia Crele?" Rasba demanded.

"Why—I—they said she'd landed in. She's gone, too—"

"You know her?"

"Why, yes—I—"

"So do I. Those books," he waved his hand toward the loaded shelves, "she gave them all to me for my mission boat!"

Terabon stared. He went to the shelves and looked at the volumes. In each one he found the little bookmark which she had used in cataloguing them:

Nelia Carline,
A Loved Book.
No. 87

A jealous pang seized him, in spite of his reportorial knowledge that jealousy is vanity for a literary person.

"I 'low we mout 's well drop out," Rasba suggested. "Missy Crele's down below some'rs. Her boat floated out to'd mornin', one of the boys said."

CHAPTER XXX

Carline had discovered his wife in the excitement at Palura's, and with the cunning of a drunken man had shadowed her. He followed her down to Mousa Bayou, and saw her go on board her cabin-boat. He watched, with more cunning, to see for whom she was waiting. He had in his pocket a heavy automatic pistol with which to do murder.

He had seen killing done, and the thing was fascinating; some consciousness that the policeman had done the right thing seemed now to justify his own intention of killing a man, or somebody.

Disappointment lingered in his mind when the lights went out on board Nelia's boat, and for a long time he meditated as to what he should do. He saw skiffs, motorboats, shanty-boats pulling hastily down the slough into the Mississippi. It was the Exodus of Sin. Mendova's rectitude had asserted its strength and power, and now the exits of the city were flickering with the shadows of departing hordes of the night and of the dark, all of whom had two fears: one of daylight, the other of sudden death.

Their departure before his eyes, with darkened boats, gave Carline an idea at last. He wanted to get away off somewhere, where he could be alone, without any interruption. Bitter anger surged in his breast because his wife had shamed him, left him, led him this any-thing-but-merry chase down the Mississippi. A proud Carline had no call to be treated thataway by any woman, especially by the daughter of an old ne'er-do-well whom he had condescended to marry.

He had always been a hunter and outdoor man, and it was no particular trick for him to cast off the lines of Nelia's boat and push it out into the sluggish current, and it was as easy for him to take his own boat and drop down into the river. He brought the two boats quietly together and lashed them fast with rope fenders to prevent rubbing and bumping—did it with surprising skill.

The Mississippi carried them down the reach into the crossing, and around a bend out of sight of even the glow of the Mendova lights. Here was one of those lonesome stretches of the winding Mississippi, with wooded bank, sandbar, sky-high and river-deep loneliness.

Carline, with alcoholic persistency, held to his scheme. He drank the liquor which he had salvaged in the riotous night. He thought he knew how to bring people to time, especially women. He had seen a big policeman set the pace, and the sound of the club breaking skull bones was still a shock in his brain, oft repeated.

The sudden dawn caught him by surprise, and he stared rather nonplussed by the sunrise, but when he looked around and saw that he was in mid-stream and miles from anywhere and from any one, he knew that there was no better place in the world for taming one's wife, and extorting from her the apologies which seemed to Carline appropriate, all things considered, for the occasion.

The time had arrived for action. He rose with dignity and buttoned up his waistcoat; he pulled down his coat and gave his cravat a hitch; he rubbed a tentative hand on the lump where the pirates had bumped him; he scrambled over the side onto the cabin-boat deck, and entered upon the scene of his conquest.

He found himself confronted by Nelia in a white-faced, low-voiced fury instead of in the mood he had expected. She wasn't sorry; she wasn't apologetic; she wasn't even amiable or conciliatory.

"Gus Carline! Drunk, as usual. What do you mean by this?"

"S'all right!" he assured her, flapping his hands. "Y're m'wife; I'm your husban'! S'all right!"

She drew her pistol and fired a bullet past him.

"Go!" she cried.

Before he knew what had happened he had backed out upon the bow deck, and she bundled him up onto his own craft. She cast off the bow line and ran to the stern to cast off the line there. As she did so, she discovered Terabon's skiff around at the far side where Carline could not see it.

Her husband was still shaking his fist in her direction, but the two boats were well apart as she rowed away with her sweeps. He stood there, undecided. He had not expected the sudden and effective resistance. Before he knew it, she was lost in a whole fleet of little houseboats which were, to his eyes, both in the sky, underwater, and scattered all over the tip-tilting surfaces.

The current, under the impulse of her rowing, carried Nelia into an eddy and she saw the cruiser rocking down a crossing into the mirage of the distance. She sat on the bow deck while her boat made a long swing in the eddy. Things did not happen down the river as she planned or expected.

She regarded the previous night's entertainment with less indifference now; something about the calm of that broad river affected her. She realized that watching the killing of Palura had given her a shock so deep that now she was trembling with the weakness of horror.

She had seen Gus Carline stumble into her cabin, and with angry defiance she had acted with the intention of doing to him what she had done to Prebol—but she had missed deliberately when she shot. When she recalled the matter, she saw that for weeks she had been living in a false frame of mind; that she was desperate, and not contented; that she was afraid—and that she hated fear.

Her pistol was sign of her bravado, and her shots were the indication of her desperation. The memory of the wan face of Prebol brought down by her bullet was now an accusation, not a pride.

Old Mississip' had received her gently in her most furious mood, but now that immense, active calm of vast power was working on the untamed soul which she owned. The river swept along, and its majesty no longer gave her the feeling that nothing mattered. Far from it! Though she rebelled against the idea, her mind knew that she was in rebellion, that she was going against the current. And the river's mood was dangerous, now, to the wanton feelings to which she had desperately yielded but unsuccessfully.

The old, familiar, sharp division between right and wrong was presented to her gaze as if the river itself were calling her attention to it. She could not escape the necessity of a choice, with evil so persuasive and delightful and virtue so depressing and necessary.

She investigated Terabon's outfit with curiosity and questioning. His typewriter, his maps, his few books, his stack of notes neatly compiled in loose-leaf files, were the materials which caught and held her fancy. She took them on board her shanty-boat and read the record which he had made, from day to day, from his inspection of Commission records at St. Louis to the purchase of his boat in shanty-boat town, and his departure down the river.

His words were intimate and revealing:

> Oct. 5; In mid-stream among a lot of islands; rafts of ducks; a dull, blue day, still those great limestone hills, with hollows through which the wind comes when opposite—coolies?—; in the far distance a rowboat. On the Missouri side, the hills; on the other the flats, with landing sheds.

> Ducks in great flocks—look like sea serpents when flying close to the water; like islands on it—wary birds.

That was above the part of the river which she knew; she turned to Kaskaskia, and read facts familiar to her:

> I met Crele, an old hunter-trapper, in a slough below St. Genevieve. He was talkative, and said he had the prettiest girl on a hundred miles of river. She had married a man of the name of Carline, real rich and a big bug. "But my gal's got the looks, yes, indeed!" If I find her, I must be sure and tell her to write to her folks—river romance!

Nelia's face warmed as she read those phrases as well it might. She wondered what other things he had written in his book of notes, and her eye caught a page:

> House boatmen are a bad lot. Once a young man came to work for a farmer back on the hills. He'd been there a month, when one night he disappeared; a set of double harness went with him. Another man hung around a week, and raided a grocery store, filling washtubs with groceries, cloth, and shoes—went away in a skiff.

She turned to where he travelled down the Mississippi with her husband and read the description of Gus Carline's whiskey skiff man, his purchase of a gallon of whiskey; the result, which her imagination needed but few words to visualize; then Terabon's drifting away down stream, leaving the sot to his own insensibilities.

Breathlessly she read his snatching sentences from bend to shoal, from reach to reach, until he described her red-hull, white cabin-boat, described the "young river woman" who occupied it; and then, page after page of memoranda, telling almost her own words, and his own words, as he had remembered them. What he wrote here had not been intended for her eyes.

> She's dropping down this river all alone; pirates nor scoundrels nor river storms nor jeopardies seem to disturb her in the least. She even welcomes me, as an interesting sort of intellectual specimen, who can talk about books and birds and a multitude of things. She may well rest assured that none of us river rats have any designs, whatever, on a lady who shoots quick, shoots straight, and dropped Prebol at thirty yards off-hand with an automatic!

She read the paragraph with interest and then with care; she did not know whether to be pleased or not by that brutally frank statement that he was afraid of her—suppose he hadn't been afraid? Then, of what was he really afraid—not of her pistol! She read on through the pages of notes. The description of the walk with her up the sandbar and back, there at Island No. 10, thrilled her, for it told the apparently trifling details—the different kinds of sands, the sounds, the night gloom, the quick sense of the river presence, the glow of distant New Madrid. He had lived it, and he wrote it in terms that she realized were the words she might have used to describe her own observations and sensations.

She searched through his notes in vain for any suggestion of the emotions which she had felt. She shrugged her shoulders, because he had not written anything to indicate that he had discovered her allurement. He had written in bald words the fact of her sending him on the errand of rescue, to save her husband—and she was obliged to digest in her mind the bare but significant phrase:

And, because she has sent me, I am glad to go!

His notes made her understand him better, but they did not reveal all his own feelings. He wrote her down as an object of curiosity, as he spoke of the sour face and similitude of good humour in the whiskey boater's expression. In the same painstaking way he described her own friendliness for a passing skiff boater. The impersonality of his remarks about himself surprised while it perplexed her.

The mass of material which he had gathered for making articles and stories amazed her. The stack of pages, closely typewritten, was more than two inches thick. A few pages disclosed consecutive paragraphs with subjects, predicates, and complete sense, but other pages showed only disjointed phrases, words, and flashes of ideas.

The changing notes, the questioning, the observations, the minute recording were fascinating to her. It revealed a phase of writers' lives of which she had known nothing—the gathering of myriads of details, in order to free the mind for accurate rendering of pictures and conditions. She wished she could see some of the finished product of Terabon's use of these notes, and the wish revealed a chasm, an abyss that confronted her. She felt deserted, as though she had need of Terabon to give her a view of his own life, that she might be diverted into something not sordid, and decidedly not according to Augustus Carline's ideals!

After a time, seeing that Carline's boat had disappeared down river, she threw over her anchor, and rested in the eddy. It was on the west side, with a chute entrance through a sandbar and willow-grown island points opposite. She brought out her map book to see if she could learn where she was anchored, but the printed map, with the bright red lines of recent surveys, helped her not at all. She turned from sheet to sheet down to Memphis, without finding what she wanted to know.

She saw some shanty-boats down the river; she saw some up the river; but there was none near her till just before dark a motor skiff came down in the day's gray gloom, and passed within a few yards of her. When she looked at the two men in the boats she learned to know what fear is—river terror—horror of mankind in its last extremities of depravity and heartlessness.

She saw men stooped and slinking, whose glance was sidelong and whose expression was venomous, casting covert looks toward her as they passed by into the gray mist of falling night. They entered a narrow waterway among the sandbars, and left behind the feeling that along that waterway was the abiding place of lost souls. She wanted to take up the anchor and flee out onto the river, but when she looked into the darkening breadths, she felt the menace of the miles, of the mists, of the wooded shores. Foreboding was in her tired soul.

She examined her pistol, to make sure that it was ready to use; she locked the stern door, and drew the curtains; she went to the bow and looked carefully at the anchor-line fastenings. With no light on board to blind her gaze, she scrutinized all the surroundings, to make sure of her locality. In that blank gloom she was dubious but brave. Not a thing visible, not a sound audible, nothing but her remote and little understood sensation of premonitory dread explained her perturbation. She entered the cabin, locked the door, set the window catches and sticks, lighted the lamp, and sat down to—think. Her bookshelves were empty, and she was glad that she had emptied them in a good cause. It occurred to her that she ought to make up another list for her own service, and with pencil and paper she began that most fascinating work, the compilation of one's own library. As she made her selections, she forgot the menace which she had observed.

In the stillness she thought her own ears were ringing and paid no attention to the humming that increased in volume moment by moment. It was a flash of lightning without thunder that stirred her senses. She looked up from her absorption.

She heard a distant rumble, a near-by stirring. The wavelets along the side of the boat were noisy; they rattled like paper. Something fell clattering on the roof of the cabin, and a tearing, ripping, crashing struck the boat and fairly tossed it skipping along the surface of the water. The lamp blew out as a window pane broke, and the woman was thrown to the floor in a confusion of chairs, table, and other loose objects. Happily, the stove was screwed fast to the floor. The anchor line broke with a loud twang, and the black confusion was lighted with flares and flashes of gray-blue glaring.

The river had made Nelia Crele believe that she was in jeopardy from man; but it was a little hurricane, or, as the river people call them, cyclones, that menaced. Dire as was the confusion and imminent as was the peril, Nelia felt a sense of relief from what would have been harder to bear—an attack by men. She had searched the map for information, but it was the river which inspired her to understand that the hurricane was her deliverance rather than her assailant.

She did not know whether she would live or die during those seconds when the gale crashed like maul blows and wind and rain poured and whistled in at the broken window pane. She laughed at her predicament, tumbling in dishevelment around the bouncing cabin floor, and when the suck and send of the storm crater passed by, leaving a driving wind, she stepped out on the bows, and caught up her sweeps to ride the waves and face the gale that set steadily in from the north.

It was gray, impenetrable black—that night. She could see nothing, neither the waves nor the sky nor the river banks; but singing aloud, she steadied the boat, bow to the wind, holding it to the gale by dipping the sweeps deep and strong.

Beaten steadily back, unable to know how far or in what direction, she found her soul, serenely above the mere physical danger, loving that vast torrent more than ever.

The Mississippi trains its own to be brave.

CHAPTER XXXI

Parson Rasba and Terabon floated out into the main river current and ran with the stream. They were passing through the famous, changeable channels among the great sandbars from Island No. 34 down to Hopefield Bend. They rounded Dean Island Bend in the darkness, for they had floated all day and far into the night, driven by an anxiety which was inexplicable.

They wanted to be going; they felt an urge which they commented upon; it was a voice in their hearts, and not audible in their ears. Yet when they stood nervously at the great sweeps of the mission boat, to pull the occasional strokes necessary to clear a bar or flank a bend, they could almost declare that the river was talking.

They strained their ears in vain, trying to distinguish the meanings of the distant murmurings. Terabon, now well familiar with the river, could easily believe that he was listening to the River Spirit, and his feelings were melancholy.

For months he had strained every power of his mind to record the exact facts about the Mississippi, and he put down tens of thousands of words describing and stating what he saw, heard, and knew. With one stroke he had been separated from his work, and he feared that he had lost his precious notes for all time.

Either Carline or river pirates had carried them away. He hoped, he believed, that he would find them, but there was an uncertainty. He shivered apprehensively when he recalled with what frankness he had put down details, names, acts, rumours, reports—all the countless things which go to make up the "histories" of a voyage down from St. Louis in skiff, shanty-boat, and launch. What would they say if they read his notes?

He had notepaper, blank books, and ink, and he set about the weary task of keeping up his records, and putting down all that he could recall of the contents of his lost loose-leaf system. It was a staggering task.

In one record he wrote the habitual hour-to-hour description, comment, talk, and fact; in his "memory journal" he put down all the things he could recall about the contents of his lost record. He had written the things down to save him the difficulty of trying to remember, but now he discovered that he had remembered. A thousand times faster than he could write the countless scenes and things he had witnessed flocked back into the consciousness of his mind, pressing for recognition and another chance to go down in black and white.

As he wrote, Parson Rasba, in the intervals of navigating the big mission boat, would stand by gazing at the furious energy of his companion. Rasba had seized upon a few great facts of life, and dwelt in silent contemplation of them, until a young woman with a library disturbed the echoing halls of his mind, and brought into them the bric-à-brac of the thought of the ages. Now, from that brief experience, he could gaze with nearer understanding at this young man who regarded the pathway of the moon reflecting in a narrow line across a sandbar and in a wide dancing of cold blue flames upon the waters, as an important thing to remember; who recorded the wavering flight of the nigger geese, or cormorants, as compared to the magnificent V-figure, straight drive of the Canadians and the other huge water fowl; who paused to seize such simple terms as "jump line," "dough-bait," "snag line," "reef line," as though his life might depend on his verbal accuracy.

The Prophet pondered. The Mississippi had taught him many lessons. He was beginning to look for the lesson in casual phenomena, and when he said so to Terabon, the writer stared at him with open mouth.

"Why—that explains!" Terabon gasped.

"Explains what?"

"The heathen who was awed by the myriad impressions of Nature, and who learned, by hard experience, that he must not neglect even the apparently trivial things lest he suffer disaster."

Then Terabon fell to writing even more furiously in his day-by-day journal, for that was something of this moment, although he has just jotted down the renewed impression of coming into the bottoms at Cape Girardeau. Rasba took up the pages of the notes which Terabon was rewriting. Happily, Terabon's writing was like copper-plate script, however fast he wrote, and the mountain man read:

> Big hickory tree grove—Columbus Hickories—Largest cane in some bend down below Helena—Spanish Moss bend—famous river bend—Fisherman at Brickey's Mill told of hoop nets, trammels, seines (stillwater bayous), jump, hand, snag, reef, lines—Jugging for catfish down

the crossings, half pound pork, or meat, for bait, also called "blocking" for catfish.

"What will you do with all this?" Rasba asked.

"Why, I'll—" Terabon hesitated, and then continued: "It's like building a house. I gather all this material: lumber, stone, logs, cement, shingles, lathes, quick-lime, bricks, and everything. I store it all up in this notebook; that's my lumber yard. Then when I dig the foundation, I'll come in here and I'll find the things I need to build my house, or mansion. Of course, to start with, I'll just build little shacks and cabins. See what I mean? I am going to write articles first and they're kind of like barns and shacks, and even mere fences. But by and by I'll write fiction stories, and they will be like the mansions, and the material will all fit in: all about a fisherman, all about a market hunter, all about a drifter, all about a river—"

"All about a river woman?" Rasba asked, as he hesitated.

"I wasn't thinking that." Terabon shook his head, his colour coming a little. "I had in mind, all about a River Prophet!"

"Sho!" Rasba exclaimed. "What could you all find to write about a Riveh Prophet?"

Terabon looked at the stern, kindly, friendly, picturesque mountaineer who had come so far to find one man, for that man's mother, and he rejoiced in his heart to think that the parson did not know, could never know, because of the honest simplicity of his heart, how extraordinarily interesting he was.

So they drifted with the current, absorbed in their immediate present. It seemed as though they found their comprehension expanding and widening till it encompassed the answers to a thousand questions. Rasba, dazed by his own accretion of new interests, discovery of undreamed-of powers, seizure of opportunities never known before, could but gaze with awe and thankfulness at the evidences of his great good fortune, the blessings that were his in spite of his wondering why one of so little desert had received such bountiful favour. Terabon, remembering what he feared was irrevocably lost, knew that he had escaped disaster, and that the pile of notes which he had made only to be deprived of them were after all of less importance than that he should have suffered the deep emotion of seeing so much of his toil and time vanish.

Here it was again—Rasba might well wonder at that gathering and hoarding of trifles. They were not the important things, those minute words and facts and points; no, indeed.

At last Terabon knew that most important fact of all that it was the emotions that counted. As a mere spectator, he could never hope to know the Mississippi, to describe and write it truly; the river had forced him into the activities of the river life, and had done him by that act its finest service.

He was in the fervour of his most recent discovery when Rasba went out on the bow deck and looked into the night. He called Terabon a minute later, and the two looked at a phenomenon. The west was aglow, like a sunset, but with flarings and flashings instead of slowly changing lights and hues. The light under the clouds at the horizon extended through 90 degrees of the compass, and in the centre of the bright greenish flare there was a compact, black, apparently solid mass from which streaks of lightning constantly exuded on all sides.

For a minute Terabon stared, cold chills goose-pimpling his flesh. Then he cried:

"Cyclone, Parson! Get ready!"

They were opposite the head of a long bend near the end of a big sandbar, and skirting the edge of an eddy, near its foot. Terabon sprang into the gasolene launch, started the motor, and steered for the shelter of the west bank. In the quiet he and Rasba told each other what to do.

Rasba ran out two big anchors with big mooring lines tied to them. He closed the bow door but opened all the windows and other doors. Then, as they heard the storm coming, they covered the launch with the heavy canvas, heaved over the anchors into a fathom of water, let out long lines, and played the launch out over the stern on a heavy line fast to towing bits.

A sweep of hail and rain was followed by a moment of calm. Then a blast of wind, which scraped over the cabin roof, was succeeded by the suck of the tornado, which swept, a waterspout, across the river a quarter of a mile down stream, struck a sandbar, and carried up a golden yellow cloud of dust, which disappeared in the gray blackness of a terrific downpour of rain.

They stretched out on their anchor lines till the whole fabric of the cabin hummed and crackled with the strain, but the lines held, and the windows being open, prevented the semi-vacuum created by the storm's passing from "exploding" the boat, and tearing off the cabin, or the roof.

After the varying gusts and blasts the wind settled down, colder by forty degrees, and with the steady white of a norther. It meant days and nights of waiting while the storm blew itself out. And when the danger had passed and the boats were safe against the lines, the two men turned in to sleep, more tired after their adventures than they remembered ever being before.

In the morning rain was falling intermittently with some sleet, but toward afternoon there was just a cold wind. They built hot fires in their heater, burning coal with which the gamblers had filled bow and stern bins from coal barges somewhere up the river. Having plenty to eat on board, there was nothing to worry them.

Terabon, his fountain pen racing, wrote for his own distant Sunday Editor a narrative which excited the compiler of the Magazine Supplement to deep oaths of admiration for the fertile, prolific imagination of the wandering writer—for who would believe in a romance ready made?

The night of the big wind was followed by a day and a night of gusts of wind and sleety rain; then followed a day and a night of rising clouds, then a day when the clouds were scattered and the sun was cold. That day the sunset was grim, white, and freezing cold.

In the morning there was a bright, warm sunrise, a breath of sweet, soft air, and unimaginable brightness and buoyancy, birds singing, squirrels barking, and all the dismal pangs banished.

Shanty-boats shot out into the gay river and dotted the wide surface up and down the current for miles. The ears of the parson and the writer, keener with the acuteness of distant sounds, could hear music from a boat so far away that they could not see it, a wonderfully enchanting experience.

They, too, ran out into the flood of sunshine to float down with the rest.

At the foot of Brandywine Bar a little cabin-boat suddenly rowed out into the current and signalled them; somebody recognized and wanted to speak to the mission boat. They were rapidly sucking down the swift chute current, but Terabon turned over the motor, and flanked the big houseboat across the current so that the hail could be answered.

The little cabin-boat, almost lost to view astern, rapidly gained, and as they ran down Beef Island chute, where the current is slow, they were overtaken.

"Sho!" Parson Rasba cried aloud, "hit's Missy Carline, Missy Nelia, shore as I'm borned!"

Terabon had known it for half an hour. He had been noticing river details, and he could not fail to recognize that little boat. His hands trembled as he steered the launch to take advantage of slack current and dead water, and his throat choked with an emotion which he controlled with difficulty. He looked fearfully at the gaunt River Prophet whose own cheeks were staining with warm blood, and whose eyes gazed so keenly at the young woman who was coming, leaning to her sweeps with Viking grace and abandon.

She was coming to *them*, with the fatalistic certainty that is so astonishing to the student observer. Carried away by her sottish husband; threatened by the tornado; rescued, perhaps, by the storm from worse jeopardy, caught in safety under an island sandbar; her eyes, sweeping the lonesome breadths of the flowing river-sea, had seen and recognized her friend's boat, the floating mission, and pulled to join safe company.

She rowed up, with her eyes on the Prophet. He stood there in his majesty while Terabon stooped unnoticed in the engine pit of the motorboat. Not till she had run down near enough to throw a line did she take her eyes off the mountain parson, and then she turned and looked into the eyes, dumb with misery, of the other man, Terabon.

Her cheeks, red with her exertions, turned white. Three days she had read that heap of notes in loose-leaf file which Terabon had written. She had read the lines and between the lines, facts and ideas, descriptions and reminiscence, dialogue and history, statistics and appreciation of a thousand river things, all viewpoints, including her own.

She knew, now, how wicked she was. She knew, now, the wilfulness of her sins, and the merciful interposition of the river's inviolable strength. Her sight of the mission boat had awakened in her soul the knowledge that she must go out and talk to the good man on board, confess her naughtiness, and beg the Prophet for instruction. Woman-like, she knew what the outcome would be.

He would take her, protect her, and there would be some way out of the predicament in which they both found themselves. But again she reckoned without the river. How could she know that Terabon and he had come down the Mississippi together?

But there he was, chauffeuring for the Prophet!

She threw the line, Rasba caught it, drew the two boats together and made them fast. He welcomed her as a father might have welcomed a favourite child. He threw over the anchor, and Terabon dropped the launch back to the stern, and hung it there on a light line.

When he entered the big cabin Nelia was sitting beside a table, and Rasba was leaning against the shelves which he had put up for the books. Nelia, dumbfounded, had said little or nothing. When she glanced up at Terabon, she looked away again, quickly, flushing.

She was lost now. That was her feeling. Her defiance and her courage seemed to have utterly left her, and in those bitter days of cold wind and clammy rain, sleet and discomfort had changed the outlook of everything.

Married, without a husband; capable of great love, and yet sure that she must never love; two lovers and an unhappy marriage between her and happiness; a mind made up to sin, wantonly, and a soul that taunted her with a life-time of struggle against sordidness. The two men saw her burst into tears and cry out in an agony of spirit.

Dumbly they stood there, man-like, not knowing what to do, or what thought was in the woman's mind. The Prophet Rasba, his face full of compassion, turned from her and went aft through the alley into the kitchen, closing the doors behind him. He knew, and with knowledge he accepted the river fate.

Terabon went to her, and gave her comfort. He talked to her as a lover should when his sweetheart is in misery, her heart breaking. And she accepted his gentleness, and sobbed out the impossibility of everything, while she clung to him.

Within the hour they had plighted troth, regardless. She confessed to her lover, instead of to the Prophet. He said he didn't care, and she said she didn't care, either—which was mutually satisfactory.

When they went out to Parson Rasba, they found him calmly reading one of the books which she had given him. He looked up at their red faces and smiled with indulgence. They would never know what went on inside his heart, what was in his mind behind that kindly smile. That he knew and understood everything was clear to them, but they did not and would not have believed that he had, for a minute, hated Terabon as standing between him and happiness.

"What are we going to do?" Terabon cried, when he had told the Parson that they loved each other, that they would complete the voyage down the river together, that her husband still lived, and that they could get a $17.50 divorce at Memphis.

"Hit wouldn't be no 'count, that divorce." The Prophet shrugged his shoulders, and the two hung their heads. They knew it, and yet they had been willing to plead ignorance as an excuse for sin.

He seemed to close the incident by suggesting that it was time to eat something, and the three turned to getting a square meal. They cooked a bountiful dinner, and sat down to it, the Prophet asking a blessing that seared the hearts of the two because of its fervour.

Rasba asked her to read to them after they had cleared up the dishes, and she took down the familiar volumes and read. Rasba sat with his eyes closed, listening. Terabon watched her face. She seemed to choose the pages at random, and read haphazardly, but it was all delight and all poetry.

She was reading, which was strange, the Humphrey-Abbott book about the Mississippi River levees, the classic report on river facts, all fascinating to the mind that grasps with pleasure any river fact. When Rasba looked up and smiled, the two were absorbed in their occupations, one reading, the other watching her read. She stopped in conscious confusion.

"Yas, suh!" he smiled aloud. "I 'low we uns can leave hit to Old Mississip', these yeah things that trouble us: I, my triflin' doubts, and you children yo' own don't-know-yets."

What made him say that, if he wasn't a River Prophet? Who told him, what voice informed him, at that moment? Who can say?

The following morning the big mission boat and Missy Nelia's boat landed in at Memphis wharf, and the three went up town to buy groceries, newspapers and magazines to read, and to help Nelia choose another set of books from the shelves of local book stores. Old Rasba had never been in a book store before, and he stared at the hundreds of feet of shelves, with books of all sizes, kinds, and makes.

"Sho!" he cried aloud, and then, again, "Sho! Sho!"

It was fairyland for him, a land of enchantment, of impossible satisfaction and glory-be! Terabon and Nelia saw that they had given him another pleasure, and Rasba was happy to know that he would always be able to visit such places, and add to his own store of literature, when he had read the books which he had, as he would do, page by page, and word by word, his dictionary at hand.

Magazines and newspapers had little interest for him. Nelia and Terabon could not help but wish to keep closer in touch with the world. They picked up a copy of the *Trade-Appealer*, and then a copy of the *Evening Battle Ax*, just out.

They read one headline:

UNKNOWN DROWNS IN CRUISER

It was a brutally frank description of a motorboat cruiser which had floated down Hopefield Bend, awash and waterlogged, but held afloat by air-tight tanks:

> In the cabin was the body of a man, apparently about 30 years of age, with a whiskey jug clasped in one hand by the handle. He was face downward, and had been dead two or three days. It is supposed he was caught in the heavy wind-storm of Wednesday night and drowned.

The river had planned again. The river had acted again. They went to look at the boat, which was pumped out and in Ash Slough. It was Carline's cruiser. Then they went to the morgue, and it was Carline's body.

Nelia broke down and cried. After all, one's husband is one's husband. She did the right thing. She owned him, now, and she carried his remains back home to Gage, and there she buried him, and wept on his grave.

She put on widow's weeds for him, and though she might have claimed his property, she ignored the will which left her all of it, and gave to his relatives and to her own poor people what was theirs. She gave Parson Rasba, whom she had brought home with her to bury her husband, $5,000 for his services.

Then, after the estate was all settled up, she returned to Memphis, and Terabon met her at the Union Station, dutifully, as she had told him to do. Together they went to the City Clerk's and obtained a marriage license, and the River Prophet, Rasba, with firm voice and unflinching gaze, united them in wedlock.

They went aboard their own little shanty-boat, and while the rice and old shoes of a host of river people rattled and clattered on their cabin, they drifted out into the current and rapidly slipped away toward President's Island. Parson Rasba, as they drifted clear, said to them:

"I 'lowed we uns could leave hit to Old Mississip'!"